M000159136

TEACH ME

OLIVIA DADE

Copyright © 2019 by Olivia Dade

All rights reserved.

No part of this book may be reproduced in any form or by any electronic or mechanical means, including information storage and retrieval systems, without written permission from the author, except for the use of brief quotations in a book review.

ISBN: 978-1-945836-02-2

ABOUT TEACH ME

Their lesson plans didn't include love. But that's about to change…

When Martin Krause arrives at Rose Owens's high school, she's determined to remain chilly with her new colleague. Unfriendly? Maybe. Understandable? Yes, since a loathsome administrator gave Rose's beloved world history classes to Martin, knowing it would hurt her.

But keeping her distance from someone as warm and kind as Martin will prove challenging, even for a stubborn, guarded ice queen. Especially when she begins to see him for what he truly is: a man who's never been taught his own value. Martin could use a good teacher—and luckily, Rose is the best.

Rose has her own lessons—about trust, about vulnerability, about her past—to learn. And over the course of a single school year, the two of them will find out just how hot it can get when an ice queen melts.

PRAISE FOR OLIVIA DADE

With richly drawn characters you'll love to root for, Olivia Dade's books are a gem of the genre—full of humor, heart, and heat.

KATE CLAYBORN

With her warm and witty voice and wry humor, Dade weaves a story with shrewd observations about human nature, workplace dynamics, second chances, and the inner strength to overcome fear and take back control. *Teach Me* is a happiness-inducing, funny, clever, and empathetic book, and I'm very much looking forward to whatever Dade writes next.

LUCY PARKER

CONTENTS

Chapter 1	1
Chapter 2	12
Chapter 3	27
Chapter 4	35
Chapter 5	43
Chapter 6	55
Chapter 7	68
Chapter 8	79
Chapter 9	90
Chapter 10	103
Chapter 11	120
Chapter 12	130
Chapter 13	145
Chapter 14	159
Chapter 15	169
Chapter 16	179
Chapter 17	190
Chapter 18	201
Chapter 19	214
Epilogue	227
Also by Olivia Dade	241
Preview of Desire and the Deep Blue Sea	243
Chapter One	244
Chapter Two	258
About Olivia	263
Acknowledgments	265

For all the teachers. This book is a romance, but it's also a love letter to you.

And to the Swedes who welcomed my family with open arms, generous hearts, and endless (ENDLESS) quantities of béarnaise sauce: tack tack!

ONE

ROSE HAD BEEN BRACED FOR CALAMITY OVER A week, ever since she'd received the e-mail from Keisha. No department chair mandated a late-afternoon meeting with one of her teachers during the summer—especially not a week before they were due to report back to school—to relay welcome news.

So Rose didn't expect to hear about improved student test scores, or new funding for the AP U.S. History program, or even the availability of that corner classroom she'd been coveting for years.

The problem: She didn't know what she *should* expect.

No clues revealed themselves in the social studies department office. No memos rested on the counters lining each side of the space, and no new signs relayed red-underlined warnings on the cork bulletin board. No administrator lay in wait to reprimand her or demand her resignation, for whatever reason.

She straightened her pencil skirt over her thighs and checked her hairline for renegade strands, but everything remained in place. To the outside observer, she should appear unflustered. Unconcerned. And no matter what happened here today, that wouldn't change.

She would not invite other people's pity or spite into her life. Never again.

A rapid *tap-tap-tap* down the hall grew louder. A moment later, Keisha bustled into the office, her sunflower-patterned dress swishing with her every movement. She held up one finger, requesting patience, as she sorted through the pile of papers she held.

"Just a minute." A frown creasing her forehead, she deposited the pile on the nearest counter. "I need to find…"

Rose settled back to wait. Keisha, without fail, shouldered responsibilities others shirked, which meant she was always busy. Always in a hurry. Always at least a few minutes late.

Under other circumstances, Rose would have befriended her without hesitation. But a smart, private woman didn't cross-contaminate her professional and personal lives.

Unwilling to interrupt or rush her coworker, Rose bit back a greeting and surveyed the office again. Over the summer, the narrow room had attained a state of pristine cleanliness it would not achieve again until late June. Usually, piles of papers butted up against stacks of supplies and notebooks and textbooks and all the other detritus attendant with their profession, since at least two social studies teachers per year didn't have their own classroom. Instead, they'd float from room to room with their carts, which they parked in the office during their planning periods.

Once the school year began, this space would seem to shrink to stifling proportions, and the quiet of this afternoon would seem a false memory. Thank Christ she'd been given her own classroom over fifteen years ago. With great deliberation, she'd positioned her desk in a corner of the room where no one could see her from the door's little window. During her planning periods, she could slip off her heels, remove her jacket, and relax. Maybe listen to some low-volume music as she graded. Maybe cry, if she needed to.

Her first year of teaching, she'd cried all the time, usually in the staff restroom. After twenty years, weeping jags were rare, but they happened. Even veteran teachers had hard days.

Keisha jotted a note on one of her papers, then plopped herself down onto one of the worn swivel chairs and faced Rose with a sigh. "Sorry to keep you waiting. And sorry I had to call you in during your break. But I wanted you to hear this from me as soon as possible."

Shit. Definitely bad news.

"I appreciate that." Rose laced her fingers loosely in her lap, the picture of calm unconcern. "What's going on?"

Keisha's glasses slipped, as they inevitably did, down her nose, and she peered solemnly over the top of them. "Betty retired over the summer."

Rose inclined her head. "I heard."

"We've hired her replacement. Martin Krause. He's a great pickup, and I think you two will work well together. But..." Keisha's lips pursed in a brief grimace. "Dale got involved."

The head of secondary social studies, based at Central Office. One of the few remaining throwbacks to the time when the school system had operated like a men's-only country club, he occasionally elbowed his way into department matters, blustery and pompous and very, very aware of himself as a man with power over dozens of lower-paid, mostly female underlings.

His involvement definitely portended disaster in some form, still unknown.

"I see." *Keep your fingers relaxed. No clenching.*

Keisha pushed up her glasses. "I imagine you do. Once

Dale saw Mr. Krause's pedigree, he insisted we take measures to retain our new teacher for more than a year or two."

Their school, like many, had trouble keeping good teachers. Any teachers, actually. Some fled within weeks, leaving the department scrambling for long-term subs. Others departed over the summers, initiating yet more rounds of interviews and training.

Getting paid an amount commensurate with the hours they worked and the difficulty of their assigned tasks would probably help staff retention. But that wasn't the point of this meeting, whatever the point might be.

Neither was her next question, but she had to know. "What's his pedigree?"

Satisfaction softened Keisha's expression. "Master's in world history. Specialization in ancient civilizations. Twenty-five years of experience. Fifteen years of teaching AP World History with exemplary pass rates for the exam."

Well, shit. That *was* a pedigree.

Rose had a master's degree too, in U.S. history, as well as twenty years of experience. But very few job candidates could say the same.

Enough. Time to peel away the prickly outer layers and get to the heart of this particular artichoke. "How does Dale plan to retain him? And what does it have to do with me?"

Very little, one hoped.

"Mr. Krause will teach AP World History, of course. But Dale didn't want to give him the rest of Betty's schedule. He thought three periods of Regular World History would scare Mr. Krause away." The creases across Keisha's forehead reappeared. "So Dale gave him your Honors World History classes."

At last, there was the choke. Inedible, a fuzzy, breath-stealing lump in her throat.

And like an artichoke, her anger and despair contained

layers. "Teaching Regular World History wouldn't scare away a good teacher. Some of the most committed, kindest students I've ever taught—"

Keisha held up her hand. "You know that. I know that. But you and I also know Dale doesn't agree. As evidenced by the term he employs for those kids."

DOA. Dumb on arrival.

The first time he'd used that phrase in Rose's presence, she'd nearly imploded with rage.

Over her two decades of teaching, she'd been assigned every possible U.S. and world history prep. Regular classes, for kids whose interests or skills might not involve history—or who might not have the time or energy to enroll in harder, more work-intensive classes. Honors classes, for kids willing to cover history in more depth and with more demanding assignments. And finally, Advanced Placement classes, for kids interested in potential college credit—and kids curious or ambitious enough to handle frequent, time-consuming homework and assignments that would stretch their analytical and writing skills.

She might not have taught regular history in a while, but that didn't mean she'd disliked that prep. Every single one of the history classes had worth. Meaning. Importance. As did every single one of the students in those classes.

Dale didn't see that. He never would.

In a just world, he'd have found a profession that didn't involve schools. A job that didn't give him any authority over students or teachers.

The world wasn't just, though. She'd understood that before she'd even understood what *just* meant.

She measured each word. Mentally rehearsed until they emerged low and calm, not volcanic with emotion. "What will I be teaching, then?"

"You'll keep your three AP U.S. History classes. The other

two will be Regular U.S. History." Keisha's warm gaze offered sympathy that Rose couldn't—wouldn't—accept. "I realize you haven't taught that prep in a while. I'm sorry."

Rose didn't give a shit about teaching a different prep. Losing her Honors World History kids, though...

That gutted her. For more reasons than Keisha would ever know.

With an effort, Rose relaxed her jaw. A long, slow inhalation brought her temper back under her command and her common sense within grasp.

School hadn't started yet. She could fix this, if only she found the right argument. "How exactly does Dale expect me to keep our AP U.S. enrollment high if I don't teach Honors World History?"

Keisha took off her glasses and rested them on the counter, then rubbed her hands over her face. "I mentioned that concern. Dale wasn't in a mood to listen."

Rose's AP U.S. History numbers were going to tank next year. No doubt about it.

Kids who took AP World History in tenth grade were going to take AP U.S. History as juniors, assuming the new teacher didn't traumatize them. But that was thirty-five or forty kids, max. They couldn't fill three AP U.S. classes, the number she usually taught.

Her Honors World History students made up the difference.

The administration called most of them "untraditional AP students." Which meant, as far as she could tell, that they came from the same sorts of trailer parks and dilapidated apartment complexes she'd inhabited as a child.

Those kids had never taken an AP course. Had no intention of taking one. But they were motivated enough to enroll in an honors course. After a year in her class, the ones who respected and liked her also trusted her. Trusted her good intentions, her teaching ability, and her promise that she'd meet their efforts with her own.

They held their breath—knowing she would assign much more homework than they were accustomed to getting, knowing they'd have to juggle after-school jobs and responsibilities to their younger siblings, knowing they'd relinquish time spent asleep or with friends to complete assignments —and leapt.

And those tenth-grade Honors World History kids became eleventh-grade AP U.S. History kids. Lots of them. Her first few years, she'd had about forty students enroll in her AP classes. The year after she'd been assigned to teach Honors World History classes? Over a hundred kids had signed up for AP U.S. History.

She'd had to duck into the faculty restroom after seeing those class lists, spotting those familiar names, and realizing the trust her students had bestowed on her. The trust she'd earned.

Afterwards, the makeup repairs had been challenging, and her colleagues had probably seen the evidence of her tears.

For once, she hadn't cared.

Nothing in her adult life, other than her few close female friendships, had ever felt like that. Like a cloak settling on her shoulders, light and warm and *hers*.

Nothing. Not her wedding ring. Not her lavish home. Not her disorienting wealth. Not the man who'd bestowed the ring and the home and the wealth upon her, and then taken them all back.

That full-to-the-brim feeling, repeated each year, had helped sustain her over the last decade of teaching, despite long hours and piles of essays and staff turnover and administrative vagaries and the not-inconsiderable fury Dale evoked in her.

And now he was taking that feeling away.

After this year, a hundred AP U.S. History kids would dwindle to thirty or forty "traditional AP students" once more. Disproportionately wealthy, given the school population. Disproportionately white, too.

Her pulse pounded in her head in a violent *thump-thump-thump*, and her thoughts raced and scattered like sophomores after the last bell.

Deep breath. "If my enrollment drops substantially, I may not be given the resources I need to teach even a handful of AP kids. You know the superintendent is looking to cut costs."

Keisha didn't argue. "Unfortunately, I have more unwelcome news. As another enticement for Mr. Krause to stay, Dale wanted to give him your classroom, since you've had one the longest of anyone here. He said your becoming a floater might help"—she made air quotes—"*shake up stale pedagogical practices* and lead to greater student success in the long run."

The school didn't contain enough oxygen for the number of deep breaths Rose needed to take. Neither did the entirety of the Earth's atmosphere.

Fortunately for the universe's oxygen supply, Keisha immediately added, "But that's not happening. I told Dale giving the new teacher your room would cause chaos within our ranks. Classrooms have to be allotted by seniority within our department, period. Otherwise, I'd spend all year fielding requests and complaints."

Thank god for Keisha Williams, rightful queen of the department chairs.

"So our new teacher will be a floater, as usual." After another rub of her face, Keisha put on her glasses again. "But Dale wants to minimize the number of places Mr. Krause has to go, so he'll be teaching in your room during both of your planning periods."

Both of them? She'd have zero quiet, private time in her classroom during the school day? For an entire school year, and possibly longer?

Her face, frozen in an expression of equanimity, felt as if it might shatter.

"If I could have convinced Dale to change his mind, I would have. I certainly tried." Keisha's shoulders slumped almost imperceptibly. "But he'd already given in on the issue of ceding your classroom entirely, so he couldn't be swayed. I'm sorry, Ms. Owens. I know having your own space is…" She hesitated. "I know it's very important to you. I wouldn't take your classroom for both your planning periods if I had any other choice."

Rose's jaw made an odd popping sound. "I know. I appreciate it." She attempted to marshal her thoughts. "Perhaps Mr. Krause could—"

"Excuse me." A quiet knock sounded from the cracked door, matching a quiet male voice. "I apologize for interrupting, but I wanted to let you know I was here. A bit early, I'm afraid."

After mouthing a silent *I'm sorry* to Rose, Keisha got to her feet. "Please come in, Mr. Krause."

Rose did the same, watching as the door swung open.

And there stood the paragon. Martin, apparently. The man who'd inadvertently taken her Honors World History classes and—at least part of the time—her classroom.

For a paragon, he was awfully nondescript. Maybe mid-forties. White, with a slight tan. Lean frame. Brown hair sprinkled with a little gray. Watchful blue eyes. Standard button-down and striped tie above a pair of standard dark pants. Unremarkable features. Not ugly, not particularly handsome.

Hating such an unexceptional face might prove difficult, but she'd persevere.

Keisha looked between the two of them. "Mr. Krause, this is Ms. Owens, your colleague. You'll be teaching in her classroom for two periods, and you'll be working together on issues related to the AP program in our department."

When he moved closer, Rose took a certain grim satisfaction in the realization that she stood taller than him, at least when wearing heels.

She was a forty-two-year-old professional, and she'd act like a forty-two-year-old professional. And forty-two-year-old professionals shook hands with new colleagues and offered help, no matter how violently frustration and fury hammered at their temples.

She extended her hand, and he took it.

"I'm Martin." The handshake was brief, his hand dry and warm, his gaze direct. "It's a pleasure to meet you."

Under his scrutiny, she struggled to remain as smooth and impervious as a polished diamond. "And I'm Rose. If you'd like, I can stay until after your meeting with Keisha and answer any questions you might have about our Honors World History curriculum and our AP program."

Keisha answered for him, her smile rife with both relief and gratitude. "That would be lovely. Thank you, Ms. Owens."

Martin echoed Keisha's thanks in a low murmur.

As Rose left the office, the department chair followed her out and shut the door.

"I mean it," Keisha whispered. "Thank you. I won't forget how well you handled this. E-mail me if you want to discuss these changes again before our report date."

Rose forced her tongue to form the words. "I'm fine. Just send Martin to my—" Oh, Jesus. This was going to sting. "Just send Martin to our classroom when you two are done."

Keisha nodded and spoke at her normal volume. "Thank

you again, Ms. Owens. I hope you have a relaxing last week of vacation."

The other woman reentered the office and closed the door behind her, leaving Rose alone in the empty, echoing hallway, waiting to assist the paragon.

Sometimes being a forty-two-year-old professional sucked enormous, hairy kiwis.

TWO

"THE STATE'S STANDARDIZED TESTING HAPPENS the week after the AP exam?" Martin double-checked the schedule Rose had printed in the department office, hoping he'd gotten the dates wrong. "Those kids will be exhausted."

She tapped a gleaming nail on the paper. "They are. But the AP prep usually covers everything they need to know for the state test, so it's not quite as terrible as it sounds."

"By the time all the testing ends, I imagine you're exhausted too." He offered her a small, forced smile. "Maybe more than the students."

She turned away with a noncommittal hum. "Let's designate some areas for you to store your supplies in my room."

Nope. Nothing there except pure professionalism. No connection whatsoever.

He let his expression revert to his normal—as his ex-wife used to call it—Resting Proctologist Face. Why proctologists, he didn't know. But as over four decades of candid photos could confirm, his default expression did not tend toward jollity, no matter what he was actually feeling. In class field trip photos, he'd been the sternest, most worried-looking second-grader in school history.

To be fair, however, right now he had good reason to be concerned.

After an entire adult life spent swimming in the turbulent waters of department politics, Martin recognized its dangers, even those concealed beneath a mirror-like surface. So he knew for a fact: When he'd entered the social studies department office, he'd somehow ventured into water so cold and deep, he risked becoming a human popsicle.

Not because of his new supervisor, Keisha. She seemed genuinely pleased to have him in her department, and she'd welcomed him with natural—if harried—warmth.

Rose Owens...she was a different matter entirely.

She wasn't actively repugnant or a bully, like the head of secondary-level social studies for the school system. During the interview process, Dale Locke had behaved like an unmitigated dick to the women and underlings around him. The type of dick Martin had tried to avoid his entire childhood, with notably limited success.

It was hard to avoid pompous blowhard assholes when they were your immediate family, he'd found.

Rose, in contrast to Locke, couldn't have been more professional or generous with her help over the last hour or two. She'd shown him the textbooks he'd be using. Explained the school's schedule. Taken him to her classroom, still empty for the summer. Discussed the information students would be expected to master for the end-of-year state tests.

But the chill surrounding her was so palpable, he'd half-wondered during their handshake whether his fingers might stick to hers as they would an ice cube.

No, not a cube. A smooth sphere of ice, like the ones at that fancy, way-too-pricey bar he and Sabrina had visited during their last-ditch, let's-try-to-save-this-marriage getaway in Manhattan several years ago.

Like those spheres, Rose looked expensive. Beautifully rounded. Slippery in her perfection. And cold. Jesus, so cold.

She wore unrelieved black and dressed in sleek lines. Her shiny patent leather heels emphasized her impressive height, especially the length of her pale, strong legs. From a stick-straight center part, her hair was slicked back into a gleaming twist the color of bitter coffee.

Not a single word from her mouth was objectionable. Not a single word from her mouth was personal, either. She didn't ask him about himself. She didn't tell him about herself. She didn't smile. She didn't do anything but give him necessary, job-related information.

And that was absolutely, unequivocally her choice. She didn't owe him, a near-stranger, smiles or warmth or personal information or interest.

He'd told his daughter Bea the same thing many, many times over the years. Being a woman didn't obligate her to make men—or anyone—comfortable in her presence. People who said otherwise could contemplate their terrible life choices while she shoved their arrogant presumption some-where exceedingly painful.

Rose's chilliness didn't offend him. Not at all.

It did worry him, though.

He could guess that she wasn't thrilled about giving up her room for both her planning periods, since any rational human would feel the same way. And if he'd understood Keisha correctly, he was also taking Rose's Honors World History classes. Again, since getting a new prep involved untold hours of work for even longtime teachers, he had to assume she hadn't kicked up those slick, midnight heels in a jig of joy.

He hadn't chosen to invade her classroom, of course. He

hadn't assigned her a different prep, either. But he'd been the unwitting cause of all the upheaval she was experiencing, and only an automaton could fail to resent him for it.

The problem: They needed to work together. And he needed to make a place for himself at this school. At least for a year, and maybe longer if Bea chose to attend Marysburg University.

So if that chill was directed at him, specifically, rather than the world at large, he should try to mitigate the damage as soon as possible. Because making an enemy in his department before the first day of school? Awkward at best, career-damaging at worst.

And knowing someone was angry at him, in whatever context, made him twitchy. Always had.

Too bad Rose Owens didn't seem interested in any overtures of friendship.

He shook his head, impatient with himself. *Give her time, man.*

"I think the storage areas you indicated will fit more than enough of my supplies." He rested a hand on the cabinet she'd designated as his. "Thank you. And thank you for all your help."

"You're welcome."

No expression whatsoever. That might as well serve as his signal to go.

"I'd better get—" he started to say, just as his daughter walked into the room.

"Hey, Dad. There you are." Bea pulled out one of her earbuds, letting it dangle against her faded WHERE ARE WE GOING? AND WHY AM I IN THIS HANDBASKET? tee. "You ready to head out?" Turning to Rose, she offered a shrug and a smile. "Sorry to interrupt, but I'm hungry enough that the guidance counselor started to resemble curly fries."

Good timing. "Ms. Owens, this is my daughter Beatrice, who'll be a senior here this year. Bea, this is Ms. Owens, who teaches U.S. history. I'll be sharing her room for two of my classes. And we'll get out of her hair now, so she can get home or..." What did a woman that gorgeous, that statuesque, and that chilly do in her spare time? Freelance ice sculpture impersonation? "...or whatever."

Then the miraculous happened.

Rose swiveled toward his daughter and...Jesus.

She smiled.

Black clothing be damned, everything about her—everything—illuminated. That flawless pale skin transformed from opaque to luminescent. Her wide-set eyes crinkled at the corners, and for the first time, he noticed they were lovely. Not just brown, but the translucent, rich amber of dark maple syrup. And that mouth...

He'd vaguely registered her lips as pale and pinched and thin. But now he knew better. Her mouth was generous, her lips glossy and pink, as plump and stunning as the rest of her.

None of that—none of the warmth, none of the liveliness —was for him. It was all for Bea, his sweet girl. And he couldn't have been happier.

Because this meant Rose probably didn't treat her students the same way she treated him. Plus, anyone who smiled like that at his daughter couldn't be *too* unforgiving.

"I love your shirt," Rose told Bea. "Do you know whether it comes in black?"

His daughter had been wearing that tee on an almost daily basis for months now. At some point, he'd inquired as to whether it indicated her state of mind since the divorce, and Bea had scoffed at him.

"It's just comfortable, Dad. And I wash it between wears." She'd flicked her fingers in the direction of his head.

"I'm not traumatized and stinky and subtly revealing my pain through overuse of quippy tees, so stop with the proctologist face."

Such an adorable smartass.

He loved having her in his new house every other week, even when she talked enough for three people, ate all his favorite Pop-Tarts, and clogged the shower drain with long, soggy strands of her blond hair. How she wasn't bald when she shed like that, he had no idea. And when she left for college, he didn't know what he was going—

No. He wouldn't think about that. Couldn't think about that.

Bea removed her other earbud and beamed at Rose. "I can check. If it comes in black, I'll have Dad send you the link."

"That would be amazing. My wardrobe was clearly missing a key element. Snark." Rose gestured at the brochures in Bea's grasp. "You're deciding on colleges?"

"Yup. Dad's car is in the shop, so I drove him here and looked at a few options while I was waiting." She shook the stack of papers. "I've split them into three piles. Really expensive, prohibitively expensive, and I'd-better-see-about-cashing-in-Dad's-life-insurance-policy expensive." Her voice lowered to a faux-whisper. "I'm leaning toward the latter."

At that, Rose actually snorted, and he would have hugged his daughter if he hadn't known she'd shove him away and tell him he was being gross and mushy.

"We're touring UVA this weekend." Bea's elbow jabbed his ribs, and he smothered a grunt. "I know he looks like he's about to deliver a fatal prognosis most of the time, but Old Sobersides here is actually pretty fun on a road trip. We do taste tests of gas station snacks."

At the mention of his ex's other favorite nickname for him, he shifted his weight, and his daughter shot a glance in his direction.

He didn't mind the sobriquet. Not usually. Not when it was said with such obvious affection.

But a part of him wished Bea hadn't used it in front of Rose.

"Gas station snacks? Really?" Rose cast a skeptical—but not unfriendly—glance his way. "He doesn't seem like someone who consumes a lot of Little Debbie Oatmeal Crème Pies."

She knew about Little Debbie? Enough to name a specific product? Odd. He'd have bet a good chunk of his inadequate salary that she'd never stepped impeccably shod foot in any store less highbrow than Whole Foods.

Bea grinned, her blue eyes bright. "Don't let the lean frame fool you. He can pound the Ho Hos like nobody's—"

Okay, enough about pounding Ho Hos. "All right, Beatrice. Off we go. Say goodbye to Ms. Owens."

"Goodbye to Ms. Owens," Bea parroted.

Rose met his eyes, and for the first time, he saw warmth —at least a little of it—directed his way. "You've done well with this one, Krause."

When he laughed, she stilled for a moment, her smile dying.

He didn't understand what had happened. But he wanted that smile back, so he worked for it. "Funny. I was just thinking I should return her to the cabbage patch and tell them there'd been a clerical error."

And there it was again. That incandescent curve of her lips. This time, because of something he'd said. Him, Old Sobersides with the Resting Proctologist Face.

Why that made his shoulders straighten a fraction, he couldn't have explained. But it did, and the adjustment felt... different. Good different.

His daughter poked him again. "You'd miss me, and you know it."

He would. He already did, every other week.

"Possibly. But your college fund would buy a lot of therapeutic Ho Hos." With that, he aimed for the door. "Thank you for all your time and help, Ms. Owens. I feel much more prepared for the school year after having talked with you."

"That was the intent."

A cool dismissal. But when he glanced over his shoulder, she was studying him with his daughter, her brow creased in an expression he had no way of interpreting correctly.

"Good night, Ms. Owens," he said.

Bea paused in the doorway and looked at Rose. "See you when school starts. I'll let you know about the tee."

"Thanks, Bea. Come by anytime."

Rose, still and silent, watched his daughter disappear into the hallway. The setting sun bathed her skin with rosy light, but that light wouldn't last much longer. And if something about leaving his new colleague alone in the gathering shadows of her classroom tugged at his chest, he wasn't paying the pull a bit of attention.

"Good night, Mr. Krause." With Bea's departure, Rose was opaque again. Still lovely, but a definite chill had descended. "See you in a week. Please close the door behind you when you leave."

After one final, unhappy survey of the rapidly darkening, nearly empty parking lot outside her classroom windows, he did. Jogging to catch up with Bea, he fell into step beside her as they trundled down the stairs and toward the main school entrance.

For once, his daughter remained silent, even without her earbuds in place. And in that brief oasis of quiet, his brain picked through images from the afternoon. The vivid sunflowers on Keisha's dress and the charming way she kind of crossed her eyes when making a point she considered vital. The personality-free patch of the department office where he'd spend his own planning periods, a space containing only a countertop, a chair, a cart, and a few shelves overhead. Lists of test dates and schedules and learning objectives.

Rose Owens. Ivory covered in ebony, polished from crown to pointed toe. Tall. Lush. Controlled. Scrupulously polite, undeniably helpful, and unfathomably distant.

A frozen monarch, melted by a teenager in a quippy tee.

Funny how he'd enjoyed both the ice and its temporary thaw. How he'd found both impressive. How something inside him had awakened when his nonsense earned her smile.

As they settled into her car and buckled their belts, his daughter finally spoke. "I'm sorry, Dad."

Despite the dusk, Bea's hair still gleamed from the driver's seat. His golden girl, now staring at him with beetled brow, clearly remorseful. Why, he couldn't guess.

"What about, sweet Bea?"

The childhood nickname didn't elicit a protest, which was evidence enough of her distress. She didn't say anything for a minute, and he tried not to cringe as she reversed the car out of the parking space with a speed he'd never have attempted and zipped out of the lot.

"I thought..." She came to a full halt at a stop sign and looked both ways before proceeding through the intersection, and he sent a silent thanks to the ever-patient instructors at her former driving school. "I didn't think you minded the names."

"The names?"

He knew which names. But she needed time and space to work through what she wanted to say, and he wouldn't insert his own words into the process.

"Old Sobersides. Resting Proctologist Face. I thought they were kind of like...I don't know." Her throat shifted in a hard swallow. "Family jokes, or something."

"They were." He hesitated. "They are."

"But we're not a family anymore." At his immediate protest, she raised a staying hand from the steering wheel, eyes still on the road. "I know, I know, you and I are still family. Mom and I are still family. But the three of us aren't. Not since the divorce. And definitely not since Mom got engaged to Reggie and came here."

"Sweet Bea…" He gave her arm a brief, gentle squeeze. "I moved to Marysburg to be near you for at least one more year. You're my family, no matter what. Never doubt that."

"I don't doubt that. That's what I just said." His daughter's voice contained an uncharacteristic snap. "Please listen to me."

He subsided back into his seat. "Okay. Okay. I'm listening."

Her voice lowered. "This isn't about whether you love me, Dad. You do. I know that. This is about whether you ever really liked those nicknames, or whether you put up with them because Mom and I thought they were funny. And if you didn't like them, you shouldn't have had to hear them. Not when we were all a family, and definitely not now."

Befuddled, he squinted against the glare from another car's headlights. "What brought this on, Bea?"

She licked her lips. "When I called you Old Sobersides in front of Ms. Owens, you looked…I don't know. Uncomfortable, I guess. Maybe a little embarrassed. And I got worried that I'd hurt your feelings. That we'd hurt your feelings, for all these years."

"You didn't hurt my feelings in front of Ms. Owens." He shifted in the seat until he was facing her profile. "Please don't be concerned about that."

Bea, true to her stubborn nature, was not mollified. "But do you actually think those nicknames are funny? Do you like them?"

That…that was a hard question. "I guess I've had similar nicknames most of my life, so I don't think too much about them."

He'd certainly had worse ones, especially as a kid. Casper, for how invisible he'd tried to become. Mute Boy, for how seldom he'd spoken at home. Pansy, for how he'd proven a liability in organized sports and hated playing the violent, mean games his older brother Kurt and Kurt's asshole friends had preferred. How he'd cried that time their father used the spatula on him.

"But do you like them?" Bea flicked him an impatient glance. "Come on, Dad, answer the question."

There was really no simple answer. That was going to be true of many questions in Bea's life, so she might as well learn it now.

"Sometimes I think those names are funny. Because *you're* funny, and because you say them with affection." Just as Bea had no doubt of her place in his heart, he didn't worry for a moment about whether she loved him back. "But other times, maybe not."

He certainly hadn't appreciated them the last few years of his marriage. Not when the fondness in Sabrina's tone had become edged with scorn. Not when she'd flung those nicknames between them like a gauntlet, a challenge to be better. Less boring. A worthwhile husband, one not so preoccupied with grading and other people's children.

Then, the edge in those familiar phrases had left him bleeding but unable to complain about the slice of pain. Because it was just a joke, after all. Just a family joke.

Bea cut to the point. "Not when Mom uses them."

Not in the last decade, no.

He chose his words with the care of a man disarming an explosive. "That's a matter for your mother and me to address, if we ever find it necessary. It's not something you need to worry about."

Bea's lips thinned. "Whatever. Either way, I won't use those nicknames again."

"That's up to you." He tried to convey his sincerity, but wasn't sure he succeeded. "My feelings won't be hurt if you do."

"Hmmm." In that moment, his daughter sounded very much like Rose had earlier.

Long minutes passed, and Bea had pulled into the fast food drive-through line, grabbed his wallet to pay the cashier, handed over their food, and started for home before she spoke again. "Ms. Owens is pretty. She seems nice, too."

He almost laughed. *Pretty* and *nice* were such pallid terms for the woman he'd met that day, and neither strictly applied.

Gorgeous. Generous. Self-contained. Inscrutable. Those words captured Rose Owens.

But Rose *had* been nice to his daughter, and he didn't care to reveal his thoughts about his colleague to Bea. Not when this conversation already had him skirting landmines.

So, sure. He could agree to Bea's assessment. "Yes. I'm glad you liked her."

"She's really different from Mom."

In so many ways. Thick and curvaceous where Sabrina had been slight and athletic in frame. Regally tall, rather than petite. Dark-haired, instead of blond. Monochromatic when Sabrina had loved bright colors.

Above all else, Rose was closed, while Sabrina had been a dwelling with the door flung wide open. Too open to contain either her happiness or her discontent, and too open to effectively conceal her extramarital activities from him, although she'd managed to shield Bea. They both had, and they both would. On that they agreed.

But again: landmines.

"Your mother and Ms. Owens both like kids. They have that in common." He didn't really want to know, but he had to ask. "Bea, why are you comparing them?"

They'd reached their driveway. She turned the key in the ignition, and the car's rumble abruptly ceased.

"Mom has Reggie. I'm leaving for college next year." She unbuckled her seat belt and angled her body toward him. "Dad, you need to start dating. The thought of you in this house all alone—" Her hands fisted in her lap. "I hate it."

Her concern warmed him, but—*dating*. The word alone made his heart clench in terror.

He'd been awful at dating. Awkward and too quiet and…boring.

In academic settings, he'd communicated capably. Outside of them, he'd become someone else. Old Sobersides. Mute Boy. Casper. Only he'd been the one ghosted again and again as a teenager.

Sabrina had been his first girlfriend. Likely his last, too.

"I don't need to date. I'm fine." He touched her chin with a gentle finger. "And sweet Bea, you should know something. You can be more alone in a bad relationship than if you'd never dated anyone at all."

Her mouth trembled. "Maybe I should go to Marysburg University."

God, he'd love that.

"No, Bea." He spoke over her protest. "*No*. You are not responsible for me. I can take care of myself, and you'll have your own independent life to create. So you're only going to Marysburg U if that's the college you most want to attend. Period."

His daughter slumped in her seat. "I just want you to be happy."

"I am. I will be." He got out of the car, rounded the

bumper, and opened her door. "Come on out. I'm claiming my moment of mush for the day."

It took her a moment, but she eventually rolled her eyes and accepted his hand as she climbed to her feet. Then he pulled her into the tightest hug he could give without hurting her.

For a moment, he simply breathed in the familiar scent of her apple shampoo. Focused on the familiar sight of blond curls at the crown of her head. Soaked in the familiar feel of her, his baby girl, nestled against him.

But not everything was so familiar. Not her lanky limbs. Not her height.

Soon, her head wouldn't even rest on his chest anymore.

His throat ached. He closed his eyes for a moment, bereft.

Still, he let her go as soon as she loosened her grip, and he worked hard to keep his tone teasing. "Did I ever tell you you're my favorite daughter?"

She didn't seem to notice how hoarse he'd become. "Ha-ha, Dad."

The rest of the evening passed normally. At least until bedtime, when she gave him another brief hug and then lingered in her doorway, silhouetted by her bedside light. The oversized tee Bea used for a nightie was becoming threadbare, but she refused to let him buy new ones. So stubborn, his girl.

Without warning, she prodded his chest with a fingertip. "Ms. Owens likes you, you know. She smiled at your dumb jokes, and she was watching you when you weren't looking at her. Which you were totally doing all the time. You should ask her out."

His daughter needed practice interpreting body language, because his new colleague did *not* like him. Not in the slightest. But it was sweet that Bea considered her middle-aged father someone who could interest a woman like Rose Owens.

"I'm not going to date Ms. Owens. Or anyone, for that matter." He kissed Bea's forehead and nudged her inside her room. "But I love you. Good night, sweet Bea."

"So stubborn," he heard her mutter as he closed the door. "Love you too, Dad."

THREE

Rose sipped from her enormous mug of black coffee and surveyed her classroom.

As always, she'd arrived over an hour early, before almost everyone else, to make sure she had time for any last-minute adjustments and to enjoy the final few minutes of quiet she'd have until late that evening.

Her desk, cabinets, and shelves contained all the supplies and papers she should need for the foreseeable future. The student desks and chairs had been arranged in neat rows, and the seating chart—useful for taking attendance until she learned all the kids' names—was posted in several places around the room. Stacked copies of the day's schedule rested on a side table, laying out what would happen during class and roughly how long each activity would take, as well as the state objectives met by the lesson and any homework she might assign.

For all their avowed laziness, kids liked to know what to expect each day, and they responded well to structure, as long as that structure came coupled with a sense that their teacher actually cared about both her students and her subject.

She did. She loved both.

As soon as kids entered her room each day, they received a task to complete. Usually annotating a document, in the case of the AP students, or answering a review question or two, in the case of the regular history students. Otherwise, the beginning of class could devolve into chaos within moments.

Today, they'd immediately fill out introductory paperwork about their interests, their contact information, etc. All standard. And then she'd go over the syllabus and introduce another getting-to-know-you activity, one she'd formulated last month with photographs from the National Archives.

Every year, even if she kept the same preps, she tweaked her lesson plans. They could always be better. *She* could always be better. Pedagogical research and historical research both advanced inexorably over time, and she needed to do the same. Otherwise, she'd be a substandard teacher, not to mention a bored one.

She was neither. So everything lay in wait, ready for the whirlwind of students that would shortly blow into the building, and the rapidity of her heartbeat told her she needed to slow her coffee roll before she shook herself to pieces.

A light knock on her half-open door heralded company. She straightened in her chair, setting aside her mug. "Yes?"

A now-familiar head of neatly combed brown hair poked through the door. "Good morning, Rose. Sorry to bother you, but I was hoping to drop off some of the papers I'll need for second period."

One of her two planning periods, which she could no longer spend in her classroom. Lovely.

She stood and gestured for him to enter the room. "Come in."

Then there he was, lingering just inside the doorway. Martin Krause, the paragon. Such a paragon she couldn't really even hate him anymore, although she was petty enough to try. But hating a man who listened so intently, spoke quietly but intelligently, and never seemed to impose himself on others had proven more difficult than she'd hoped.

Almost two weeks of teacher workdays and staff meetings and department gatherings, and she still hadn't spotted anything loathsome about him. Sure, she'd tried to despise his ever-present blue button-downs and striped ties and dark pants, and the careful side part of his hair, but that was a stretch even for her.

He didn't bluster. He didn't presume his authority over her or anyone else.

He was just another teacher put in an awkward situation by Dale Fuckwad Locke.

So as long as Martin minded his own business, she'd mind hers, and they'd get along fine.

Preferably, he'd also refrain from laughing or smiling while in her presence, because when he did either, he became entirely too attractive for her peace of mind. She couldn't exactly make that demand, though, much as she wanted to.

He wasn't smiling now. But why was he still lingering near the door, studying her like that?

She raised her brows. "Do you want me to remind you which shelves and cabinets we designated as yours?"

"No." He tilted his head to the side, a pile of papers tucked between his arm and his body. "You just...never mind. I'll drop these off and get out of your way."

She didn't want to know. She didn't want to know. She didn't, didn't, didn't want to know.

Christ, she wanted to know. "What?"

He put his papers on his allotted shelf, turned back to her, and seemed to consider his words carefully. A habit of his, she'd noticed, and not an unwelcome one.

"Are you okay?" He crossed and uncrossed his arms over his chest. Strong arms, as she'd discovered the day he helped haul textbooks to various department classrooms. "Because you seem a little...not yourself."

She looked down at herself. Black velvet blazer, in deference to the overactive school air conditioning. Black silk blouse, knotted with a flourish at the side of her neck. Her favorite black trousers, made from polished cotton and cuffed at the hem. Black heels with pewter accents on the toe. No coffee spills. No hangings threads.

Nothing that should have tipped him off as to her mental state.

But maybe he'd meant something else. Maybe he was criticizing her appearance, and she'd finally find something to hate about him. A woman could only hope.

She narrowed her eyes at him. "What, precisely, does *not yourself* mean?"

At that look, he took a half-step backward.

He pursed his lips before slowly, reluctantly answering. "Your foot. It's, uh, tapping."

"Maybe I'm impatient." She enunciated the words very, very clearly.

He inclined his head. "Maybe. But your foot didn't tap once during that marathon three-hour staff meeting, not even when the consultant used the term *growth mindset* for the seventeenth time."

Taken by surprise at the unexpected snark, she couldn't help herself. She snorted.

Her ex had tried to break her of that habit, the last remaining tic from her childhood as Brandi Rose Owens, trailer park princess. Barton had cringed at the sound every time, curling up on himself with irritation and distaste. But out of sheer contrariness, she'd chosen to retain that piece of her old self, unlike all the other telltale bits she'd so ruthlessly erased.

Martin, however, didn't cringe at the noise. Didn't look away in disgust. Instead, he transformed in an entirely different manner. His arms eased from across his chest, and he propped his fists on his hips as he grinned at her.

Dammit. Not again.

His smile and pose transformed him from a nondescript former Boy Scout into the sort of man you saw gazing off into an ocean sunset in an expensive cologne advertisement. His face creased, his blue eyes lit, and a woman would have to be either gay or dead not to respond.

His age had burnished him, not bowed him. He was...

Christ, he was lickable.

He moved a step closer. "Your hands are shaking a bit too. And I don't think I've ever seen such an enormous mug of coffee in my life, outside of cartoons."

She blinked at him, unable to recall the context for his observations.

He waited for a response. When it didn't materialize, he concluded, "So I was wondering if you were okay. If you needed anything. Because the first day of school is always hard, no matter how long you've taught. I usually have trouble sleeping the night before."

Her pride demanded that she spurn his concern. Refuse to be seen as anything less than capable and independent and impervious.

But then he gave a self-deprecating shake of his head and confessed, "One time, I dreamed I came into the classroom for the first day and had been unexpectedly assigned to teach the history of the steamboat. I had no lesson plans. No class rosters. Nothing. I was horrified."

Her lips moved without her permission. "Do you know a lot about steamboats?"

"Hell, no," he said, and they both laughed.

In truth, she'd barely slept the night before. And during the little rest she did manage, she dreamed of a classroom full of kids staring blankly at her as she belatedly realized she hadn't created lesson plans or handouts or anything —*anything*—that would fill the time.

She'd thought those nightmares would cease after a decade or two in the profession, but nope. A few former colleagues who'd retired long ago told her they still had similar anxiety dreams on occasion, so she anticipated many nights in the future spent tossing and turning over mysteriously missing syllabi and seating charts she couldn't decipher.

But she hadn't anticipated talking about her first-day jitters with anyone at school. "I may not have slept quite as well as I normally do."

"Thus the caffeine." His blue eyes were so warm, her knees didn't want to support her. For the sake of self-preservation, she dropped into the chair behind her desk. "Is there anything I can do to help?"

She cleared her throat, gathering the mantle of pride around herself once more. "I'm fine. But thank you for the kind offer."

He dropped the subject without another word. Again, a paragon. It was insupportable.

"The room looks great." With a slow turn, he took in every corner of the space. He had a very, *very* nice rear view, which was a revelation she could have done without. "I love the Shakespeare quote on the bulletin board."

"*What's past is prologue.*" She drummed her fingers on her desk, now nervous for reasons that had nothing to do with either caffeine or first-day jitters. "I spend a lot of time during the year trying to show my students how our history still influences so much of our daily existence. Our government, our culture, our economy, everything."

"Are those…" His lips curved. "They are. You've laminated articles from *Our Dumb Century* and put them up everywhere. I had no idea you read *The Onion* too."

She lifted a shoulder. "Students respond well to satire. Besides, the articles are hilarious, and it's all grounded in real history. If you don't know the history, you don't get the joke."

"You're absolutely right." His eyes caught on the wall to the right of the door. "And thank you for putting up a few world history posters for my classes." He strode to study one more closely. "This is a stunning photo of the Great Wall of China."

There. That stab of grief as she remembered what she'd lost at his unwitting hands. That was just the reminder she needed.

Distance. Keep your distance.

"Students should be arriving shortly, and I have a few more things to do before first period. Did you need anything else, Mr. Krause?"

Unlike almost every other man she'd known, Martin got hints. After a final, awkward half-bow, he left and partially shut the door behind him.

But once he was gone, she didn't check her lesson plans for the umpteenth time or straighten the student desks by a micron or two. Instead, she thought about Martin. Took the observation she'd just made about him and spun it out.

Martin got hints. Martin was watchful. Martin could read and interpret body language.

Most well-off, cishet white men couldn't do either. Didn't need to do either, unlike the people in their orbit, because they held the power. They created the weather, while others languished in the rain or cringed away from the lightning.

Maybe he'd grown up poor, like her. Maybe he'd learned empathy and watchfulness from his years of teaching. But the way he'd stepped back from a simple glare...she'd seen that kind of reaction before. In some of the neighbor kids at the trailer park. In the wife of one of Barton's colleagues. In some of her students, the ones she watched for bruises.

And she wondered. About his childhood. About his marriage.

It was foolish. She barely knew the man. She could be entirely wrong in every way.

Still, what she was wondering burned in her chest like coals. The sudden, shocking anger didn't leave her until the first student arrived at the door, slouching and feigning casual disinterest to the best of his young abilities.

Then she became Ms. Owens, not Rose.

Right now, Martin didn't matter. Couldn't matter.

She stood. Smiled at her student. Told him where to find the class schedule, the syllabus, and his seat. Swung the door wide and waited for the next arrivals.

Her hands weren't shaking anymore.

The new school year had begun, and she was ready to kick some pedagogical ass.

FOUR

MARTIN ENCOUNTERED ROSE SEVERAL MORE TIMES throughout the day, as one would expect, but only for brief instants as they entered or exited her classroom or passed in the hall. He had no idea whether they shared the same lunch block, since he'd brought his food and hurriedly eaten it inside the social studies office next to the other department floater, a twenty-something woman named Dakota Brown.

Dakota was eager and chipper and damned young. She'd arrived in the office right after he'd left Rose's classroom that morning, and the vast gulf between the two women had disoriented him for a minute. If Dakota were confetti ice cream, sweet, cheerful, and straightforward, Rose would be bittersweet chocolate gelato. Dense. Complexly, intensely flavored. Not to everyone's taste.

The grocery store closest to his house carried pints of gelato. Maybe he and Bea could do a taste test of those someday and pretend they were classier than they really were.

But Dakota was good company for lunch, and the students were...well, students. Not too different from the kids at his previous school. Some chatty, some quiet. Some awkward, some posturing. They'd relax and become more themselves once they learned the routine and trusted him.

By the end of the year, if all went as planned, each class would become sort of an extended, temporary family. An evolving but unitary organism, working toward the same purposes: factual knowledge, greater ease with critical thinking and writing, increased ability to make connections between different ideas, different time periods, and different subjects, and—above all—comfort in the educational environment.

He couldn't always make his students happy to be in his class. But he could make them feel safe while they were there, and he knew all too well the importance of safe spaces.

When the last bell rang, and his seventh-period students rushed toward the door clutching backpacks and fistfuls of forms to complete, he dropped down into one of their chairs for a moment. Just a moment. Just until the adrenaline crash inevitable at the end of a long, important, stressful day subsided.

Rose strode through the door, and then came to a sudden halt upon spotting him.

She opened her mouth. Closed it. Gave her head an impatient little shake, but somehow it seemed more self-directed than an indication of displeasure with him. "Are you ill, Mr. Krause?"

He wondered idly if the school administered coffee in IV form at the nurse's office. "Not sick, just tired. Sorry. I'll move momentarily."

"Take your time." She swept toward the desk, her heels clicking with each long stride. "But as a reminder, we have a faculty meeting in the cafeteria in ten minutes."

And he needed to talk to Bea before then, to confirm their

dinner plans. He rose to his feet with a groan, which Rose didn't acknowledge.

But as he reached her doorway, her voice stopped him. "The beginning of the year is exhausting enough, even if this weren't a new school for you. Be sure not to run yourself into the ground."

A quick glance backward revealed an impassive face, angled down toward her papers.

"I won't." He sighed. "I mean, I will."

When she didn't say anything more, he left and shut the door behind him. Because she deserved at least a couple minutes of privacy after a long day, even if she hadn't asked for them.

During the faculty meeting, he saw her across the cafeteria. Spine straight, not a strand of her hair out of place. Sitting next to other faculty members, but entirely removed from them. There were no whispers or furtive laughs. No idle conversations between speakers. No smiles, much less adorable snorts.

He didn't get it. At all.

He'd have said she considered herself above the rest of them, but that didn't ring true. Not given her friendliness with Bea, and the brief glimpses he'd garnered of how she interacted with students. With them, she was all lively, charismatic warmth, rather than the chill of an empress. And even with him, all her coldness didn't negate her generosity.

She'd given him her time and guidance during the summer. She'd given him a substantial portion of her classroom storage. She'd put up posters for his students. She'd even reminded him to take care of himself, albeit in an affectless way.

As Churchill might have said, Rose Owens was a riddle, wrapped in a mystery, inside a really soft-looking black blouse.

After the meeting, he lingered to introduce himself to a few of Bea's teachers. By the time he left the cafeteria, Rose was long gone. But along the way to the department office, he glanced into her closed door's little window.

He couldn't see her. The placement of her desk meant she wasn't visible from the door, which he imagined was not accidental. But there, on the floor beside her desk, he could just see a pair of breathtakingly high black heels, tumbled onto their sides. And over the back of a nearby student chair, a black velvet blazer lay carefully folded in half.

She was in there barefoot, in that silky confection of a shirt.

For her, he guessed that was basically one step from naked.

He stumbled over his own feet. Then made himself keep moving down the hall.

But three hours later, as shadows crept into the corners of the department office, and he couldn't seem to focus his eyes anymore, he couldn't help himself. He had to know. So he slipped his school-issued laptop inside his briefcase and slung the strap over his shoulder, gathered a stack of freshly-copied papers, and headed toward her classroom.

Nothing had changed. Shoes on the floor, jacket on the chair.

He knocked softly.

"Just a moment," she called out.

Then, from the window, he watched a long-fingered, capable hand gather those shoes. After a moment, a black-clad arm reached for her jacket. Another few moments, and the tap of her heels came toward him.

He shouldn't be disappointed. He really shouldn't.

She opened the door and seemed unsurprised at the sight of him.

"Come in, Mr. Krause." She clicked back to her desk with

all due speed, but her descent into her desk chair lacked a soupçon of her usual grace. It was a revealing hitch, although it didn't tell him anything her enormous trough of coffee that morning hadn't.

"Just dropping off handouts for tomorrow." He entered the room, leaving the door cracked behind him. "You're tired too, huh?"

She'd placed an intricately pierced ceramic lamp, like one he might choose for his nightstand, on the corner of her desk. The light, warmer than the fluorescents overhead, gilded the smooth curve of her hair and cast a glowing, dappled circle on the floor. Her long fingers sorted through student papers one by one, each motion precise and beautiful.

He could have watched her forever.

"Not especially," she murmured.

Such a liar. A good one. No tells that he could ascertain.

For some reason, he didn't move. Didn't speak. He just followed her movements as she sorted, then typed, then jotted a few notes to herself on a sticky pad. When she finally lifted her eyes to him again, he blinked like a man awakened from a trance.

Her lips, now pale and dry, thinned. "You need sleep. Go home and go to bed."

She was right, but he didn't move. Couldn't move.

"How did your classes go today?" he asked.

"They were fine." She closed her eyes for a brief moment, her lashes a sweep of darkness. "If you're not going to get home to your daughter and rest, at least sit down, Mr. Krause. Before you collapse."

The same student chair as earlier was calling his name, so he dropped into it with a sigh. "I know you're teaching all U.S. history this year, including AP, but I don't know how many of each prep."

He looked down at himself, listening to his own words—emerging, somehow, from his own mouth—with mingled awe and horror.

Had he truly just sat down in her classroom again? While she was trying to work? And he really just inquired about her schedule? Him, Mute Boy?

She wanted him gone. He didn't make idle conversation, *especially* with people who wanted him gone. So what the hell was Old Sobersides doing? Did he crave another of her smiles that badly?

She rested her elbows on her desk. "I'm teaching two periods of Regular U.S. History and three periods of AP U.S. History."

He leaned forward, astonished. "Three periods? How many students are in each class?"

"Right now, around thirty. But that number will drop a bit, as some of the kids flee from all the homework." She lifted a hand toward her forehead, then dropped it back to the desk. "Which might be for the best, since we don't have enough textbooks for everyone."

He had no explanation for those numbers. None.

"But how is that possible? I only have two periods of AP World, and those classes aren't even completely full." His mouth was open and fish-like, but he couldn't help it. "How in the world did you attract that many kids to your AP classes?"

She met his gaze directly, those dark-amber eyes solemn but not bitter. "Until recently, I taught two periods of Honors World History every year."

Now his own eyes closed for a moment, as everything coalesced in his beleaguered brain.

"And those kids followed you to AP," he finished for her. "Shit. Shit, Rose. I'm sorry."

He wasn't just fucking with her schedule this year. His

presence would change what and whom she taught next year, and possibly for years to come.

She lifted a shoulder in a fluid shrug. "It's fine."

Oh, God, that meeting of AP teachers last week. "The funding for AP programs will drop if our numbers drop. Which they will, since you're not attracting the Honors World History kids to AP U.S."

She didn't deny it. "Only if they drop too much. I'm brainstorming different ways to recruit those kids to my AP classes."

"That's not solely your responsibility. I'm part of the AP program too, and it's my arrival that caused this whole problem." He dropped his chin to his chest, distress shortening his breath. "When my brain is functioning more effectively, I'll come up with some strategies to fix this and run them past you. Rose, I'm so sorry. But I'll come up with something good. I promise."

God, she had to hate him. She must be furious.

But when he forced himself to look up, to face her anger, she didn't look angry at all. Instead, she was holding up a hand, palm forward.

"Martin." Her voice was low. Soothing. "It's okay. None of this is your fault. You didn't choose your preps. And no matter what happens, everything will be fine."

Her gaze was as soft and warm as a quilt fresh from the dryer. The kind he'd once swaddled Bea with when she was sick, or when she'd been outside too long in the snow. Back when Bea needed him.

But for Christ's sake, why was Rose comforting *him*?

Pansy, he could hear his father spit. *Boy's got no spine. Look at him snivel.*

No. He wouldn't listen.

He'd spent too many years erasing that voice with better, kinder, more truthful ones. The voice of his therapist. His daughter. His oldest friends. His students, as they hugged him after graduation and thanked him for caring. His ex-wife, once upon a time.

He breathed as he'd been taught, and his father abruptly went silent.

But he still had no idea how Rose, a woman and colleague he barely knew, could bring back that old panic. That old fear that he'd disappointed and angered someone powerful in his life. Someone important. Someone he—

He needed to go. Now.

When he stood abruptly, her hand fell to her desk.

"Sorry again." With an effort, he kept his voice steady. "I'll make this right somehow. But for now, I'd better get home to Bea, just like you said."

He left her sitting there in her classroom, a halo of golden light surrounding her like a nimbus as she wordlessly watched him go. Then he hustled to the parking lot as fast as he could, the dogs of his past growling and lunging for his heels with every step.

FIVE

When Rose entered the department office, Martin didn't turn her way. Instead, he kept speaking into the clunky office phone, his voice hoarse but impassioned.

"Kevin, I know you have a lot of things going on right now. But I promise you, dropping out now won't help you get where you want to—" Martin paused and rubbed his eyes with his free hand. "I'm so sorry she's sick. Why don't we discuss your options with the guidance counselor? If Marysburg High doesn't work for you, there are alternative sch—"

This time, he went silent for a while as he listened to the agitated voice on the phone.

Rose closed the door quietly behind herself, so quietly she wasn't sure he even heard her.

He was hunched over the counter, elbows resting on the laminate surface, eyes closed. For once, his age had inscribed itself over his features, creasing his brow and bracketing his mouth.

The supply cabinet adjoined the small desk area he'd been given, and she tried not to disturb him as she searched for a ream of colored paper. But he must have heard her heels on the tiles underfoot, because he opened his eyes and gave her a tired little wave.

Waves and passing wishes for a good day were about the extent of the interactions they'd had that week, to her surprise. After his conversational overtures the first day of school, she'd half-expected him to drop by her room more often. First thing in the morning. After the final bell. For a casual chat, or to discuss the AP program, or...

Something. Anything.

She shouldn't be disappointed. She wasn't disappointed. She was merely...nonplussed.

His features relaxed a fraction. "I'll talk to the counselor and have her call you about setting up an appointment. If you want me there, I can attend the meeting too. And remember, you can contact me anytime. Now, next year, whenever. I'll help you the best I can." Another pause. "I'll be thinking of her and wishing her the best. Same for you and your younger brothers and sisters."

She caught his eye, and he didn't look away.

"Take care, Kevin. Remember what I said. I'm here. Just make sure you get to that appointment." His lips curved in a brief, sad smile. "You're more than welcome. Bye."

He hung up the office phone, that blue gaze still holding hers, and she waited.

When he spoke, his voice was quiet. Gravelly with weariness and frustration. "He showed up to class the first couple of days, but not the rest of the week. No note. No phone call. Turns out, his mom is sick. Dying. And someone needs to hold the family together. He was thinking maybe he could do that and still go to school, but now he doesn't think he can."

She nodded, a silent encouragement for him to continue.

His pen bounced when he threw it onto the counter. "He's a kid, Rose. Sixteen. He shouldn't have to watch his mother die. He shouldn't have to take care of his siblings. He shouldn't feel like he has to quit school to do all that."

"You're one hundred percent right," she told him. "It's not fair."

"I'm going to talk to the guidance counselor to set up an appointment and see if there's something else to be done. Some type of help Kevin doesn't know about." He jotted himself a note. "I'm not familiar with all the resources available in this state and this county. But whatever they are, they're probably not enough. I may not be able to fix this."

When her own mother was dying, she'd have sacrificed anything for a figure like Martin in her life. For unselfish concern and an unconditional offer of support. She'd been older than his student at the time, but still rudderless. Still desperate. Still alone, in every essential way.

He was a good man. A good, good man, and he was expecting too much of himself.

"Martin." After a moment, he raised his head. "That kid knows you're waiting to help him. Whatever happens, whatever the guidance counselor says, however the meeting goes, you did the best you could. You're doing the best you can."

He exhaled slowly through his nose, his shoulders visibly relaxing.

Another minute passed before he spoke. "Thank you. I needed to hear that."

Tuesday afternoon, he'd staggered into her office, half-drunk with exhaustion. He'd left wracked by guilt over what his arrival in Marysburg meant for her and the AP program. Too much guilt. So much guilt that she had to wonder yet again who had hurt that man, and how badly.

Whenever she thought about it, those coals in her chest roared to life once more.

How could she keep trying to hate a man who worked that hard? Who cared that much?

She couldn't. She'd given up the fight.

And at this moment, she had to admit it: She liked him. Which made sense, because he was a very likeable person. Thoughtful. Smart. Funny. A great dad. Committed to his students.

Devoid of a wedding ring. Hmmm.

"I've been thinking about ways to keep your AP U.S. History enrollment high." A notebook appeared in his hand, and if anything, those lines scoring his forehead had deepened. "My main thought is that we need to familiarize my Honors World History kids with you and your class before they have to choose their schedule for the next year."

She propped her butt against the counter and rested one slouchy boot-clad ankle over the other. "In the hopes they'll be irresistibly enticed by my teaching prowess, I take it."

His sober mien cracked, and the cologne model reappeared with a smile. "Helpless against your pedagogical wiles."

"How do you want that to work?" She crossed her arms and drummed her fingers against her biceps. "Do you want me to guest-teach your honors classes a day or two? Because we'd need to ask Keisha for permission. You'd have to fill in for my classes, too, and I don't know how comfortable you are with U.S. History."

He dismissed that concern with a flick of his hand. "I taught U.S. history at my old school for a long time, so don't worry about that."

"I could put together a world history lesson that would approximate what they'd experience in my AP class. Primary sources. Critical thinking exercises. Assigned reading and note taking." She squinted in thought. "Maybe something about mummies. Kids love desiccated human remains."

He straightened, blue eyes going bright. "The ancient Egypt unit is my favorite."

"When it comes to world history, mine too." She let herself smile at him without reserve. "So that's the plan?"

"That's the beginning of the plan," he corrected. "During the year, we'll do other crossover lessons and brainstorm some different strategies."

"In case my classroom allure proves insufficient?" The click of her tongue chided him. "Ye of little faith."

"I have great faith in your allure." His smile faltered, and his cheeks turned ruddy. "When it comes to teaching, I mean."

Adorable. Simply adorable. So sweet she might as well call him dessert.

She considered him for a long moment.

His hair might boast a conservative cut and remain an unremarkable gray-templed brown, but it was thick and shiny, and when pieces fell onto his forehead, they somehow emphasized the startling blue of his eyes. He might possess the world's most boring wardrobe and wear a button-down and tie even on teacher workdays, but those clothes covered a lean, capable frame replete with surprising strength. He might wear reading glasses when grading or working on his laptop, but they lent him a sexy professor vibe she didn't mind in the slightest.

And when he smiled, that lean, ascetic face transformed in a way where no one in her right mind could doubt it: The man was sexy. Not to mention educated, intelligent, funny, perceptive, hardworking, and kind.

But none of that would have swayed her, not on its own. She'd turned aside handsome men before, smart ones, even pleasant ones that made her laugh. But Martin did something for her none of those men ever had or could.

With him, she felt...safe.

The man he'd shown himself to be, she couldn't picture trying to make her feel small. Pitying her, rather than sympathizing with her. Hurting her with derision or snide judgment. Talking down to her.

And she could swear he was into her, at least a little bit. He watched her when he thought she didn't notice, and it wasn't always the casual glance of a friendly but professional colleague. He'd blushed when talking about her allure just now. As far as she could tell, he hadn't visited anyone else's classroom for casual chats, not even on that first day.

No one needed to know if they became more than coworkers and casual friends. Not a single soul. Martin seemed more than capable of discretion, and maintaining strict, protective boundaries around her privacy required absolutely no effort on her part. Not after all these years.

So she was doing this, even though her entire history cautioned against it. But the defenses that had kept her inviolate for so long also kept him out, so she was willing to breach them, at least a little bit. At least enough to ask one simple question.

"Martin?" She met his eyes, beat back her incipient panic, and offered a ladder to her tower. "Would you like to go on a date with me?"

MARTIN'S MUSCLES LOST ALL ABILITY TO MOVE, including his tongue.

Which was fine for the moment, because every conceivable answer to her inconceivable question was ricocheting around his overtaxed mind.

Yes! Holy fuck, yes!

No. Nononono.

Excuse me, were you talking to me? Old Sobersides? Are you certain?

She was waiting there patiently for his response, her

round bottom resting against the countertop, her arms crossed. But it didn't seem to be a defensive gesture, oddly enough.

As soon as she'd entered the department office today, he'd noticed the change, despite his preoccupation with the heart-breaking phone call to Kevin.

She'd come to him a woman exposed.

Still impeccably dressed, in a black blouse with big bell-shaped sleeves dipped in gold at the ends and a matching skirt that faithfully molded itself to her bountiful thighs. His mouth had gone dry when he'd first spotted that skirt, those thighs, in the morning.

Her hair sleeked back into a flawless ponytail in the back, and her face formed a perfect ivory-and-pink oval, punctuated by big brown eyes and lush lips. But that face...

That face.

For the first time, she'd granted him the same face she showed her students, his daughter. Expressive. Warm with humor and affection and tolerance. And she'd revealed it not for just a moment, or in response to some stupid joke he'd made. He'd received the gift—and it was a gift, he knew that —of a Rose Owens freed of her self-imposed restraints for the entirety of his phone call and their subsequent conversation.

Then...then she'd asked him on a date.

Again: holy fuck.

Now those crossed arms seemed more a gesture of self-warming than defensiveness, since the department office got chilly at times. He wanted to offer his jacket, but he didn't think it would fit her. Besides, that would involve muscle movement, which was beyond his capabilities at the moment.

"Martin?" Still no impatience.

He wanted to say yes to the woman who'd appeared today. Hell, he wanted to say yes to the woman who'd greeted him in the same department office three weeks ago, icy remove intact. Both those women intrigued him, impressed him, and—unprofessional though it might be—aroused him.

But he'd fled her room in a panic earlier that week for good reason.

He wasn't worthless or weak or mute, or anything else his father and brother had called him. But he'd just emerged from a twenty-four-year marriage with the one and only girl-friend he'd ever had. A simple, straightforward woman, with simple, straightforward needs.

He hadn't been able to meet them. He'd bored the living hell out of her.

So how the fuck could he even pretend he'd be able to give Rose what *she* needed? She was two women in one, and he didn't truly understand either of them, much as he admired both. Her motivations, her desires, her capabilities all eluded his grasp.

Maybe more time spent together would remedy his befud-dlement. But even if he understood her, what exactly could he offer her? A middle-aged, divorced man with Resting Proc-tologist Face mourning the imminent departure of his daughter to college?

Rose was a powerhouse. Gorgeous and complicated and vibrating with authority. She could do better than him. She'd realize that at some point, if the date blossomed into some-thing more.

At the thought of her disappointment, her anger, as he failed to offer what she deserved, all the wild hope that had pinwheeled to life the moment she'd asked him for a date shrank and shriveled into nothingness. He shriveled. Became small and awkward and quiet.

Bullies, he could now handle. A potential lover, not so much.

He tried to swallow. Failed. "Um...thank you so much, Rose."

From his first, halting syllable, her amber eyes sharpened on him, and her spine returned to its usual pin-straight posture. But she was still waiting, still silent, so he needed to continue fumbling through this and offer her an explanation she'd understand. One with a certain amount of truth in it. One that wouldn't humiliate him quite as much as the entire truth.

"I wish I could," he added.

He really did, although her expression didn't seem to indicate an inordinate amount of faith in his sincerity. Dammit.

Then he was talking, talking, talking, desperate for any words that might erase the momentary flash of hurt he'd seen in those amber eyes before they turned frigid. "It's just that I only moved here last month, and I'm still settling into the house. And into Marysburg, for that matter, and the school." He offered her a smile with more teeth than sincerity. "The beginning of the school year is so hard and so exhausting, I don't know how I'd find time for dating. Especially since I have Bea every other week, and she's searching for the right college. Not to mention what might happen if things didn't work out, and we still had to share your classroom and coexist in the same depart—"

She raised a queenly hand. "Enough. I understand."

Uncrossing her ankles, she rose to her full height. She inclined her head, fully encased by whatever restraints she'd snapped into place around herself.

"Please rest assured that this conversation won't need to be repeated." Her fingers, wrapped around a ream of blue paper from the supply closet, didn't tremble, and her eyes didn't lower from his. "I apologize if I've made our working relationship awkward."

She was apologizing? In what world did she need to apologize?

"You didn't." He let out a slow breath, regret seeping into his instinctive panic. "Rose, I don't—"

But she was already turning for the door. Which remained cracked the entire conversation, he now realized. And was opening, inch by inch, to reveal—

Oh, no.

The vulpine face of Dale Locke, suffused with the eager glee of a man who'd finally, finally cornered his prey. Keisha stood beside him, brows drawn in distress.

Martin would like to believe they'd just arrived at the door. That they'd heard nothing.

Dale's first, overloud words smashed that hope. "You'd catch more flies with honey than vinegar, Brandi. Thought you were old enough to know that."

Brandi? Was he talking to Rose?

She held Dale's stare, silent.

To her credit, Keisha tried to intervene. "Dale, she goes by Rose, which you've known for fifteen years. Please call her that. And we can look at the numbers later. We should let them finish their conversation in peace."

But Dale didn't move. Didn't look away from Rose.

God, he must hate her. Loathe her with every fiber of his unfortunate being, every beat of his piggish heart. A woman like her would be a waving red flag to a bully, an invitation to charge and break through that pride, that pristine self-containment.

No wonder he'd fucked with her schedule. No wonder he'd struck at the heart of her AP program. No wonder he'd taken away her classroom for both planning periods.

There she stood, a woman. To be blunt—although Martin didn't consider it an insult, not by any means—a fat woman.

No longer a young woman. Dale's inferior, if only in organizational terms.

But she wasn't conceding an inch. Not in height, not in dignity. Wasn't deigning to acknowledge his faux-jocular insult with a single sound.

Somehow, Dale didn't realize he'd already been beaten. Already declared irrelevant.

"Sorry we overheard your conversation with Mr. Krause." Dale offered a sly grin. "Hope you're not embarrassed."

Each sentence meant its opposite, and they all knew it.

Then Rose smiled, and Martin realized he hadn't truly seen her before now. Not even a sliver of her.

Because that smile was bright and terrifying and cold enough to shatter them all into glittering shards. She'd gone beyond ice. She was absolute zero in female form, so frigid no life could survive in her presence. Certainly not a prick of Dale's insignificance.

"I'm not. Please excuse me." With another glorious, annihilating smile, she left the office.

Dale stepped out of her way, the glee scrubbed from his face as if it had never existed.

And then, for the first time, Martin understood. Not everything, but enough.

He should have realized it before, but he'd been too deep in his own muddled head to piece together an accurate representation of hers.

A woman capable of such sincere, bone-dissolving warmth toward the young and vulnerable didn't armor herself with fierce, chilly composure for no reason.

Rose had dealt with bullies before.

Rose had been hurt. Badly.

Rose would likely understand his own fears. Might have even been patient with them. Might have helped him overcome them.

And because of those fears, he'd just turned down her unguarded overture of interest, hurt her feelings, and pricked her pride. All in front of the last person she'd ever want to see her vulnerable.

His guess? He'd never get another chance. Never see her unveiled and unprotected again. Not as a friend, and certainly not as a potential lover. Not even if they worked together until retirement.

If he could find a spare time machine, he'd go back ten minutes, extract his head from his ass, and then kick that ass until he shouted his acceptance of her invitation, bloody and exultant. But unless the science department had progressed far beyond the state's standards of learning, he had no access to a time machine.

He'd have to find another way into her tower, even though his head swam at great heights, and he imagined there would be thorns aplenty along his climb.

It would require time. Patience. Faith in himself.

He had plenty of the first two, less of the latter.

But he was a teacher, goddammit. He'd learn.

SIX

He'd said no. Of course he'd said no.

To Martin's credit, he'd fumbled through the flustered refusal with seemingly genuine regret, and only after a long, fraught hesitation. But in the end, after all the labored explanations, the answer was simple.

No.

Suddenly, Rose didn't feel so safe after all. Especially after that encounter with Dale.

Vulnerability meant pain. Pity. Judgment. Humiliation. Snide pleasure at her downfall.

She should have known. She *had* known.

Due to her own misjudgments, her privacy had been compromised, her pride wounded. And she knew what she needed to do, to be, now.

Just as she reached her door, Martin exited the department office. Chin high, she stepped inside her classroom with deliberate slowness—he wouldn't see her run or hide from him, ever—only to hear a horrible, horrible sound. Footsteps. Familiar ones, originating from the direction of the office.

Shit. A man like him couldn't let it lie, could he? He'd want to smooth things over. Make sure they left matters on the right note. Reassure himself that she was okay, they were okay, everything was just perfectly, unequivocally okay.

Sure enough, he appeared in her doorway a moment later, his face set in an expression she couldn't quite decipher. She didn't try, either. His emotions did not concern her, and hers had been deposited safely out of his reach.

He glanced at the purse on her desk and her closed laptop. "You're almost done for the evening?"

A lie would reveal too much. "Yes."

"Then I'll walk you to the parking lot."

A direct refusal would do the same. "Won't Dale want to speak with you? Shouldn't you go back to the office?"

"Probably."

He appeared neither bothered by the prospect of Dale's displeasure nor intimidated by her hauteur. Instead, he just stood there and waited for her to gather her belongings.

Once she had, he preceded her out the door, stood quietly when she locked it behind them, and kept her brisk pace down the stairs and toward the main entrance. Once they reached the nearly-empty parking lot, he scanned their surroundings as they walked.

A few feet from her car door—so close to freedom—he finally spoke. "Does Dale have much influence over your career?"

His voice remained low enough not to carry, a gesture she reluctantly appreciated.

She was too tired for subtlety. "Are you asking me how I've avoided disciplinary measures when Dale and I obviously despise one another, and I barely speak to him?"

"I suppose I am." Martin watched her unlock her car with her remote. "If you're willing to answer."

He didn't need to know. Then again, she'd seen no

evidence that he gossiped. So if it would ease that worried furrow in his brow—although she didn't care anymore whether he was anxious, not in the slightest—she could give him the faintest outlines of the truth.

She swung open the driver's side door, and he held it wide. "I have influential friends."

Her former in-laws might have raised an egocentric, pompous ass of a son, but from the beginning, they'd treated her with the generous kindness of doting relatives. Sent cards and called on her birthday. Had thoughtful gifts—midnight-dark cashmere gloves during a cold winter, or DVDs of historical documentaries they thought she might enjoy—delivered to the home she shared with Barton. Taught her how to navigate through the iceberg-studded waters of moneyed society. Inquired about her career and supported her training to become an AP teacher.

After the divorce, she'd assumed that would cease. That they'd turn on her, as almost everyone else in Barton's social circle had. Instead, they invited her to dinner at places where the menus had no listed prices. Suggested shopping trips to stores she could no longer afford and offered to pay for everything. Made their advocacy of her and her career clear to the upper echelons of the school system.

At some point, she'd started accepting a few of those dinner invitations, because Annette and Alfred said they liked good food, and they knew she did too. They said hundred-dollar entrees seemed a small price to pay for such excellent company. They said they might only be first-generation rich because of early, lucky investments in now-giant tech companies—a fact their social circle never allowed them to forget—but they had more than enough money for a few plates of truffle risotto. So occasionally Rose swallowed her pride, along with a glass or two of excellent wine, and let them pick up the check.

A few times a year, she agreed to shopping trips too, because Annette needed someone other than those well-coiffed, ill-intentioned piranhas at the country club telling her what suited her coloring and slight frame. But despite Annette's pleas to buy clothing for them both, post-divorce Rose only accepted gifts on her birthday and at Christmas. She'd rather take impeccable care of the clothing purchased during her marriage and scour consignment shops in expensive neighborhoods than accept charity.

She'd never bothered fighting her former in-laws' attempts at professional protection, though. Margie Owens hadn't raised a fool. Without the Buckham family at her back, Dale would have driven her to a different school district long, long ago. After the first time she ignored his boorish attempts to belittle her. Or maybe when she told him if he hugged her one more time, she'd neuter him where he stood.

Plus, the only time Rose had ever mentioned to Annette and Alfred that she could perhaps handle her own work difficulties, their faces had dropped in unison.

With wounded dismay in every quavering syllable, Annette had whispered, "Rose, my dearest, Barton may no longer be your husband, but we still consider you our daughter. Please let us help you."

And yes, Rose noticed that Annette's stick-straight back suddenly acquired a decided hunch, and Alfred—who ran 5Ks in his spare time—wavered and reached for the back of a nearby chair as if he required a cane. They were incorrigible, and she'd called them on their shenanigans more than once over the years.

But if she'd tried to respond to Annette's words with more than a nod, she'd have wept, not laughed.

They'd served as her protectors for over a decade now, and she had to assume they'd continue to perform that role until the moment they died. Dale could only push Rose so far, and then her former in-laws would push back.

Martin tilted his head, still holding the car door. "Couldn't those influential friends have helped you keep your Honors World History prep and at least one planning period in your own classroom?"

"Perhaps."

She hadn't told her former parents-in-law about either affront. Such powerful weapons as the Buckhams had more impact when sparingly used. Furthermore, she was a damn adult. She'd solve her own problems, as long as those problems didn't involve her having to change school systems.

And above all else, she wanted to stymie Dale's latest machinations on her own, and she wanted him to *know* she'd done it on her own, no outside help needed.

Martin eyed her curiously, but didn't pursue the topic. "I'll see you Monday?"

Only because I have no other choice. "Of course."

Enough. She tugged the door shut, clicked her seatbelt into place, and started her car. He wisely stepped aside as she pulled out of her space. Then she drove home, where a bottle of good Riesling, a wedge of Grana Padano, a crusty baguette, gossamer-thin slices of prosciutto, and a well-worn paperback mystery awaited her return. All the supplies required to help her erase this misbegotten afternoon and repair the stupid, stupid breach she'd made in her own defenses.

Come Monday, those defenses would be as impenetrable as ever.

The Owens girls might take a few punches, but as long as they drew breath, they didn't stay down for long.

Two weeks later, the first intra-department observation assignments arrived via e-mail.

She got Martin. Naturally.

Eventually, of course, she would be observing every other teacher in her department for half an hour at a time, and they would do the same. And she understood the goals behind the initiative—exposure to new pedagogical methods and potential connections with other teachers and across subject areas —but still. Now? As her first observation?

She needed more time with Martin like she needed to sponsor another student organization in addition to the social studies club and the literary magazine. Which was to say, not at all.

To her continued befuddlement, he'd reinstituted his early-morning and late-afternoon visits to her classroom. Sometimes to drop off materials for the next day, sometimes to make certain she knew about some important last-minute meeting or memo, and sometimes for what appeared to be no reason at all.

He just...loitered. Talked in his usual quiet, thoughtful way about his students or his lesson plans or even his daughter. About his impressions of UVA and Charlottesville. About his former student Kevin's grief-stricken decision to earn a GED instead of returning to Marysburg High.

The chatter wasn't overwhelming. Martin was comfortable with silence—which was fortunate for him, since she didn't respond much to his conversational overtures. He also seemed to know when she really needed to concentrate, departing from the room promptly and with a quiet click of the door behind him.

And at least a couple times a week, he somehow figured out when she was about to leave for the night. Because she'd reach for her classroom door handle, purse and briefcase on her shoulder, and voilà! Like magic—the bad kind, where the magician reached into his hat and produced a rubber cock-roach instead of a cute baby bunny—Martin would appear, ready to walk with her to the parking lot.

She could have refused his company. If she did, she knew he'd promptly leave.

But...well...

As far as his classroom visits, she refused to let him know they—he—affected her in the slightest. A request to end the visitations would reveal too much. And when it came to their parking lot walks, the days were getting shorter, and the lot *did* need more overhead lights.

Plus, when her briefcase got heavy with books and grad-ing, he wordlessly held out his hand for it. Hefted it for her. Set it inside her car and waited until she left the lot before he did the same.

Again, she could have denied him his gallantry. She lifted weights at the nearby gym before school three days a week, after all, and she'd been walking alone to the parking lot for umpteen years.

But whenever she handed over her burdens, he didn't become bowed by them. Instead, his shoulders seemed a bit straighter. Whenever he walked beside her, his stride loos-ened and lengthened.

So she'd let him be chivalrous. But she still wasn't chatting.

Once burned, twice no-way-in-hell.

That resolution became harder to maintain once she saw him teach, however.

During her planning period, sitting at her own desk, she watched him greet his AP World History students at the door with a smile, just as she did. Direct them toward an itinerary listing the day's activities, just as she did. Get them going on a start-of-class activity, just as she did.

He'd prepared for the lesson, clearly. His notes rested in

front of him, all the other necessary materials close at hand. His laptop lay open, prepared to project images onto the interactive whiteboard. Again: exactly as she'd have done.

The bell rang, he opened his mouth to discuss ancient Egypt, and that was where the similarity ended.

Where she would gesture with her hands to emphasize a point, he went still.

Where she would get loud, gaining students' attention with liveliness or a bit of sarcasm, he got quieter. More intense. He leaned forward, and his class mirrored the movement.

He was sincere. Knowledgeable. Passionate. Compassionate.

The students were mesmerized. And for good reason.

Martin Krause was a fucking phenomenal teacher.

At the sight of such brilliance, such unmitigated competence, she had to shift a bit in her desk chair. Martin had never, *never* seemed sexier to her.

It really sucked.

And as she soon discovered, so did her reaction to the day's main lesson.

Once he'd finished the class's introductory activities, Martin projected an image of a large granite sphinx onto the board, complete with a human head, a lion's body, and a long, false, angular beard.

He let the students study the image before speaking. "This ancient Egyptian sphinx was made to represent someone named Hatshepsut. Simply from looking at this image, what can you tell me about that person?"

They raised their hands instead of shouting out answers, a sure sign of a well-managed classroom. Those hands belonged to all types of kids, too. Good.

The young woman he called on tilted her head as she eyed

the sphinx. "He must have been powerful. I mean, someone built this for him. And doesn't the lion indicate strength?"

"It does, and you're right. This sphinx represents someone very powerful." Martin smiled at her. "But you made an assumption just then, without noticing. Can you figure out what that was?"

Several other hands shot into the air, but he gave the girl a chance to think.

It took her a few moments, and then a smile slowly broke across her elfin face. "That sphinx isn't a man. It's a woman. With a beard."

"Well, technically, a half-woman. Don't forget the lion bits." When Martin grinned, the class laughed. "But you're right. Hatshepsut was one of several female pharaohs. She ruled from 1478 to 1458 BC, and her reign began a lengthy peaceful, prosperous era in Egyptian history. After a few early, successful battles, she concentrated on forming international trading relationships and overseeing building projects that advanced Egyptian architecture so much, no other country in the world could match it for a thousand years."

His students jotted a few notes, only to glance up when Martin spoke again.

"Now let's compare two other images of her. One from early in her reign, and one from later." The image on the board changed. "This is a statue of Hatshepsut at the Metropolitan Museum of Art." Another picture. "This statue was made later. What are the differences?"

More hands. Lots of them.

"In the early statue, she doesn't have a beard." The young man hesitated. "And she kind of has...uh..."

Martin took pity on him. "She has noticeable breasts."

"Yeah." The boy exhaled. "In the later statue, she's a dude."

"How is that represented?"

"The beard. And she doesn't have"—the boy gestured at his upper body—"those."

Martin nodded. "Other things are different, too. Her chest is broader, her proportions more traditionally masculine. So tell me this: Why do you think the representations of Hatshepsut changed over time?" The image of the pharaoh as a sphinx reappeared. "Why show her like this later in her reign? And why aren't there more images of her as a woman?"

A hand shot up in the back of the room, the student no longer slouched over the desk. "Maybe Hatshepsut was transgender."

"That's an interesting thought, Sam." Martin contemplated the matter for a moment. "Transgender people have certainly existed throughout history, although I haven't heard any evidence in support of Hatshepsut transitioning to become a man. That said, historians can overlook things they don't expect to find. They're products of their era, just like the people they're studying."

Sam nodded, looking...not happy, but something close. Affirmed, maybe?

Whatever it was, Rose wanted to kiss Martin for it.

"Any other ideas?" Martin looked around. "Dante?"

"Did she figure out she had to dress like a man to be taken seriously?" The boy frowned. "You know, because of the way people thought about women back then?"

"Another great thought." Martin acknowledged Dante's comments with an approving tip of his head. "There are certainly many times and places in world history during which a convincing male appearance would have afforded women more power and authority."

His forehead creased in thought. "One thing you'll notice over the course of our year together, though, is that history isn't an inevitable march toward greater freedoms for women and various marginalized groups. Rights can be granted and then removed, and then given again at some point in the future. Or not." He swept a glance over his class. "At this point in Egyptian history, women owned their own property, worked outside the home, received equal pay for equal work, and had equal status under the law. Ancient Egyptians didn't even prefer the word *mankind*. They used *humankind*, written with both male and female figures."

More frantic notetaking by his students.

He spoke slowly and clearly. "In its simplest terms, representing Hatshepsut with a false beard and a male form followed tradition. All pharaohs wanted to resemble Osiris, as a way of emphasizing their connection to him and their power as rulers. Also, evidence shows pharaohs were cleanly shaved, so even male rulers tied on their beards."

A brief pause let his students catch up to him and shake out their cramping hands.

"But many representations of Hatshepsut as a woman didn't just disappear of her own volition. They were razed after her death and replaced by images of her dead husband, who'd been pharaoh before her."

His voice lowered even further, and even the normal shuffling of feet and papers ceased. "Throughout world history, for a variety of reasons, people have erased powerful women, both literally and figuratively, both during their lifetimes and after their deaths. In Hatshepsut's case, her late husband's son did it by destroying her statues. Literal erasure. Other female pharaohs remained undiscovered for centuries because archaeologists assumed they must be men. Figurative erasure. One could even argue that Hatshepsut erased herself in the later statues she commissioned, although I think the issue is more complicated than that."

As his students scrawled once more across their notebooks, Martin bowed his head in apparent thought. Then he looked up and spoke again with quiet emphasis, conviction in every word.

"Which brings up a related point. Sometimes, powerful women throughout history have altered their appearance—in person, or in art." Martin's blue eyes were solemn. "They want to send a certain message. To reinforce their authority. To protect themselves or their legacy. To erase or curate some aspect of themselves to prevent being erased by others."

She refused to look down at her clothing.

The sharp heels. The unrelieved black. The lustrous fabrics. The impeccable tailoring.

"What does curate mean?" one of the kids asked.

"If you curate something, you're choosing what to display and considering how others will see it. You're making sure what gets seen has the intended effect. Does that make sense?"

The girl nodded.

"Men do the same thing, of course. Appearances are important to pretty much everyone," Martin told his students. "But my larger point is this: Powerful women— some famous, some not—have always existed in world history, just as they exist today. There were influential women in every culture, in every time."

He closed his laptop. "In my class, I don't save discussions of women for women's history month, because if we don't talk about women, we're not addressing half the population. If you don't know what they were doing, what rights they did or didn't have, how they affected their culture and government and economy, you don't know history. Period."

After letting that declaration sit for a few seconds, he continued. "The same principle applies to other marginalized groups. History is written by those in power, but those deprived of power deserve to be seen too. For the sake of their humanity, but also because their stories are crucial in understanding world history. Our job this year is to see everyone, not just great leaders. Even leaders as great as Hatshepsut."

In that moment, Rose definitely felt seen by Martin. Whether she enjoyed the feeling or not was less certain.

When her thirty minutes of observation ended, she slipped out of the classroom and returned to the social studies office. She typed a brief but glowing observation report and e-mailed it to Keisha and Martin. Then she pulled out a stack of grading and stared at it, green pen motionless.

She'd just watched Martin—who knew full well she was observing him that particular period—walk his high-school class through a well-considered discussion of gender, power, and the historical erasure of women and the marginalized. Heard him declare with quiet passion that their stories mattered.

That, by inference, her story mattered. That *she* mattered.

Brandi Rose Owens. Born female and poor. Unlikely to appear in any history textbook.

She understood her own worth and power. The choices she'd made to honor the former and preserve the latter.

Now she knew he did too.

But what he'd intended by the lesson, she hadn't the slightest idea.

SEVEN

THE MARYSBURG HIGH SCHOOL SEASONS'
Greetings Festival, as far as Martin could tell, was experiencing a full-fledged identity crisis.

On the one hand, the mid-December gathering featured an inflatable Santa, a giant wooden dreidel, and a colorful, beaded unity cup, not to mention all the baked goods one would expect from a winter fundraising festival. Fudge, fruitcakes, rugelach, sugared doughnuts, sweet potato pies, and more types of cookies than he could count.

His stomach growled, and he tried to remember how much cash remained in his wallet. Not enough, that was for certain.

A veritable blizzard of paper snowflakes hung overhead, and colored strings of light draped over every booth. All appropriate for winter. Fair enough.

But there also appeared to be a limbo contest occurring off to the right. Plastic bags of cotton candy jostled for retail space next to pumpkin pies. An enormous fake palm tree hovered over a selection of grilled burgers and hot dogs for sale. And if he wasn't mistaken, a cluster of girls dressed all in black was gathered around…

A dunk tank? Really? In December?

From behind the circle of girls, he heard a distinct *thunk*. Then a breathless squeak, quickly followed by a splash and gleeful cackles from the surrounding crowd.

Yup. A dunk tank. In December.

"The girls' softball team holds a mean grudge." Keisha appeared next to him, braids swaying with the shake of her head. "It's been two years, and they still haven't forgiven her."

He blinked at her, confused. "Excuse me?"

"You'll see." Keisha grinned. "But you may not believe what you're seeing."

Whatever. He had more pressing questions to ask. For instance: What the actual fuck?

"I don't…" He swiveled his head to survey his surroundings, spotting a hula lesson in the far corner next to a pin-the-red-nose-on-Rudolph game. "I don't quite understand the theme of this festival."

"It's exactly what it says. A Seasons' Greetings Festival. Seasonzzzzz," Keisha emphasized. "Plural."

His brows rose. "I thought that was a typo."

She recoiled. "Are you kidding? The English department would slaughter us all in our sleep if we abused our apostrophes so badly." Her eyes had gone wide, and after darting a look around them, she pointed an accusing finger. "Don't even joke about that."

He raised his hands. "I won't. I promise."

The English department did seem rather intense, now that he thought about it. He should have noticed during the whole Frankenstein Is *Not* the Monster Initiative earlier in the year, given all their posters and morning announcements and costumes and yelling during staff meetings. Not to mention the assembly.

A quality production, but the hand puppets had been overkill.

Keisha directed a hard stare his way. "Good. Anyway, we used to have two festivals. One for winter, another for summer. But we had trouble getting enough volunteers for both, so we merged them into one big fundraiser in the middle of the year. Then the decision had to be made about which season to celebrate, and no one could choose. So Principal Dunn said screw it, let's do both."

"Thus the caroling snow-cone purveyors." He rocked back on his heels. "This festival truly has it all."

"It does." Keisha patted him on his arm. "I need to get eggnog in a coconut before they run out of those little umbrellas. While I do so, I suggest you study the dunk tank a bit more closely."

Bea would want pictures of the festival, since she and her mother were visiting Virginia Tech that weekend, so he got out his cell and wandered in the direction of the splashes and a veritable army of black-clad young women.

After greeting a few of his students and taking several photos—notably, of an island-themed menorah—he finally edged his way through the crowd surrounding the dunk tank. Only to discover a waterlogged, laughing mermaid inside that tank, her red-and-green tail impeding her progress up the ladder to her little wooden seat.

He didn't even recognize her at first. Not with her face devoid of noticeable makeup and her hair plastered to her cheeks and along her neck. Not wearing what appeared to be the top of a short-sleeved wetsuit and a long, fishy tail, both clinging to the generous curves of her body.

Rose. But not the same Rose he'd seen to that point.

"C'mon, Bianca." She finally managed to plop herself back onto the wooden platform. "Take your best shot."

The apparent ringleader of the girls had dyed her curly hair a shade of black that absorbed all light. Her eye makeup did the same, and what he'd guess was naturally golden skin had been powdered to a deathly ivory. A goth, just like all the young women arrayed around her.

Queen of the goths, he amended, as she gestured peremptorily for another softball.

"Give the guy more money," the girl ordered one of her minions. "Ten balls."

The shorter girl dug through an odd-looking wallet—was that black duct tape?—and went to talk to the amused-looking parent manning the outside of the booth.

Rose shrugged. "Hey, I'm here no matter what. My shift doesn't end for another hour." Her nose crinkled in a teasing smile. "Hey, Bianca, did anyone ever tell you your name is kind of ironic? You know, given your wardrobe choices?"

"Like you can judge, Elvira." A fleeting curve of the girl's lips was quickly buried under a forced-looking scowl. "And no, you're totally the first. What an original observation."

"Thank you. What a sincere compliment." Rose peeled a wet strand of hair from in front of her eyes. "Question: Have you considered using your superior softball skills for good, rather than evil?"

Bianca considered that for a moment, tapping a long, shiny black nail against her chin. "No."

Rose laughed. "Fair enough. Although maybe, if you practiced enough, your team could be state champions. Just saying."

"We've been state champions all three years I've been captain, and you know it." Bianca's eyes had narrowed in trumped-up outrage, until all he could see were two black blots in their vicinity. "Get ready to get wet. Again. And when I run out of money, my shortstop is up."

Martin blinked.

Wait. The school's state-champion girls' softball team consisted entirely of goths? Ones who, if he recalled Keisha's offhand comment correctly, harbored some sort of half-joking vendetta against Rose?

No wonder they'd lobbied to change the Marysburg High mascot to a raven last month at the school board meeting.

"More cash for the school, and for our AP programs." Rose flipped her tail in a cheerful taunt. "Bring it on, Perez."

He edged farther to the side, half-behind a sturdy young woman with a nose stud and black boots. If Rose spotted him in the crowd, she might stiffen as she always did in his presence, even three months after his refusal of a date. And he was too fascinated by the scene, by the sight of her grinning and informal and loose, to risk ending it prematurely.

For those three months, he'd been working to regain her trust. Visiting her in the morning and after school. Walking her to her car. Waiting for her to thaw and let him behind her defenses again, so he could return her invitation.

It had sort of worked. A little.

She hadn't asked him to stop his visits, which he'd half-expected and dreaded. And she would now talk to him easily enough about professional matters, if nothing else.

They'd switched classes twice already, in what he considered a very successful tactic to interest his honors kids in AP U.S. History next year. The students had returned from her classroom happy and intrigued, although they still had doubts about the AP workload. But he and Rose had several more months to execute their plans, and he possessed full confidence in her ability to sway his students in her direction.

She'd managed to sway him, after all, despite all his doubts.

Too bad he couldn't seem to do the same for her.

That late afternoon in the social studies office, that brief stretch of time when she'd appeared before him unguarded and soft, had begun to seem more and more like the fever dream of a man obsessed. It wasn't that her regal composure didn't stir and attract him. It did.

He just wanted all of her. Not simply the parts of herself she deemed safe for exposure.

So, no, he wasn't going to interrupt the dunking-in-progress. Because right now, right here, the rest of her sat before him, soaked and laughing and glowing with both cleverness and warmth.

Although, now that he looked more closely, she appeared to be shivering a little.

Dammit, what kind of fools rented a dunk tank in December?

Bianca selected a ball from her minion's fresh supply. "Enjoy your bath, Ms. Owens."

Once she'd retreated behind the designated line, she wound up and threw a perfect pitch. It hit the circular metal plunger with a solid *thunk*, and down went Rose, who descended into the water with a smile and a little gasp.

He got close to the edge of the tank as she surfaced, studying her bare lower arms. Goosebumps. And that ruddy color staining her cheeks didn't come from embarrassment or the tepid warmth of the gymnasium.

She spotted him in the same moment as he spotted the freckles on her nose.

Christ, they were a punch in the gut. Adorable and…well, *vulnerable*. He wanted to kiss every exposed speckle, then move downward. Then downward again, until she was gasping for reasons other than submersion in chilly waters.

"Mr. Krause." She slicked her hair back from her face, her smile fading. "I didn't see you."

"I know." If she'd seen him, she'd have hidden herself. Like she was doing now, without ever moving a single millimeter.

Quick conversations before and after the school day clearly weren't sufficient to complete the quest he'd undertaken. More extreme measures would have to be taken.

He emptied his pockets and put their contents in a dim corner behind the tank, removed his watch, and toed off his shoes. "I came to relieve you. Your shift in the dunk tank is over."

Her lips parted, revealing chattering teeth, and he was suddenly, fiercely glad he was preparing to take an icy dip. Whether she ever softened toward him again or not didn't matter. The sight of Rose chilled and shivering was unbearable.

She dashed water from her eyes and squinted at him. "No one told me you'd volunteered for this. Besides, I've only been here for an hour."

He loosened his tie, but didn't bother to remove it. The amusement inherent in dunking a teacher fully dressed in work clothes should provide incentive for students to stay, despite Rose's departure.

"It's December." He held out a hand, waiting for her to ascend the little metal ladder and climb out with his assistance. "Sixty-minute shifts, max."

"But I wanted to dunk her nine more times," Bianca protested. "Then sic a few of my girls on her. Otherwise, what's the point of having a vendetta?"

"I can't disappoint the students, Mr. Krause." Rose struggled back up to her seat, ignoring his hand. "Consider yourself off-duty."

He dropped his arm to his side and thought for a

moment. Clearly, his extreme measures required additional research. As a historian by training, he should have known.

He swiveled to study Bianca. "Why are you so determined to dunk Ms. Owens, anyway?"

A snort sounded behind him, a noise he hadn't heard for over three months. To his ears, it might as well have been a recital by the school's handbell choir.

"Yes, Bianca." Rose flapped her tail. "Tell Mr. Krause why you've carried a grudge for two years and graciously shared that grudge with your entire softball team."

The girl with the nose stud swung to face her captain. "You've never actually told us the full story, Bianca."

Bianca shifted, black-painted lips tightening.

"Yeah," her minion with cornrows and a skull t-shirt said. "I've always wondered."

After five seconds of silence, Bianca broke.

"Fine." She sighed heavily. "Fine. I was in Ms. Owens's world history class sophomore year, and we could pick the subject of our end-of-year research project. She said we could choose any topic important to world history. *Any.*"

Her pause stretched and stretched, and he couldn't wait. He had to know. "What did you pick?"

"Slendermffffff," she muttered.

"What did she say?" Nose Stud looked to him. "I didn't hear it."

Another period of fraught silence ensued.

"Slender Man, all right?" Bianca finally said. "I wanted to do my end-of-year project on Slender Man, and Ms. Owens said no. Which was totally a betrayal, because look at her. She's clearly a goth who got locked in a Nordstrom and wasn't allowed to leave until they assimilated her somehow. Probably at the MAC counter."

Skull Tee wrinkled her nose. "Didn't you get those ripped black jeans with the safety pins from Nordstrom? I thought your parents took you for your birthday. You wouldn't shut up about their café and their stupid bread pudding for like a week."

"Slender Man?" Nose Stud shook her head. "That's so over. What the heck, Bianca?"

"It was two years ago." Bianca crossed her arms, her lower lip extending. "Slender Man was a thing."

Skull Tee tapped the toe of her Chucks. "Dude. Get over it. Do you know how many real-life massacres and murders you could have researched instead? I mean, Lizzie Borden?"

Yet more silence.

"Fine." Bianca dropped her arms and glared at Rose. "Consider the vendetta cancelled."

And there it was. Victory.

He smiled and turned to Rose. "If there's no more vendetta, they can dunk me instead of you. Come on out."

Her brow had beetled, and she didn't climb out of the tank. Instead, she tilted her head toward Bianca, eyes pleading with him for...something.

Dammit.

A single glance at the young woman revealed everything. She seemed deflated. No longer gleeful. And her team shifted behind her, uneasy.

Fine. He could fix this too.

"Hey, Bianca." He rolled up his sleeves, not that it would matter in a minute. "Let's talk about how overrated Tim Burton's films are."

Her shoulders slowly pulled back. "What did you just say?"

Once again, he extended a hand to Rose. This time she took it, and the explosion of prideful glee inside him might have been disproportionate, but he didn't care. A win was a win.

"You heard me. Quirk does not always equal quality."

Once Rose was dripping safely on the polished wood floor of the gym, the parent manning the booth handed over a plush towel and a bundle of clothing. Martin draped the towel over Rose's shoulders, using its corners to blot her eyes and cheeks in careful dabs.

"Oh, I heard you. Ladies?" Bianca stretched her pitching arm. "Did you hear Mr. Krause too?"

Nose Stud cracked her knuckles. "Oh, yeah."

"You're mine, Mr. Krause. I'm watching you." Skull Tee pointed two fingers at her eyes, then at his. "I call next turn."

"No one insults Tim Burton." Bianca paused. "Except about issues of diversity and maybe gender dynamics." Another pause, and then she recovered herself. "No one."

A pool had formed beneath Rose, and her tail squished as she widened her stance.

"Don't fall on the wet floor," he told her, unable to stop himself.

Seventeen-plus years of Dad training. He couldn't abandon it at a moment's notice.

She sighed, but her lips curved. "Thanks for that necessary tip, Mr. Krause."

One more swipe of those adorable freckles. Then he forced his fingers to release the towel, handed her the clothing bundle, and entered the tank.

The wooden seat below him tilted a bit to the front, ready to drop, and droplets of chilly water soaked through his pants. The bluish pool waited beneath. Its chlorinated water smelled like triumph.

He grinned at Rose, who'd wrapped the ends of her hair in her towel and commandeered another cloth to wipe the floor. She smiled back, amber eyes warm and unguarded.

"Thank you," she mouthed.

His chest expanded in a heady rush, but he forced his attention back to the softball team's captain. "I'll repeat:

Burton's movies are overrated. Especially *Edward Scissorhands*. What are you going to do about it, Perez?"

"I'll give you one guess."

Her smirk preceded another perfect pitch, and down he went.

Fuuuuuuck. That water...Jesus. How had Rose survived an hour of this?

But she was still waiting, still watching, still smiling when he resurfaced with a shudder, and nothing, nothing in his recent past had felt so horrible but so good.

He'd splash into freezing water for that.

Ruin a perfectly good silk tie for that.

Above all, continue believing—in himself and what he could offer her—for that.

For her.

Only, only for her.

EIGHT

ROSE FROWNED AT HER REFLECTION IN THE window. Then once more, at the sight of her Audi parked snugly beside Martin's Subaru in the darkness beyond the plate glass.

Somehow, she seemed to have waited for his shift in the dunk tank to finish and given him clean towels and sweats she'd scrounged from the boys' locker room. Somehow, she seemed to have accompanied him to a coffee shop after the festival.

Somehow, she seemed to have forgotten the importance of a safe distance from him. From everyone except her students, her former in-laws, and a few trusted friends from college.

Because somehow, there she sat, her hair still damp and tucked behind her ears, no makeup on. Wearing a gray sweatshirt and sweatpants, also appropriated from the boys' locker room lost and found box, because he'd stared at her original choice of clothing—suitably chic, suitably black, maybe not so suitably lightweight—with such horrified dismay and so many inquiries about possible hypothermia.

Her spike heels added a little something extra to the outfit, she imagined.

She cradled her mug of coffee and blew on its steaming surface. Across from her, Martin did the same, his blue eyes intent on her bare face.

Yes, something had clearly misfired in her brain.

But the man was a terrible liar. Just awful. There was absolutely no way in hell he'd ever intended to staff the dunk tank until he'd seen her plunge into the icy water. He'd come to the booth with no towel. No bathing trunks or wetsuit. No extra changes of clothing. No excuses to offer when Keisha found him in the tank and loudly wondered what in the world he was doing.

No, he'd clearly intended to watch the festivities and consume mango salsa-topped latkes—very tasty—and go home just as bone-dry as when he'd arrived.

One look at her goosebumps, and he'd taken off his shoes and prepared for submersion.

And the way he'd dabbed at her face with that towel, his brow furrowed in concentration, his touch as light and soft and warm as a cashmere throw…

No. She wouldn't think it again. Wouldn't feel it again.

He didn't make her feel safe.

Not in the slightest.

But she supposed maybe they could be friends. Of a sort. With strict boundaries to protect her from any undesired emotional consequences.

And friends had coffee together, right? No big deal. No panic necessary.

"Black, huh?"

She blinked, abruptly aware that she'd been so busy thinking about Martin Krause that she'd paid no attention to the actual, physical man two feet away. "Uh, what?"

His fingertip nudged her mug. "You take your coffee black. I should have known."

"Black and bitter." She couldn't resist adding, "Like my heart."

He raised a skeptical brow. "Right. Because people with black and bitter hearts often staff dunk tanks to fundraise for their schools and provide vendetta-based amusement for students."

"All part of one of my evil schemes." She battled to keep her face solemn. "A complicated one involving mermaid tails and goth softball teams."

With a tip of his mug, he saluted her. "That does sound complicated. Good luck."

"I don't need luck. Merely guile and misanthropy."

Cologne Ad Man reappeared with a grin. "No wonder you wear all black. You're clearly the villain in this particular melodrama."

"The cliché is correct: Villains get all the best lines. Besides, they drive the plot." The long night had definitely caught up with her. She had few filters remaining between her brain and mouth. "And women often get cast as villains for trying to be the heroes of their own stories, so better to embrace the role from the start. Make it your own."

He bowed his head to blow on his coffee once more, shielding his expression. "That's the reason for all the black clothing?"

"Well, I'm not on the girls' softball team, so it's not that." A long sip of her coffee bought her a moment to think. "The best black clothing doesn't ask to be liked. It's uncompromising." She exhaled in a long sigh. "There's a lot of black clothing for women my size, but most of it was created to facilitate the disappearance of the woman wearing it. To erase her from sight in apology for her existence as a fat woman. That's not the kind of black clothing I wear. Mine has metallic accents. Bold lines. Quality fabrics. Good tailoring. All unmistakable markers that I'm not apologizing or looking to disappear."

"Those heels don't hurt the cause either."

She extended one silver-veined stiletto under the café lights. "No, they don't."

His brow furrowed. "Or maybe they do hurt. They don't look particularly comfortable."

"I don't intend to present a more comfortable version of myself for anyone. Even me."

Yes, sometimes her feet ached, and she longed to relax into flip-flops or Crocs or Uggs or whatever comfortable, hideous shoes were currently popular. But discomfort was a small price to pay for the safety of an inviolate, immaculate shell.

He spoke slowly. "Yet here you are. In sweats."

For him.

Her breath hitched, and her hand jerked in the direction of her purse.

Shit. Shit, this was a mistake.

"I'm worried about Sam," he abruptly announced. "I was hoping to talk to you about them."

She'd had a few concerns herself, simply because of the student's situation, so she settled back into the pleather-tufted chair. "Go on."

"I haven't seen any bruises. But we both know kids like them can have a rough time at home, depending on the parents. They have a single dad, and he hasn't returned my messages for months." He grimaced. "I've talked to Sherry in guidance, but she hasn't had any more luck than me. As long as Sam keeps coming to school on time and getting decent grades, there's not much more I can do."

Another sip of her coffee helped corral her thoughts. "Have you spotted any signs of abuse?"

"I don't know." His mouth twisted. "They're guarded. All I can say is that when they arrive in the morning, they look unhappy. And they stay late after school. For yearbook a couple days a week, but sometimes for no particular reason I can figure out."

"Any idea whether they're being bullied in school?"

"I've asked. Sam says no, and they seem sincere." He slumped backward in his chair. "There could be nothing wrong. Sam could just be a teenager going through a rough patch for all the typical teenage reasons, compounded by the emotional upheaval of transitioning. But if there's a problem, I think it's at home."

His leg was bouncing. He was agitated, clearly concerned for his student.

But she couldn't help but wonder whether there was more going on than that.

"Did Sam's father come to a parent-teacher meeting?"

Bounce, bounce, bounce. "Once. Right after school began."

"How did he seem?"

"Fine. Friendly enough. But parents can fake it for quick meetings." His jaw turned stony. "I know that from personal experience."

She shouldn't ask. Not if she intended to keep a certain distance.

Which she did. Definitely. But they were friends now, right? And a friend could ask certain questions.

Especially when those coals in her chest were aflame, and rage had darkened her vision. The thought of a parent—or anyone—abusing the man seated across from her...

If they ever showed up at Marysburg High, she'd eviscerate them. And laugh.

She imagined black could hide a lot of bloodstains.

Despite her anger, she kept her voice calm. Low. Steady.

"If you're willing to talk about it, I'd like to hear more about that personal experience."

His gaze focused on a point in the distance. She swiveled to see what had drawn his attention, but there was nothing there.

She turned back and waited, unsure which answer she really wanted from him.

After a long moment, he met her eyes again. "Sure. I'll tell you."

———

MEN DON'T WHIMPER ABOUT THEIR FUCKING FEELINGS, PANSY BOY.

But Martin's father had been wrong about that, as he was about so much else.

Swallow enough hurt in silence, and the pain either chokes you or curdles into gut-deep rage.

His dad's version of manhood would destroy you one way or the other. Which Martin, after so many years of mute suffering, had eventually realized. In the end, he'd drawn out most of the poison through talk therapy. Through acknowledgment of his emotions. Through vulnerability, rather than a pretense of strength.

His father's voice became his college counselor's. *Vulnerability is strength, Martin.*

He believed it. He could only hope Rose did too. At least when it came to others.

Her eyes were sharp on him, but not cold. Not judgmental.

So he pulled in a breath and told her...not everything. But enough for now. "My father had very specific ideas about how boys should act and think and be. About how his sons in particular should act and think and be."

She'd laced her fingers together on the table in front of

her, but not in a relaxed way. As if she were holding them back from doing something infinitely more destructive.

But her voice was soft and sweet as whipped cream. "Such as?"

"They should be good at sports. They should shout over other people. Make a mess. They should have lots of equally loud and messy friends. They should get laid early and often. Tell bitches to shut up and fuck off if they got too bossy or clingy." He sighed. "His words. Not mine."

"I know." Her fingers had turned bone-white in her own grip. "Go on."

"Boys shouldn't care much about school or grades, or anyone else's feelings. Shouldn't like keeping their mom company as she cooked. Shouldn't join Model UN. Shouldn't cry if they got hurt or try to disappear during an argument." He tried on a smile. It didn't quite fit. "Basically, they shouldn't be me."

"That sounds..." Something popped in the vicinity of her jaw. "That sounds really painful."

"My older brother took after our father. Things could get"—he chose and discarded various adjectives —"interesting."

She enunciated the quiet words one by one, each seemingly an effort. "By *interesting*, do you mean *violent*?"

"Sometimes."

But his father and Kurt hadn't required spatulas or fists to inflict pain. Their scorn for him, for everything he said and did and was, hurt worse than a few bruises.

Her nostrils had flared wide open, but the warmth in her gaze could have dissolved sugar into syrup. "Where was your mother in all this?"

At the stove, carefully not watching what happened around her. Retreating to her bedroom immediately after she'd cleaned up the remnants of their dinner, while the men watched sports and got mean. "Doing her best to stay out of the way. The same as me."

"The difference is—" She cleared her throat, the noise harsh. "The difference is that she was an adult, while you were a child. Her child."

"She did her best to protect my younger sister, Mila."

As far as he knew, no one in the family had heard from Mila for over a decade. Not even his mother. Last he'd heard, his sister was somewhere on the west coast, working in finance.

When Rose set down her mug, it clattered against the marble table. "But you didn't need your mother's protection. Because you were a boy."

Enough. This recitation of his past didn't hurt him, not anymore. But he was pretty certain she was about to grind a molar to dust.

She might bat him away, but...

He reached across the table and covered those twisting fingers with his palm. "Rose. It's okay."

Her gaze whipped to his, so full of anguish and rage his stomach twisted. "It's not. It's not okay. Not even a little bit."

"It wasn't." One by one, he disentangled her fingers before she broke something. "But it is now. I haven't seen my father or brother in over twenty years. I have an amazing daughter. I have a job I love. And if I need her again, I have a great therapist on call. Everything is fine."

Rose made an odd sort of grunting sound, clearly unappeased, and he fought the sudden urge to laugh.

All that passion and compassion, all for him. Or at least, for the boy he'd once been.

And she was the villain in this story? Like hell. Black or no black, she was no evil queen. Much as she might like to pretend otherwise.

Muscle by muscle, her hands relaxed under his. "How long have you been divorced?"

"A couple of years." He'd filed the papers after finding Sabrina's damning texts, but the process took a while. "She got engaged a few months ago and moved to Marysburg. I didn't want Bea to have to choose between us for her senior year, so I followed."

Her mouth opened, then closed. Then opened again.

He could have sworn she was about to ask for more details, and he would have shared some. Although, in all honesty, that particular wound was much rawer than his childhood terrors, not to mention much more relevant to his brief but fraught history with Rose.

If his quest to breach her walls progressed much further, she'd need to know. But he didn't think they'd reached that waypoint yet.

To his relief, she unzipped her purse instead of inquiring further.

"Need to leave a tip," she muttered. "There's a five somewhere in here."

He reached into the sweatpants pocket for his wallet. "I've got it."

She pinned him with a gimlet stare. "I thought you weren't beholden to traditional rituals of manhood."

"Apparently, therapy didn't fix everything." He adopted a helpless expression. "Blame our nation's mental health infrastructure."

Her snort drew the amused gaze of the barista. "Smartass."

"I'm hurt you would say that." He plucked out a few bills. "Very hurt."

Her squinty-eyed scrutiny narrowed even further. "If I put my own money on this table, are you going to find some way to slip it into my purse later?"

His mouth dropped open in genuine astonishment. How had she known?

"That's what I thought." She rezipped her purse. "Fine. I'll let you provide for the little lady tonight. Next time is mine."

Next time? She wanted a next time?

Why hadn't he risked hypothermia in an overly-chlorinated tank before now?

They walked to the parking lot in a comfortable silence.

When they reached her driver's side door, she turned to face him. "For now, I'd just keep an eye on Sam and tell them you're always available if they want to talk. Next time I see them, I'll try to chat and form some sort of connection too." Her lips curved in a wry smile. "I don't think being a grumpy teenager who stays late at school merits much more intervention at this point, although I understand why you're worried."

He nodded. "I agree."

But he'd be watching closely, and he knew Rose would too.

After he opened her car door, Rose eased inside and tossed her purse onto the passenger's seat. Buckling her seatbelt, she spoke without looking at him. "You know you're just as much a man as your father and brother, right?" The buckle clicked into place. "And more importantly, you're a better human."

The last bit was kind of mumbled, but he caught it.

An outright compliment. God bless winter-festival dunk tanks.

"Being a man doesn't even require a Y chromosome or a penis." Martin grinned. "So yeah, I know I'm a man despite my master's degree and shameful lack of dunking skills."

She didn't try to tug the door from his hands. Instead, she

glanced up at him as the winter wind blew a strand of her hair across her cheek. "See you Monday?"

When he carefully tucked the strand back behind her ear, he could have sworn she nuzzled into his touch for a millisecond. "See you Monday."

That dunk tank manufacturer was totally getting a thank-you note in the morning.

NINE

Halfway through seventh period, the fire alarm blared to life.

No surprise there. The school ran a drill monthly, and they'd reached the final day of January and the final period of the school day. Rose imagined someone in the front office had seen a calendar somewhere, checked for previous drills that month, muttered a silent *oh, shit*, and heaved a sigh while pulling the red handle.

In theory, she should depart the copy room and join the teachers and students streaming toward the exits. Their voices, raised in both laughter and complaint—because it was freaking cold outside—echoed in the hall just outside the closed door of her little sanctuary.

In reality, a staff meeting was starting ten minutes after the final bell. The copy room would be mobbed both before and after the meeting, so if she ceded her territory now, she'd be lucky to get her packets done before sunset. Besides, this was her damn planning period. She wasn't giving up fifteen minutes of it to tromp around school grounds.

It was cold out there. A bit slippery too. And her heels didn't have much traction.

Small though it was, the copy room contained a thread-bare but overstuffed chair she could occupy during the less labor-intensive parts of packet creation. The heat from the machines kept the space toasty, and fresh stacks of copies warmed her hands better than gloves.

Nope. No way in hell she was leaving that room.

She added more paper to the appropriate tray, forced the machine to accept her top-loaded packet—damn copier should have been replaced before the turn of the century—and fiddled with the settings. Collation, definitely. Staples. One step darker than default, as per usual. Two-sided copies required another battle, but she prevailed.

All the pages appeared to load correctly. Hallelujah.

Then she was lounging in the chair, warm and peaceful, as the machine chugged next to her. And if she tweaked the blinds just a tiny bit...

There. In full view of her window, Martin had guided his students from her classroom out to the frozen tundra. As she watched, he urged them to don their jackets and circulated among the different factions that naturally formed as soon as the kids stopped walking.

Such a good teacher. Such a good man.

She had no idea why his ex-wife had let him go, but there was no way—no fucking way—that woman's new fiancé could outshine Martin in intelligence, wry humor, or sheer human decency.

He bent over to study something on the ground, and Rose almost bit her tongue in two.

Not to mention that round, taut ass. Jesus.

She'd almost asked him about his marriage so many times over the past month or so, but always stopped herself before the words could emerge.

That night in the coffee shop last month, he'd exposed himself to her judgment, to her potential ridicule or incomprehension, as he told the story of his childhood. He'd trusted her to listen and understand, and she hoped to God she'd done a decent job of both, despite her raging hatred of almost his entire fucking family.

She understood the weight and gift of that trust. The strength required to make such a valuable, fragile offering.

But for all the friendly, private conversations and coffeehouse visits they'd had since then, she hadn't offered her own trust, her own history, in return. So she didn't have the right to ask for more intimate revelations about his marriage, his relationship with his ex-wife, or anything else.

Still, she wanted to know. She wanted it more than she wanted the truffle risotto at Milano, and that was saying a lot.

Without warning, Martin straightened, about-faced, shielded his eyes from the sun, and looked directly at her window. With a small, secret smile creasing his face, he gave his head a disapproving shake. *Naughty, naughty, naughty.*

She offered him a taunting, wiggling wave of her fingers in return.

With exaggerated gestures, he wrapped his arms around his torso and shivered. Shuddered, actually, his expression so pitiful she actually laughed out loud in the copy room. In response, she plucked at the sleeves of her fitted sateen jacket and slid her arms free, removing it in a slow, deliberate glide to show just how warm she was. Warm enough to lounge in just a thin, silky blouse.

Below her, he went absolutely still on the frozen grass.

Which was weird, because why would removing her jacket—

Hold on. Had she just stripped for him? In the copy room?

It was just a jacket, but still. What about stripping said *friendly distance*?

Then, to her horror, their principal wandered into view. Tess said something to Martin, but he didn't appear to hear. Instead, he was still staring up at the copy room window. Tess swiveled to follow his stare.

Somehow, before Rose gathered enough wits to leap away from the damned window, he'd maneuvered himself and Tess so he stood between her and the sight of a teacher who'd ignored a mandatory fire drill.

Rose snapped the blinds shut, exhaling with a whoosh.

Get your head straight, Owens.

She would. She would. Just as soon as she figured out how.

At the staff meeting, she waved at Martin when he entered the cafeteria, and he settled in the seat next to hers. While she skimmed the handout on the table, he dug through his briefcase for something.

At the bottom of the paper, she noticed a thumbnail picture of the presenter. Ed Barnes.

Shit. Should've gulped down more coffee before coming.

"It's the same consultant we saw before the start of the school year," she whispered. "The superintendent's latest overpaid pet. We're in for a loooooong afternoon."

From the depths of his briefcase, Martin produced a metallic thermal bottle. The generous lid popped right off, and he flipped it over. A cup.

Clearly, he'd planned better for this meeting than she had.

He hefted the bottle and carefully poured his steaming coffee into the cup, and she almost wept in envy.

Then he nudged the cup directly in front of her.

Oh, she wanted it. But she couldn't. She couldn't.

"It's yours. You should have it." With sorrow in her soul, she slid it back in front of him. "If I fall asleep, please elbow me. And if I die of boredom, please scatter my ashes directly in front of the presenter, so he accidentally breathes me into his sinuses and gets an infection."

He grinned and moved the cup beneath her nose. She tried not to moan in need.

"I had plenty of coffee after the fire drill. Because some of us needed to warm up more than others." His lips quirked. "This is dark roast, by the way. Black and bitter."

"Like my heart." She snorted, still amused at the running joke. "Anyway, I'm only warm due to my superior metabolism. I went outside, of course, just like you."

He inclined his head. "Of course."

It was his coffee, and she really shouldn't rely on him for anything. But it smelled like the sort of coffee a god might offer when he swooped down from Mt. Olympus and impregnated some mortals. Caffeinated ambrosia. Seduction in liquid form.

Martin leaned close and whispered, "Rose, stop eye-fucking the coffee and just drink it."

His breath, a waft of warm air. His mouth, so close to her ear...

She shivered as a tingle of arousal eased down her spine.

At the first tap of the microphone on the impromptu dais, she pulled herself together. "Language, Mr. Krause."

But she drank his coffee, and as she did, she could see him watching her mouth.

Once she'd gulped down the heavenly contents of his cup —and then the second cup he poured for her—her thoughts cleared enough to remember the special treat she'd prepared for the meeting. Although she hadn't known the name of the presenter beforehand, anytime their superintendent hired a consultant, certain things were a given.

As Principal Dunn reminded everyone of the presenter's qualifications with the polite but unenthusiastic tone of a woman who'd been ordered to waste an hour of a staff meeting for no good reason, Rose produced two small squares of paper from her own briefcase. Then folded them in half so no one else at their table could read the print on the grid.

Discreetly, she tapped Martin's knee under the table.

He jumped, turning to her in a startled rush, and she rolled her eyes and removed her hand.

Real smooth, Krause.

When their curious colleagues had turned back to the presenter, she tapped his knee again—this time, he managed to remain composed—and tipped her head downward, indicating that he should look beneath the table. Once he did, he eased a hand down below, and she pressed the folded paper in his palm.

At the ridiculously brief contact of skin to bare skin, she almost jumped herself.

Hunched, protecting the sight of the paper with his arms and hands, he unfolded her little project. It took him a moment, but then Handsome Cologne Man reappeared with a slow, pleased smile. His hand disappeared beneath the table, and he wiggled his fingers, gesturing for her own paper. She passed it over, and he read that too, the creases at the corners of his eyes deepening with his amusement.

"Bingo?" he mouthed. "Really?"

She scrawled in her notebook and turned it so he could see. *Loser buys coffee next time.*

After a moment, he wrote a response on his legal pad. His gaze steady, he watched her read his message. *What does the winner get?*

Whatever he or she wants, her fingers wrote, entirely without direction from her brain.

Like he had at the sight of her copy room striptease, he went very still for a moment.

His lips parted, and his handwriting became a bit choppy. *High stakes indeed.*

They were. Higher than any she'd allowed for a long, long time.

Resolutely, she turned back to the presenter and attempted to pay attention. For the sake of professionalism, naturally, but also so she wouldn't miss any of the educational buzzwords on her bingo sheet.

Some of the concepts Barnes espoused were helpful, but they weren't anything she or Martin hadn't heard a million times before. In some cases, decades before, only couched in different terminology. So a little frivolousness at this meeting wouldn't hurt either of them. And as everyone knew, teachers made absolutely terrible students, so she and Martin weren't doing anything worse than, say, Mildred over there, with her crossword puzzle in her lap. Or Becky and Rasheed, who were whispering to each other. Or Jia, whose discreet game of cell phone solitaire seemed to be progressing nicely.

"Let's discuss the most important parameters for student success," Barnes began.

The game was afoot.

She'd chosen *growth mindset* as the center square for both boards, so it was essentially a free space. Within a minute after the presentation began, she and Martin had marked it off.

Differentiation. Stakeholders. Entrepreneurial.

Dammit. Those were words she'd given Martin, and he made a low, pleased hum as he crossed through each of them.

Fifteen minutes later, Martin was silently exulting in his imminent triumph. Either of two separate phrases would give him bingo: *high-impact* or *research-driven*. And since Barnes was about to start discussing assignments, she was probably fucked.

So thoroughly fucked.

She shifted in her seat as her imagination ran with that image, ran until it was flushed and breathless and sweaty.

With effort, she dragged herself back to the tasks at hand. Professional development. Bingo. And then, to her pleased shock, Barnes took it old-school.

"As you're aware," he intoned, "we need to ensure through our choice of grading rubrics and our communications with students that we encourage grit and resilience. Along with making certain our assignments require a certain amount of rigor, problem-based learning—"

Grit and *resilience*? Just for kicks, she'd included those passé buzzwords in her bingo board, but she'd never expected them to come up. It wasn't 2014, after all.

Martin glanced over at her paper, his brow creasing in newfound worry.

Well, he should be worried. Because all that stood between her and bingo now was—

"—digital literacy," Barnes said.

Bingo.

Martin's entire face sagged, and she gave his arm a quick pat of consolation.

I'm getting a trough of coffee next time, just so you know. No, a vat, she wrote.

He gazed at his notepad for a minute before writing back. *It's on me. Congratulations.* After another long pause, he added, *Is that your prize? Or do you want something else?*

His handwriting stayed within the lines. Marched across the page, precise and orderly.

She stared at it for a minute as she held onto good sense by the tips of her ebony-polished fingernails.

I think, she wrote slowly, *maybe I—*

Perfunctory applause punctured her confusion, and she quickly flipped her notebook shut. The other teachers at their table gathered belongings and stared expectantly at the temporary dais.

"Thank you so much, Mr. Barnes," Tess said. "I think everything else we need to address can be covered via e-mail, so go forth and enjoy the rest of this chilly afternoon, everyone."

More applause, this time enthusiastic, and the exodus from the cafeteria began.

Once the rest of the table had emptied, Martin watched himself slowly cap his pen. "So? What's your prize?"

His voice had turned low. A bit tentative.

Just then, Keisha appeared at their table. "Ms. Owens, I'd like to speak with you for a minute, if possible."

Shit. Had she seen the bingo game? Or realized two of her teachers were writing notes to each other during the presentation? But if so, why hadn't she requested a meeting with both of them?

"Of course." Rose deposited her papers and notebook into her briefcase, making sure the bingo board got buried in a pile of memos. "Would you like to meet in my classroom?"

Keisha shook her head. "I have a doctor's appointment. Let's talk on the way to the parking lot, if that's all right with you."

"Sure," Rose said.

As she and Keisha turned for the cafeteria door, Martin was watching them both, his pen still clutched in his hand. She offered a little wave, which he returned, and then she left.

Once they'd exited the school, Keisha repositioned her

briefcase on her shoulder and glanced at Rose. "Ms. Owens, I'm aware that this has been a difficult year for you, and I want to reiterate my thanks for your professionalism in dealing with the challenges you've faced. Especially given the source of those challenges."

Her voice was low. Too low for the handful of other teachers in the parking lot to hear.

"If there's anything I can do to help you bolster next year's AP U.S. History enrollment, please tell me. And you should know that I'm advocating for you at every level of administration. Including at Central Office. You might not always be aware of those efforts, but they're happening."

Dale. Keisha was trying to shield Rose from Dale. Had been trying for years, most likely. Which wasn't a surprise, really, but...

Dammit, sometimes keeping a safe emotional distance from her colleagues sucked.

They'd reached Keisha's shiny red compact, and Rose paused for a moment to collect herself before speaking.

Still, her voice was a bit too thick. Too husky. "Thank you. I'm very grateful for your support."

Shit. Keisha deserved more than that.

Rose forced herself to keep going. "I'm lucky to have you as my department chair, and I realize it." The truth, although she generally avoided revealing such personal information to her colleagues. "I know Martin feels the same way."

He wouldn't mind her telling Keisha that. Rose had heard him say similar things to their supervisor before.

Keisha paused with her keys in her hand. "Thank you. I've always felt fortunate to have such dedicated, caring teachers in my department. You and Martin are exemplary educators."

Okay. Enough of this.

Rose edged a few inches toward the school. "Thank you again. Is there anything else you wanted to discuss?"

Another long pause. Then Keisha exhaled through her nose and set down her briefcase.

"Nothing from a supervisory perspective. But..." She pursed her lips. "This is awkward, and I apologize for intruding on your personal concerns."

This...was not good.

Whatever Keisha intended to discuss now, Rose was pretty sure she'd have preferred a bingo-related reprimand.

"We've worked together for over a decade, so we both know I respect your privacy. But I need to say this. Not as your boss. As your—" The other woman sighed. "As a concerned spectator."

Rose swallowed over a throat that had turned dry as the Gobi. "Okay."

Keisha's eyes caught hers. "Martin doesn't have a hard shell. You know this. I know this. Adorable newborns in Malaysia probably know this."

Oh, no. No, Rose didn't want to have this conversation. Not now or ever.

Still, she remained silent, because she respected Keisha. Trusted her, if only in a limited way.

"I don't know what's happened in your past to make you what you are." Keisha pointed a forefinger at Rose. "And let me be clear. I don't want or need to know. It's not my business. Beyond that, you're an admirable person. You're a fantastic teacher and a hardworking colleague, even if you keep yourself at a distance from your colleagues." She crossed her eyes a bit in emphasis. "From all of them except Martin."

With precise movements, Rose folded in her hands in front of her. "But?"

"But you do have a hard shell. And that man is so into you, he can barely form words when you're occupying the same space." The department chair let that sink in for a moment. "I get that you may have had a hard past, and I get that he turned you down once for a date. But if you don't intend to let him inside that shell, be kind." Keisha's braids rustled as she leaned forward. "Be kind, Rose."

Rose kept her breathing steady. In. Out.

Until her department chair drove off, she needed to appear tranquil. Unruffled.

"I hear you," she said, each word a pristine pearl of calm enunciation.

"I know you do. And no matter what happens, I won't mention it again. Like I said, I apologize for the intrusion." Keisha unlocked her door and heaved her briefcase inside the car. "Now I need to convince my doctor to test my thyroid. Wish me luck."

Rose forced a smile. "Good luck."

Leave. Please leave. I need time to think before Martin appears at my door.

After folding herself into the driver's seat, the department chair squinted up at Rose.

"I almost forgot. Two more supervisory matters." Her finger pointed at Rose once more. "Cool it with the note-passing at staff meetings."

Damn, that woman had sharp eyes, even if they spent some of their time crossed.

Keisha's grin pressed dimples into her round cheeks. "And at our next consultant presentation, I get my own bingo board."

Yup. Way too sharp.

With that, Keisha closed her car door and drove away.

As soon as the other woman left, Rose rushed back to her classroom, closed and locked the door behind her, and hustled back to her precisely-placed desk. She didn't turn on her lamp. The blinds were up, so the descending dusk would provide enough illumination for a few simple tasks, and her computer provided its own light.

She kept her jacket tightly cinched, her shoes firm against her soles.

From the outside, all anyone would see was an empty, darkening classroom.

Even Martin.

Especially Martin.

When he quietly tapped at the door minutes later, she didn't answer. Same when he tapped again around dinnertime, when they both usually left for the night.

He didn't depart until much later than usual, and she snapped her blinds shut as soon as his footsteps faded down the hall. When he reached the parking lot and spotted her car, at least he wouldn't be able to see her through the window. He'd know she was still there, but there wasn't much she could do about that.

What she *could* do, however: Protect him.

From her.

Her conversation with Keisha had served as a potent reminder: A relationship with him wouldn't be truly private. Couldn't be. Which meant it couldn't happen.

Given that decision, the other woman was right. If Rose didn't intend to lower her guard, she needed to impose some distance between her and Martin.

A man without his own armor could be hurt so easily.

And she had no intention of shedding hers. Not even for him.

TEN

BEA STRAIGHTENED MARTIN'S SILK TIE OUTSIDE the restaurant. "Looking good, Dad."

"You're just saying that because you gave me the tie for Valentine's Day." At the sight of those blond curls at her crown, he couldn't help pressing a kiss to them. "Such a daughterly cliché. Didn't you have some socks you could have shoved into a gift bag? Or a razor?"

He'd just been delighted she'd thought of him, especially while spending the week at her mom's house. But telling her that would only make her roll her eyes.

"That kiss was your allotted mush for the night." Giving the tie one last yank, she stepped back and scanned him with a critical teenage glance. "Ties might be a cliché, but you ruined your best one in the dunk tank, for some reason. And the blue brings out your eyes. Suck it up and appreciate my generosity."

He eyed the ornate ironwork around Milano's entrance. "Somehow, I think your generosity will be rewarded tonight. Manifold."

"It's my birthday. I deserve good food." She heaved open

the heavy wooden door. "I heard amazing things about this place. Apparently, I need to try the truffle risotto."

Truffles? Jesus.

Why her classmates were talking about a restaurant like this, he'd never know. When he'd checked out the menu online, he'd failed to spot any prices, which was always, always a bad sign. As the old saying went: If you had to ask, you couldn't afford it.

But his girl was turning eighteen tonight, and she never asked for much. If she wanted truffle risotto, he'd eat a few more servings of cheesy mac and give her some damn truffle risotto. Next year, she'd probably be thousands of miles away and unable to empty his bank account in a single meal.

Her college applications had been mailed months ago. Other than Marysburg University, all her choices would require a significant amount of travel. Too much travel for frequent visits.

He swallowed past the thickness in his throat and followed her to the etched-glass table inside the restaurant's entrance. After a quick glance at Milano's lush, velvet curtains and tufted chairs, he revised his estimate of the night's bill a hundred dollars higher.

Then his eye caught on a familiar tilt of the head, a familiar bitter-coffee shade of hair. Only he'd never seen Rose's hair down before, except after the dunk tank. Never seen it ripple over her shoulders—*bare* shoulders, he noted with another hard swallow—in waves that shone in the candlelight.

"Krause. Reservation for two," Bea informed the maître d'.

Rose was sitting at a round table beneath a crystal chandelier, cinched into what appeared to be the classiest black bustier in existence. The tops of her breasts gleamed pale, and they rippled in a hypnotic way when she laughed.

Wait. Why was she laughing? Was she on a date?

He forced his eyes away from her magnificence, only to see—thank goodness—an older couple at her table. Physically, they didn't much resemble her, since both the man and woman were slight of build and several inches shorter than Rose, even seated. But the woman was wearing black from head to toe, her dress formed from a draped fabric that looked soft and delicate and expensive, even across the room. Her silver hair smoothed back into a flawless twist, one that looked very familiar. She was smiling at Rose with the sort of doting affection he'd seen in pictures of himself and Bea.

Obviously, these were Rose's parents. He'd known she came from money, her knowledge of Little Debbie's baking talents notwithstanding.

"Dad?" A tug at his arm.

He'd wanted to take Rose someplace like this for Valentine's Day, but he hadn't. He hadn't even asked. Ever since that staff meeting in January—where he would have sworn, *sworn*, she was flirting with him, if only a tiny bit—she'd remained friendly, but hadn't given him any indication she considered him more than a colleague and casual friend. Someone with whom she could grab coffee occasionally, but no one she'd date.

And he'd decided months ago that he couldn't tell her how he felt or ask her out. Not if he didn't know she trusted him. Not if she wouldn't share her past with him. Or her present, for that matter, which was currently sitting across from her in a restaurant he could barely afford.

Maybe that decision was just an excuse to justify his own self-doubts, but if so, it was a good one.

Another tug. "What are you—oh. Oh, that's fantastic! Hey, Ms. Owens!"

Motherfucker. He should have known.

By the time he returned his attention to Bea, he'd missed

his chance to stave off disaster. His daughter had already waved off the tuxedo-clad woman behind the desk and was rushing toward Rose's table, as Rose and her parents looked up in startlement.

He followed as quickly as he could, but there was no catching Bea in full flight. The school's damn track team had done too good a job.

Rose and her parents stood as Bea approached, and they all smiled at her with seemingly sincere welcome. But when Rose spotted him in hot pursuit of his daughter, she froze in place.

"—so I told him I wanted to come to Milano for my eighteenth birthday, because you said such incredible things about the truffle risotto, Ms. Owens, but I had no idea you'd be here tonight." Bea flung out her arms. "What an amazing coincidence!"

Apparently, his girl had spent some time with Rose, unbeknownst to him.

Next time he saw Rose at school, he was going to request that she rave about Chipotle in the future.

"I'm sorry," he mouthed to her as Bea continued to talk.

She jerked a little, then lifted a smooth, round shoulder in an elegant shrug.

"Are these your parents?" Bea bestowed her best grin on the older couple. "Because I can see where you got your amazing fashion sense."

Now that he considered it, his daughter *had* been wearing a lot of black recently. He'd half-wondered whether she wanted to make a last-ditch effort to join the softball team.

The white-haired woman lit up at Bea's comment. "Thank you, my dear. I'm afraid I missed your name? And the name of your handsome companion?"

Handsome? Obviously, Bea had chosen a truly transformative tie.

Before his daughter could interrupt Rose's dinner further, he intervened. "I'm Martin Krause, Rose's colleague in the social studies department." He placed his hands on Bea's shoulders. "This is my daughter, Beatrice, who's a senior at Marysburg High."

"I go by Bea," she interjected.

"*Anyway*," he emphasized, "we should find our own table and leave you to your meal. I hope you have a lovely evening."

"Oh, but you can't go." Rose's mom gazed at him in dismay. "You mustn't."

Rose's father spoke for the first time, his narrow face serious. "We'd love to eat dinner with one of our Rosie's colleagues and his charming daughter. Please join us."

Rosie? Martin blinked at them both and turned to Rose for guidance.

She stood staring at her parents, mouth slightly agape. So no guidance there, although the poleaxed look on that lovely face did not seem to indicate untrammeled delight.

In her eyes, this was no doubt an egregious violation of her privacy.

He needed to respect that.

With a smile that strained his cheeks, he said, "I'm afraid we couldn't—"

"That sounds great!" Bea exclaimed. "Do we ask the waiter to get more chairs, or what?"

Rose appeared to shake herself. "We shouldn't intrude on your time with your dad, honey, especially since you're leaving so soon for college. I'm sure he wants to get every minute with you he can."

Bea frowned mutinously.

"And no doubt Rose wants to spend some time alone with her parents." He nudged his daughter's shoulder. "Let's go find our table, sweet Bea."

The older woman clapped a hand over her heart. "Sweet Bea? Oh, that's so lovely."

"We're not Rosie's parents, although we wish we were." The older man seemed to age two decades before Martin's eyes, sagging back into his seat with slumped shoulders. "Are you certain you can't dine with us?"

Rose's mother—or not her mother, apparently, but obviously some sort of near relation—had transformed over the past few seconds. Was that...was that a hunch?

He could have sworn her posture had been just as impeccable as Rose's.

"Please say you and your daughter will join us for dinner." Her small, graceful hand appeared to have a newfound tremor. "Seeing such a sweet young face across the table would be so wonderful."

Oh, Jesus. Only a churl could refuse such a wistful invitation.

Bea poked him in the ribs. "*Dad.*"

Rose's not-parents blinked soulfully up at him, eyes sad but hopeful.

Martin smothered a sigh and mentally prepared for an awkward evening. But before he could speak, Rose braced her hands on her hips and turned to her dinner companions.

"Drop the act, you two," she told them, her tone affectionate but firm. "You can play the doddering-elderly-couple game with me, because I know you're both perfectly happy and healthy. But Martin and Bea don't know the rules, and they might not want to participate."

The older woman's posture improved with remarkable speed. "Excellent point, Rosie. Our apologies, Martin and Bea."

"Yes, indeed. Please excuse us." The other man offered an abashed smile, shoulders broad and square once more.

"Rosie tells us we absorbed the lessons of a long-ago acting class with lamentable enthusiasm."

Rose shook her head in fond exasperation. "Martin and Bea, please meet my former parents-in-law, Annette and Alfred Buckham. They might want you two to eat dinner at our table, but they're not in any danger of expiring during the meal if you refuse. Feel free to say no. That said, you're more than welcome to join us."

As Rose raised her brows in inquiry, Bea poked Martin again in silent entreaty.

It was his daughter's birthday. He should follow her lead.

Besides, he wanted to spend time with Rose. Wanted to know more about her personal life. Wanted to keep sneaking glances at her from across a table and bask in her presence.

"Okay." He raised his hands in surrender. "If you're sure this isn't an intrusion, we'd be delighted to have dinner with you."

While Annette, Alfred, and Bea all beamed at him, Rose swiveled to scan the restaurant. "Let me catch our server and tell him to bring us more chairs and hold our food until you've ordered."

He shook his head. "I'll take care of it."

She muttered something about *performative masculinity* and *insufficient therapy*, but she let him help seat her, as well as Annette, while Alfred directed a genial smile at the table at large. And she didn't try to stop Martin from hunting down the server, who was more than delighted to add another couple of people to his table—not to mention his tip.

As Martin rejoined the group, he studied all its members. Rose was holding out a hank of her skirt—some sort of flouncy black fabric—for Bea to touch, while his daughter studied it and chattered away. His girl seemed perfectly comfortable in Rose's presence, as if the two had talked a million times before. Maybe they had.

He'd be asking Bea about that on the way home.

The sight of Rose herself nearly hurt his eyes, she was so fucking beautiful. He had to look away, before he revealed entirely too much to both her and his daughter.

That left two people: Rose's former in-laws. He could have used Annette's spine as his classroom ruler. Alfred radiated well-seasoned strength, rather than elderly frailty.

That must have been one hell of an acting class.

Performing skills aside, they were wise enough to want Rose as their daughter and gaze at her with open pride and affection as she charmed Bea.

He liked them already.

After dinner together, he could only hope they'd feel the same way toward him.

DESSERTS FINISHED, ROSE AND BEA EXCUSED themselves for the bathroom.

He stood until they'd left the room, and then seated himself again.

"Thank you so much for allowing us to share your table." He smiled at Alfred and Annette, whose conversational ease and wholehearted welcome had made the entire evening much less awkward than it could have become. "Bea couldn't have had a lovelier birthday dinner."

Annette inclined her head in gracious acknowledgment. "She's a wonderful young woman, which is no doubt a testament to your parenting. We're delighted the two of you could join us."

"Believe me, your presence was our pleasure." Alfred arranged his fork at a precise angle on his plate. "We've never met one of Rosie's colleagues before."

No doubt they hadn't. "Rose is quite private."

Annette's shoulders visibly stiffened under that drape-y fabric, and her blue eyes narrowed on him. "She has her reasons. Anyone in her life would have to understand that and appreciate her for what she is, rather than what he'd like her to be."

Fuck. He hadn't meant that as a criticism, merely a statement of fact.

If honesty would fix this, he'd offer it.

He held Annette's gaze without flinching. "I think Rose is magnificent. Smart and kind and hardworking and witty. Do I wish I knew more about her? Yes. But that doesn't mean I resent her self-containment or that I'd ever push her to change for my own comfort."

Alfred's mouth turned down at the corners. "Which makes you a better partner for her than our son ever was."

That...that was more information about Rose's marriage than he'd expected to receive.

More than he was comfortable receiving from anyone but her.

Annette reached across the table and covered his hand with hers. It was slim and cool. "I'm going to tell you something. Rose would kill me if she found out, so don't share this with her."

More private information about Rose? No. He couldn't allow it.

"Please don't—" he began.

"She may try to appear impervious to hurt, but she's not." Annette patted his hand, then removed hers. "Cause her pain, and we'll make quite certain you regret it."

"So much regret." Alfred offered him a genial smile. "The sort of regret that would cause a man to rethink all his critical life choices to that point."

Before tonight, he'd worried that Rose had entirely isolated herself in the world. From time to time, she'd mentioned a few college friends, but no family, and no one local.

He supposed that was one worry he could retire.

These people loved Rose. Would threaten near-strangers for her. Would openly criticize their own son's behavior toward her.

Which meant they deserved more truth. "I can't promise I won't ever hurt her, because I'm human, and I also don't know enough about her to avoid any sore spots. But I can promise I will do my absolute, unequivocal best not to cause her pain. Ever."

"Good enough for me." Alfred leaned over the table to thump Martin's back. "For now, you can forget about all those terrible regrets. But we'll be watching."

"Oh, Alfred." Annette heaved a dreamy sigh, scooting her chair close to her husband's so she could rest her head on his shoulder. "Did you hear that? *Unequivocal.* He's a nerd, just like her."

"What's this about nerds?" Rose came up to the table, Bea at her side.

"Nothing important, Rosie," Alfred said.

Martin withdrew his wallet from his pocket. "It's been a wonderful evening, but Bea and I need to head home and open presents." A quick look around didn't reveal their server. "If you see our guy, can you flag him down?"

Annette's laugh tinkled through the restaurant. "My dear, Alfred paid the bill an hour ago, while you were diving face-first into your risotto."

First of all: Rose hadn't been lying about the dish. He would do terrible, terrible things for that risotto.

Second: No. He wasn't letting Rose's former in-laws pay for him and his daughter.

How much cash did he have? "Let me pay you back. How much was our portion of the bill?"

Alfred tried to stand, then collapsed back into his chair.

"Where's my cane, darling?" he asked Annette, his voice feeble. "I'll go talk to the server about how much each meal cost, even though my leg hurts so much." He aimed a despondent look at Martin. "Paying for dinner brings such pleasure to an old man's day. Are you certain you won't reconsider?"

That hunched position Annette had assumed couldn't be comfortable. "We wouldn't want him to feel uncomfortable, dearest. Even though it would make us both so, so happy to pay for the meal. Why don't I try to find the server instead?"

She clutched her spine as she inched up from the chair. "Pass me my pain pills, would you, Martin? They're in my purse." Another mournful glance his way. "Sometimes extreme disappointment makes my back seize."

If he wasn't mistaken, Bea had turned away to hide her snickering. That didn't make it much less audible. Rose, on the other hand, sent him a reassuring look.

She leaned over to whisper in his ear. "Whatever you decide is fine, Martin. Let them pay or don't. Or feel free to play their game in your own way."

A natural actor, he was not. But the rules of this game were now clear to him, and with Rose's encouragement, he was willing to play.

He squeezed his eyes shut, as if in terrible discomfort, then pinched the bridge of his nose with his thumb and forefinger. "What a coincidence. Anytime I can't pay for my part of a meal, I get a blinding migraine."

A very familiar snort almost made him smile, but he kept his composure.

"Once I hand over the right amount of money, though, I instantly feel better." Dropping his chin, he pinched harder. "Oh, my poor head. I know you don't want me to be in pain, Alfred. Please help."

Silence.

When Martin peeked through his fingers, Rose and Bea were grinning at him with seeming pride. Alfred rolled his eyes as Annette began to giggle, the sound soft and sweet.

Finally, the older man admitted defeat. "Touché, son. May we at least pay for your daughter's dinner as a birthday present?"

Headache miraculously cured, Martin dropped his hand and thought for a moment. "As long as you ask before paying the bill in the future."

He didn't anticipate dining with Rose's in-laws again, but a careful man planned for all eventualities.

Alfred heaved a sigh. "Fine."

"Then thank you very much for Bea's dinner." Martin offered the other man a handshake. "We had a lovely evening with you and your wife."

Alfred's grip was steady and strong, his eyes on Martin assessing. And when Martin handed him a wad of cash, the other man didn't protest.

"The truffle risotto was the best thing I've ever put in my mouth, including those deep-fried Twinkies at the Wisconsin State Fair." Bea bounced on her heels. "Thank you so much for dinner, Mr. and Mrs. Buckham. It was great meeting Ms. Owens's family."

Rose's hand on his arm somehow managed to heat his entire body, and her murmur tickled his ear in a shivery taunt. "Impressive acting skills, Krause. And if you're worried about them paying for Bea's meal, please remember that they have plenty of money. Besides, eating with people they like really does make them happy."

When she removed her hand, his forearm continued to burn from the contact.

"Good night, Annette." She hugged her former mother-in-law, surrounding the older woman's slight frame with both arms. "Dinner was fantastic, as always. Thank you." Then it was Alfred's turn for an embrace. "Alfred, you need some work to become a master thespian. But I really appreciate dinner, and I really appreciate you both."

The couple gazed at her, soft-eyed.

"We'll call you later this week," Annette promised. "Take care of yourself, Rosie."

"Why don't Martin and Bea walk you to your car?" Alfred suggested. "We need to visit the facilities before we leave."

Rose cast them a skeptical glance, one Martin secretly seconded.

"You live two minutes from this restaurant," she said.

Annette sagged where she stood. "When you get as old as us, dearest—"

Rose shook her head. "Never mind. We're going."

At the coat check, they reclaimed their late-winter gear. He helped Bea don her fleece jacket, and then held Rose's sleek, quilted black coat open for her.

She stared at it, then at him. "Really?"

But at that point she apparently decided to take the same approach with him as she did with her former in-laws. Without further protest, she let him ease her into the coat and draw her silky hair from beneath its collar.

When his fingertips slid along her warm, soft nape, her chin tipped back, her eyes going half-lidded, and if his daughter hadn't been standing three feet away, he honestly had no idea what he might have done next. Stroked her nape a second time. Kissed her.

Found out whether he could earn that look again. And again.

But instead, he held the door for his two favorite ladies in the world and walked beside them into the dim parking lot. After Bea settled in his Subaru, he tossed her the keys.

"Turn on the engine and get warm," he told her. "I'll be right back."

For once, she didn't offer any sass. "Sure thing. Take your time."

Rose was already seated by the time he arrived, but he held her door for a moment. "I'm sorry. I hope we didn't disrupt your entire evening."

"No worries." Under the car's interior lights, her lashes cast lacy shadows beneath her eyes. "Dinner was fun. I hope Bea enjoyed it too. And like I said, please don't think twice about letting Annette and Alfred pay for her." She paused. "However, you should probably know that their performance tonight was just a warmup."

At his alarmed look, she laughed. "Once Annette gets out her Swarovski-studded reading glasses and starts talking about whether she needs one of those adjustable beds and a walk-in bath, that's when you know you're really in deep shit."

He could only imagine. "See you tomorrow at school?"

"Yeah." She looked up at him, eyes suddenly serious. "Yeah, you will."

After shutting her door, he watched her leave the lot.

Then he returned to Bea, hustling inside his car as quickly as possible. Funny how he hadn't even felt the cold until just then.

"Did you enjoy your birthday dinner, sweet Bea?" He backed out of the parking space. "I hope you didn't regret joining Ms. Owens and her family."

She didn't hesitate. "I had a great time. The food was amazing, and Annette and Alfred were hilarious."

"And Ms. Owens?"

"I like her." A simple, firm statement. "I've always liked her."

He thought back to earlier in the evening. Discussions of truffle risotto. Black clothing. "Do you talk to her a lot?"

He didn't disapprove, by any means. But like any teenager, Bea occasionally missed social cues, and he wanted to ensure she hadn't made Rose uncomfortable or imposed on her.

Bea lifted a shoulder. "A couple times a week, maybe. Sometimes I see her in the hall, and we chat for a little while."

"About which restaurants are most likely to bankrupt your college fund?"

"About a little of everything." Bea paused for a moment, and then twisted toward him in an abrupt movement. "Even about you, the other day."

Well, that was news to frighten any man. "All right."

"I was complaining about how you always make me go to bed early so I get enough sleep, and I slipped up and called you Old Sobersides." In his peripheral vision, he caught her grimace. "I'm sorry."

He darted a quick, reassuring smile her way. "I told you not to worry about that."

"I know. But I won't do it again." His daughter wiggled, settling herself more firmly in the seat. "Anyway, that's not the interesting part. The interesting part is what she said."

He wasn't certain he wanted to know, but Bea was going to tell him one way or another. "What did she say?"

"She was really nice about it, but really serious too. She told me she didn't understand the nickname. She said you had a great sense of humor and"—she crooked her fingers—"*a sharp wit*, and she thought it was hilarious to watch you say funny things with a straight face."

That felt good. Better than good.

Maybe a bit *too* good, since he and Rose might not ever be anything more than colleagues and casual friends.

"That's when it occurred to me." Bea spread her hands. "You and Mom don't have the same sense of humor. Like, at all. She likes slapsticky stuff, and you're more into nerdy references and wordplay. That's probably why she didn't think you were funny, but you totally are. Ms. Owens is right."

He didn't know quite what to say to that. "Thank you?"

"And then she said how much she'd wished for a dad like you when she was my age. Someone to tell her she was working too hard and that she needed to get enough sleep."

Again, more information he desperately wanted, but coming from the wrong mouth.

"Ms. Owens hasn't told me about her parents, and I doubt she's told anyone else either," he said as gently as he could. "I would keep anything she says about them in confidence. Even with me."

Bea thought that over for a minute. "Good point."

He and Sabrina really had raised a good kid, even in the midst of their own disconnection.

"The last thing she said was that all her students thought their parents were unfair and annoying sometimes. But not all of them had dads who cared enough to make sure their daughters got enough sleep. Which was her roundabout way of telling me to appreciate you," Bea said. "And after that, I told her exactly what I'm about to tell you. I do appreciate you. You're a great dad, and I love you, and I don't tell you that enough."

How did Rose manage to twist his heart even when she was miles away?

And how was he going to survive dropping Bea off at college?

"I love you too." He cleared his throat. Then cleared his throat again. "You're the best daughter I can imagine having." Another hard blink, and he kept his tone as neutral as possible. "Then again, my imagination isn't very good."

She smacked his arm. "Enough with the"—more air quotes—"*sharp wit*, Dad. I have one more thing to say."

If he didn't survive it, he hoped Bea could get herself home safely.

"I told you before, and I'll tell you again: Ms. Owens likes you. I mean, *likes* you, likes you." She poked him. "I don't know why you haven't asked her out yet, but you need to stop messing around. Before some other guy figures out she's awesome and snatches her up."

How much could he say without violating Rose's privacy?

"Ms. Owens isn't always the easiest person to understand." He selected each word with care. "Sometimes it can be hard to know what she wants."

Bea made a sort of unimpressed grunt. "Doesn't seem that hard to me. Then again, you're a dude."

"I am." He turned into their driveway. "I am a dude."

"But I have faith you can overcome your dudeness." As soon as he turned off the engine, she hopped out of the door. "Crack her like a walnut, Dad."

She thumped the hood in demonstration of said cracking.

His daughter seemed to understand his intentions toward Rose already, but he supposed it couldn't hurt to make them clear.

"I'm not sure *cracking her like a walnut* is the most romantic simile I've ever heard." He shut the door behind him with a decisive thud. "But I'm certainly going to try."

With a wide grin, his daughter hummed a few bars of the Nutcracker Suite.

Such a smartass.

Emphasis on the smart.

ELEVEN

ROSE HELD OUT UNTIL FIVE MINUTES BEFORE THE
first bell.

Then, before she let herself think too hard about it, she
rushed down the hall to the social studies office to see
whether Martin had arrived yet.

Just because he hadn't visited her classroom early in the
morning for the first time in months didn't mean something
had gone wrong. That he was out sick with a terrible illness,
alone and feverish and delirious. Or that he'd crashed his car
on his way to work and was even now lying unconscious and
bleeding in some awful emergency room.

Or that he'd simply grown tired of her company. Given up
on her once and for all.

She flung open the social studies office door. No Martin.

Another dash back to her classroom, as her gathering
students watched her with startled confusion. When she
peered out her window, she didn't see his Subaru in his usual
spot. So with two minutes to spare before she needed to start
teaching, she rushed to Keisha's room.

The department chair, standing in the doorway to greet

her own students, reared back in surprise at the sight of Rose jogging toward her. "Ms. Owens, what on earth is the matter?"

Damn, running in heels sucked. Rose was panting and possibly even a bit sweaty, which would usually dismay her. But this morning, she had more important issues to consider.

"Is Martin okay?" she gasped out. "I can't find him."

Keisha's eyebrows rose. "He's having back issues. He's out today and maybe the rest of the week."

Thank God.

Although...oh, he must be in terrible pain not to come to school, given the circumstances.

"But..." Rose leaned forward, bracing her hands on her thighs. "But the AP test is coming up in a couple weeks, and I know he's trying to review as much as he can beforehand. A random sub won't be able to help much with that. Martin must be horrified."

"Be that as it may, he's in no condition to come to school, so we called a sub." Keisha glanced at the clock on the wall. "There really aren't a lot of other options."

Shit. Rose needed to go. Now.

"His AP classes are during my planning periods. I'll take them. The sub can get everything else." She hobbled toward the door. "Please e-mail me his substitute lesson plans if you can."

Keisha's eyebrows essentially disappeared into her hairline. "I will."

True to her word, Rose's supervisor had sent the lesson plans before second period began. So after approximately fifteen minutes of prep—conducted while she had her kids work independently on a review packet for the state standardized test, also coming soon—she stood in front of the AP World History class, introduced herself, and did her best to channel Martin. Then conducted more of her own classes before taking over his other AP class for seventh period.

All told, during the day, she had a twenty-five minute break for lunch. That was it.

By the time the last bell rang, she could barely move. But instead of staying at school to grade and plan, and instead of driving home to stare blankly at a wall for a few hours, she flipped through the staff directory and programmed a new address into her phone's GPS.

Martin's home.

She locked her classroom door two minutes after the students left, ran to the parking lot in hopes of beating the buses—because once they started pulling out, no one was going anywhere for a loooong time—climbed into her car, and started the engine.

Then promptly turned it off again.

Bea was probably helping to take care of him after school. Or maybe his ex-wife or his buddies or someone else from the department. Martin wasn't like Rose. He didn't isolate himself.

He didn't need her.

Of course he didn't need her.

Then again, he'd lived in Marysburg less than a year. He hated to bother people. As far as she knew, he didn't go get coffee with any of the other teachers. And Bea spent every other week at her mother's home.

Fuck it, Rose was going.

Once she pulled into his driveway, a glaring omission in her half-assed plan occurred to her. If his back was too painful for him to attend school, how the hell was he supposed to answer the door?

Bea. Bea could help.

She pulled up the girl's number—at some point during

their dinner at Milano, Bea had given it to her "just in case"—and called.

"Uh, Ms. Owens?" Bea sounded confused. "I'm just down the hall at Ms. Albright's AP Lit study session, like we talked about yesterday. Why are you calling me?"

Damn. She'd forgotten. And she hated to interrupt a study session, especially one led by Candy Albright. The ringleader of the Frankenstein Is *Not* the Monster Initiative never forgot, never forgave, and doled out vengeance the likes of which Bianca and the girls' softball team couldn't even imagine.

Didn't matter. Candy could plot Rose's death later.

"Are you staying with your father right now?" No point checking her reflection in the rearview. A disaster didn't magically repair itself when you stared at it. "Because he was out today with back issues, and Ms. Williams said he might not return this week."

"Hold on." Rustling, and the sound of a door creaking open, then closed. "I had no idea he stayed home today, Ms. Owens. I'm with Mom this week, and Dad sounded fine on the phone last night. I just figured we hadn't crossed paths today by chance."

The girl's words began to trip over each other. "I'd get over there now, but this study session counts as extra credit, and my grade is right on the edge between an A and a B. Mom and I had plans for tonight, but maybe I could—"

"Honey." When Bea kept talking, her voice getting higher and higher with stress, Rose repeated herself. "Honey. It's okay. I'll take care of your dad. I'm at your house now. My main question is: How do I get in?"

Once Bea had shared the location of their extra key—if Martin insisted on using a fake rock, he really needed to buy a more convincing specimen—she told Rose a little more about how her father's back issues usually manifested themselves.

"Sometimes when he wakes up, he instinctively tenses, and it makes things a million times worse. You should definitely just go in, instead of calling ahead or ringing the doorbell. And if he tries to tell you he's fine and you can leave, don't listen. He's a great nurse but a terrible patient." Bea paused, her tone changing in a way Rose couldn't quite define. "Also, I'm not sure I should tell you this, but..."

"What?" Rose wanted all the information she could get. "What, Bea?"

The girl immediately gave in. "Sometimes he needs stuff in the middle of the night. He gets sooo thirsty, Ms. Owens, and he has to take his muscle relaxants and ibuprofen at certain times. Is there any way you can stay there tonight? It would really ease my mind."

Rose winced. All night?

"I know that's a lot to ask. You don't have to," Bea said, her voice growing forlorn. "He'll probably be fine all alone. Or I guess I can tell my mom she can't see me tonight, even though she's made all those special plans."

What kind of monster could ignore such a sincere plea? "No, no. I'll do it."

"You promise?"

Bea sounded oddly excited. Or maybe that was relief?

"I promise," Rose said.

After ending the call, she walked up the front steps of the small, tidy home and let herself in, even though it went against all of her privacy-obsessed instincts.

At the sound of the door shutting, Martin called out from somewhere in the house, "Bea, I'm fine, and you need to be at your study session. Go back before Ms. Albright puts a hit out on you. And another on me for distracting you from your studies."

She slipped off her heels just inside the door, loath to damage his gleaming hardwood floors, and followed the sound of his voice.

"Not Bea," she called back.

Utter silence.

She passed an eat-in kitchen. Bea's messy bedroom. A gray-and-white bathroom.

Still no response.

The poor man was probably too dazed from pain and drugs to understand what was happening. "That said, Candy may still put a hit out on you and your daughter. Not to mention me, for interrupting Bea's study session." She knocked on a half-open door, the last one at the end of the hall, forcing herself not to look inside. "Are you decent in there?"

"I guess." He sounded befuddled. "Rose? Is that you?"

"It's me. Unless the robotics team has gotten really, really sophisticated. May I come in?"

He didn't hesitate. "Yeah."

Poking her head around the edge of the door, she braced herself for whatever currently awaited her within his bedroom. "See? Not a robot."

Her introductory eyeful of Martin in his natural habitat was definitely memorable.

He blinked at her with hazy blue eyes as he lay flat on the bed, strands of his brown hair flopping over his forehead in boyish disarray. But the bare chest above his white sheet, the expanse of lean muscles dusted by more dark hair, was anything but childish.

As when she'd first seen him in that suit at Milano, her lungs just gave up and devoted themselves entirely to worshipping his handsomeness. Which was inconvenient, because she could use some air in a world turned suddenly hypoxic.

"How are you feeling?" she wheezed out.

He jerked at the words, and then stiffened everywhere with a bit-off groan.

"Oh, shit." She rushed to his side. "What can I get you? More ibuprofen? Your muscle relaxants? Water? Or should I take you to the hospital?"

"No hospital." The words sounded like sandpaper. "Pillow under my knees. Please. Sorry."

A frantic glance revealed a pillow that had fallen beside the bed. She plucked it from the floor and slid her hand beneath the region of the sheet that seemed most likely to contain his knees.

If she was wrong, this was shortly going to become an extremely awkward moment.

There. The bend of his knee, the flesh there warm and velvety under a few crisp hairs. As gently as possible, she eased the pillow beneath that crook as he breathed harshly. Then the job was done, and he relaxed into the mattress while she attempted to gain control of her heartbeat.

"Thank you." His breathing slowed. "Don't worry. I'm wearing gym shorts. Didn't want to flash Bea accidentally."

She wasn't disappointed at the presence of those shorts. Definitely not.

With careful fingertips, she smoothed the hair from his brow. "Do you feel better now? With the pillow there?"

His eyelids lowered. "Yeah."

"What can I get you? Do you need a drink?" Two pill bottles rested on his nightstand, beside an empty glass. "More pain medicine?"

With seeming effort, he opened his eyes again and glanced at his bedside alarm clock. "Took ibuprofen and muscle relaxants about half an hour ago. Maybe more water?" He shifted, then winced. "Sorry. Shouldn't have to take care of me. Should take care of myself."

"You're fine." Glass in hand, she strode to the kitchen and searched the cabinets until she found a fresh cup. Cool water dispensed from the refrigerator door, so she filled the cup there and deposited the old glass in his sink. Within moments, she'd returned to his room. "Here you go."

When he tried to lift his head, she slid more pillows beneath it to support him.

"Thank you," he murmured. "Again."

He didn't seem entirely steady, so she held the cup with him as he drank, their fingers tangling over the slick glass.

Once he'd drained the liquid, she eyed his position. "Do you want me to get rid of the pillows under your head?"

"Leave them." He attempted a small smile. "Easier to talk that way."

Another comma of hair had escaped onto his brow, so she nudged it back into place. "You don't need to talk, Martin. Go back to sleep, and hopefully you'll feel better when you wake up."

"Why…" He swallowed. "Why are you here?"

That question could be answered so many ways. But if he wanted her gone, none of the more embarrassing responses mattered.

"Keisha said you were in bad shape and might be out for the rest of the week, so I wanted to check on you. Maybe help, if you needed it." She took a half-step back from the bed. "I'm sorry. I know this is an intrusion. I can g—"

"*No.*" He reached out an arm, then clenched his eyes shut and let it fall. "No, Rose. Not a complaint. Definitely not a complaint. A question."

If she didn't need to leave, and he no longer required immediate assistance, she wanted to rest her feet for a moment. Before they fell off of their own accord.

She looked around his small room, dominated entirely by

the large bed. "Could I sit down somewhere? Is there a chair I could bring in here?"

"Sit." His hand rose an inch and patted the mattress once. "King. Plenty of room."

That seemed like a terrible idea. "I'll jostle you."

He mumbled something she didn't quite catch.

"What?" She leaned closer, until a bare inch would have meant kissing him.

His eyes closed again, this time as if in defeat. "Always wanted to have someone sitting next to me. Dad said...weak."

That asshole better hope she never encountered him, because her pointy-toed shoes were good for more than just fashion. "When you were sick or hurt, you wanted someone beside you?"

He sighed. "Yeah."

"Of course you did. All kids do." His features relaxed when she stroked his brow, so she kept doing it. "Did your mom ever keep you company when you didn't feel good?"

"Sometimes. Until Dad came home."

"Hmmmm." Slowly, she eased her weight down onto the mattress at his side. "My dad left before I was born. But when she wasn't working, my mom would sit next to me whenever I got sick. Bring me juice or flat soda or whatever I needed."

Most of the time, Rose had stayed home alone when ill. But on the rare occasions when her mother insisted on calling in sick to work or missing class to nurse her daughter, she'd spread a threadbare quilt over the couch and cocoon Rose inside, positioning them so they could both watch cartoons.

In those moments, getting sick had almost felt like luxury. Like grace.

Like shame and despair too, given the likely consequences.

"Sounds... nice." His breathing had turned slow and steady. "Where does...she live?"

Rose forced her hand to keep moving. "She died while I was in college."

His hand rose to cover hers on his forehead, his palm warm and dry. "I'm sorry, Rose. So sorry."

"It's okay."

It hadn't been. Not for a long, long time. But now...yes. Mostly.

His forehead moved back and forth under their hands. "Not okay."

"Shhhhhhh." With gingerly movements, she lifted his hand and placed it back by his side. "Sleep, Martin. I'm here."

She slowly scooted back until she could prop herself against the headrest and stretch her tired legs in front of her. Then she kept stroking his forehead as his brow cleared and his chest rose and fell in the steady rhythm of sleep.

He hadn't even asked how she'd gotten inside. Hadn't questioned her right to come. Hadn't hesitated to fall asleep under her touch.

More trust from him.

Maybe it was about time to return some of it.

TWELVE

WHEN MARTIN WOKE A COUPLE HOURS LATER, HE stared at Rose as if she'd risen from the sea in an oversized scallop shell, wonder and confusion battling for supremacy in his expression.

"I thought the muscle relaxants were causing hallucinations, but I guess not." He frowned, eyes still fixed on her. "Unless this is a hallucination too."

"The nature of reality is suspect," she agreed. "But as far as I know, we're both here. I stopped by my house for a few supplies while you were asleep, which is why I look different."

"Different..." His voice was husky from sleep, his features softened. "Different doesn't begin to express how you look right now."

After she'd gathered what she needed for an overnight stay, she'd changed clothing. Instead of her usual tailored pieces, she'd chosen a pair of soft knit gaucho pants and a slouchy silk tee, along with her favorite ballerina flats. Essentially, they were really expensive pajamas and slippers. All black, of course. All clothing she'd never worn outside her home before.

Before she'd left, she'd also taken down her hair and gathered it into a loose braid, as she often did in the evening. A generous application of makeup remover took care of her usual foundation and blush and everything else that announced her readiness to do fashionable battle on a daily basis.

This was as naked as she ever got, except during actual sex. And Martin, drugged but perceptive soul that he was, appeared to realize it.

His face abruptly creased in concern. "Not that you aren't beautiful every day, because you are. Obviously. That's not what I meant at all."

He'd called her beautiful. Just said it outright, as if it were a given. An immutable fact. As if any suggestion she *wasn't* beautiful would offend him.

How had all that sweetness survived his childhood intact?

She would have said he had a heart of gold, but it must have been stronger than that. Steel. Diamond, maybe.

"I knew what you meant." Comfortably propped against his headboard once more, she smiled down at him. "Don't worry."

She couldn't help it. She had to brush that stray eyelash from his cheekbone.

His skin heated beneath her lingering touch, and he caught her hand with his. "I don't have enough functioning brain cells to worry right now."

Fire sparked beneath her skin as he gently played with her fingers, exploring the valleys between them and the ridges of her knuckles with light strokes of flesh against flesh.

She struggled to keep her tone even. Wry. "I know you too well, Martin. You will always, always have enough functioning brain cells to worry. It's one of your many charms."

He tugged her hand to his mouth, and his lips pressed against her palm. "Thank you."

"For calling you a worrier?" No oxygen again. She was going to have to evolve into a higher life form soon, one that could survive outside Earth's atmosphere. "My pleasure."

His lips were soft. So soft.

He spoke into the cup of her palm. "Thank you for caring about me. Thank you for coming to check on me." His muffled voice turned dry. "Thank you for breaking into my home to do so."

She tried to jerk her hand away, but he held on. "I didn't break into your house! Bea told me about your fake rock. Which is a disgrace to fake rock-kind, by the way. Next time, buy a key-holder that approximates something found on the actual ground."

"Thank you for sitting beside me when I was hurting," he continued, as if she hadn't spoken. "Thank you for telling me about your father and your mother."

Goddammit, she was trembling like some nervous virgin. "I didn't tell you much."

"It's enough." A tender kiss to the center of her palm, and then he folded her fingers over that spot. "Rose, I—"

His stomach growled. Loudly.

They glanced at it together.

After a slow exhalation, he started again. "Rose, I'd like to—"

Another growl, this one extended and angry.

She wanted to do this. She did. But now wasn't the right time.

"Let's get you fed." Sliding her hand free from his, she levered her weight carefully off of his mattress. "Do you have a tray I can use on the bed?"

His mouth went tight for a moment, but he didn't protest the interruption. "My back is feeling a bit better, and the

132

doctor says I'm supposed to move as much as I can. We can eat in the kitchen together. Let me just put on my shirt."

With tiny, halting movements, he removed the sheet and began to ease his way to the edge of the mattress.

Like the rest of him, his bare legs were lean. Strong.

Like the rest of him, she wanted to run her tongue over them.

"Do you need help getting out? Or getting dressed?" She really should offer to leave while he got on more clothing. But…no. Not happening.

His feet touched the floor, and he waited a second to make sure he could stand upright before moving again. "Thank you, but I'll be fine. I hope."

She hovered nearby, ready to support his weight if needed. Delighted to, actually, if that meant more contact with his strong shoulders and warm flesh.

He carefully pulled a t-shirt over his head. "God bless modern medicine."

Apart from their post–dunk booth coffee excursion, she'd never seen him without a button-down shirt, dark pants, and tie. Even on the occasional Fridays when teachers could donate to charity and wear jeans, he simply handed over his money and showed up to school in his usual outfit. She'd begun to believe he might not actually own a single piece of non-work clothing.

Which was fine. Whatever made him comfortable.

But there was something about seeing his surprisingly muscular forearms and legs…

He appeared oddly vulnerable, but also bigger somehow. More a man in his prime.

"You look different too." Apparently, she wasn't the only one who lifted weights in her free time. He had biceps. Noticeable ones. "I like that tee."

"Christmas gift from Bea." His grin brightened his eyes.

"This one is nicer than the Black Death European Tour tee she gave me last year. Although the dates were historically accurate, which I appreciated, the rat on the front kind of freaked people out."

She snorted. "I'll have to see that sometime."

"Be my guest." He started to make a sweeping gesture toward his closet, then halted with a groan. "Damn you, modern medicine."

His stomach growled again, and he stared at her pitifully.

She put an arm around his waist to support him—out of sheer altruism, not because she wanted to smell his piney shampoo or feel the press of his body against her side—and guided them toward the kitchen. "Let's get you fed. I can ransack your closet later."

His steps slowed. "I'll take that as a promise."

"You can take that any way you want."

They were almost precisely the same height, so when he turned his head, his lips came a hairsbreadth from hers. "Really?"

His lashes were surprisingly long, but they didn't shield the expression in his eyes. The yearning. The banked heat. The solemnity of a man ready to lay his soul bare.

When she licked her lips again, he followed the movement with his gaze.

Then his stomach protested with a rumble loud enough to wake neighbors.

Rolling his eyes, he sighed. "Dinner. Then we talk."

Her arm tightened around his waist. "I'll take that as a promise."

"YOUR AP STUDENTS SHOULD BE ON TRACK AS FAR

as the review lessons." Rose handed Martin the sandwich she'd concocted with the spartan contents of his refrigerator and a crusty baguette she'd brought from her own house. "The sub said the kids in your honors classes did fine too, but I couldn't determine that for myself, since I had my own classes to teach."

Sandwich forgotten, he stared at her in horror. "You sacrificed both your planning periods to teach my AP classes? Your only break all day was lunch?"

"I won't lie." She took a big bite, chewed, and swallowed. "I'm a bit tired. But I can keep covering for you until you're ready to come back."

Now that he'd recovered from the initial gut-punch of seeing Rose entirely unguarded—in both expression and garb —for the first time ever, he could spot the circles beneath those wide-set amber eyes, the lines of tension around her lush mouth.

No teacher had ever covered for him like she had.

In fact, he couldn't remember another teacher ever covering for *anyone* like that.

This much gratitude was uncomfortable. Almost unbearable. "I should say no, but I honestly don't know when I can come back, and my AP kids need a good teacher to help them review."

"I figured." She sipped from her can of Diet Coke. "It's not a problem. You'd do the same for me."

He would. But oh, God, she was going to exhaust herself every day. For the sake of his students, yes, but mostly for him. He knew that.

The sandwich now tasted like the dirt he'd inadvertently eaten the day before. "Rose, I don't know whether to apologize for the rest of my life or fall at your feet in thanks."

As he raised his glass of water to take his next dose of

ibuprofen and muscle relaxants, she eyed his careful movements. "I get the sense any falling you'll be doing for the immediate future will be involuntary."

She wasn't wrong.

"Falling is what caused this whole problem, by the way. I tripped over an exposed root while I was hiking yesterday." He grimaced. "Rookie mistake. Should have been paying attention to my feet. I thought I was fine afterwards, but I woke up with back spasms."

Her face pinched in a wince. "That's terrible. Remind me not to appreciate the wonders of nature anytime soon."

His laugh wrenched his back. "Will do."

But he hadn't been appreciating the wonders of nature, at least not in forest form.

Instead, he'd been appreciating the wonders of Rose Owens.

The way her chin tipped high whenever she exited her classroom, her complete self-possession daring onlookers to challenge her. The way those zippered boots she'd worn last week cuddled the curve of her calf, the top edge teasing the backs of her knees. The way fond exasperation tugged at her lips as she watched her former in-laws plummet into decrepitude at a moment's notice.

So, yeah, he hadn't been watching his step.

He'd been wondering if he should finally ask her for a date.

"I really do wish I could help with your honors kids too." Her fingers tightened on her sandwich, squeezing some of the mayo out from the edges. "I don't know whether I've done enough to convince them to enroll in my AP classes next year. And besides, I..."

He let the pause linger, loath to interrupt her thoughts.

Her forehead wrinkled, and she seemed to force the next

few words out. "Besides, I, uh, miss them. Miss teaching that class."

Her initial distress at being stripped of that prep hadn't simply stemmed from concern about the AP program's funding, then, or even anger at Dale's interference. He'd had no idea. None.

And he'd never heard her admit to an ounce—a micron—of emotional distress before.

If he said the wrong thing now, she'd shut down faster than an overheated copier.

He selected the words one by one. Tested them in his own mind, like a man venturing up the stairs of an abandoned home, making sure each step could bear his weight before he proceeded. "You like teaching students that age? Or is it the subject matter you miss?"

Her hands fluttered in agitated movements. They picked up the remaining half of her sandwich. Put it back down. Plucked at the hem of her silky-looking shirt. Played with the ends of her braid.

Rose was not a fidgeter. He was watching her fight every instinct she had.

Fuck, he wished he could make this easier for her. His heart hurt at the sight of such a smart, caring woman struggling so hard to share herself. All of herself, not just the bits she didn't mind others seeing.

"Both, I guess," she finally said. "I love ancient Egypt, like I told you, and I have some fun activities for the mythology unit. The plague and Joan of Arc too. And tenth grade is a fun age. The kids aren't as determined to seem cynical as my eleventh graders." She paused again. "But it's more than that."

He let his silence do the work this time.

"I grew up poor, Martin." She tore little pieces from the

crust of her baguette. "Really poor. Trailer park poor. Food stamps poor."

No visible surprise. Keep your face neutral.

"People judge you all the time when you're poor, especially if you're on welfare. They think it's their right. That you must be dumb or lazy or dishonest." Blotches appeared on her bare cheeks, pink splashes of rage. "When my mom went back to school to become a nurse, the people at the welfare office didn't believe her GPA. The woman in charge of our case kept saying, 'This can't be right. You're not that smart.'" Her long, elegant hands had formed fists on the table. "Mom and I finally figured it out. The system is meant to keep you alive, but also to punish you. To humiliate you. To make sure you would never, ever be part of it if you had a choice."

He forced himself to breathe normally. *Your outrage, your anger on her behalf, don't matter. This isn't about you.*

Her mouth pressed into a thin, white line. "Then there were the people behind us in line at the grocery store, who'd sigh and roll their eyes and make comments about what we bought with our food stamps. Who'd inform us when we'd chosen something they considered too expensive, since they didn't want their valuable tax dollars paying for anything more than the bare essentials. And all the other people who looked at us and said we obviously didn't need help, obviously shouldn't get money, because we dressed too nicely. Didn't look poor enough. Had a decent TV."

All that flinty pride. All that fuck-you defiance and refusal to show weakness.

No wonder. No wonder.

She glared in his direction, but he didn't think she saw him. "We scoured thrift stores for decent clothing, because Mom didn't want to stand out in her classes, and she didn't want other kids to mock me at school. Our hair always looked nice because we knew a good stylist, and Mom cleaned her studio sometimes in exchange for a cut and color. And we scrimped for years—*years*—to get a decent TV and cable, because God knew we weren't going to movies, weren't attending concerts, weren't eating at restaurants or visiting amusement parks. We needed some sort of amusement other than library books, much as I loved reading."

He wanted to tell her she didn't need to defend herself or her mother, not to him. Not ever.

Not about you, he repeated to himself. *Not about you.*

"We didn't have health insurance, which meant every time I got sick, every time I had to go to the doctor or Mom had to miss work to take care of me, the TV fund would go back to zero. So I'd tell her I was fine. I didn't need the doctor. She could go to work." Her voice grew distant as she sifted through her memories. "When I was little, to stop myself from crying I'd pretend she was there, just out of sight. Around the corner. In the kitchen, getting me ginger ale."

A half-rueful, half-bitter smile curved her mouth. "I hallucinated her once, when I had a high fever. Talked to her for hours. When Mom got home, she had to take me to the hospital, and the TV fund was gone. Again."

His heart. Oh, Jesus, his heart.

But the frozen dam had melted at long last, and there was no stopping the violent, churning flood of water and ice as it hurtled downstream. He didn't even try.

She'd survived a long winter. She deserved spring, even if the turn of seasons tossed some boulders and snapped a few trees in half.

Without warning, she shook her head so hard, her braid whipped against her cheek. "But that's not my point. Your AP World History kids are great. Smart, funny, generally hardworking. But very few of them need us, Martin. They'd be fine whoever their teacher was, because most of them have money. Most of them have parents with enough time and energy to ensure their kids' success."

He couldn't say she was entirely wrong, although he suspected more AP kids needed a teacher like her than she realized. He'd been one of those kids himself, desperate for affirmation and understanding and gentleness from any adult in his life.

She sprawled back in her chair without any attempt at grace. "I wasn't like them. I was a good student in school. Not great. Mom thought I could do better, but I knew I wasn't AP or college material. By the time I started ninth grade, I was already washing dishes at restaurants and getting paid under the table, so I could help contribute to our savings. I didn't have time for homework, and I wasn't smart enough for anything past high school."

Not smart enough? He would laugh, if he weren't so close to shouting or tears.

"I loved writing, though. Read anything I could find for free." She pushed away her plate restlessly. "At the end of freshman year, Ms. Jenkins met with me one day after class and said I could do more. Be more. She wanted me to skip normal tenth grade English and take her AP English Lit class that next year. *Hemingway doesn't deserve you*, she said. *But you deserve Hemingway*."

Rose's face had lit like a lantern at the first mention of her former teacher, and the beauty of it held him immobile in his chair.

"I thought she was joking at first. It required special permission from my mom, and from the school. But she wasn't joking, and I..." Her exhalation shook, just a little. "I respected her. I trusted her, when I didn't trust anyone but my mom. And somehow, after I got an A in her class and a five on the exam, I started taking other AP courses. I started applying for scholarships. I started applying for student loans. I went to college. I went to graduate school. Me, of all people. Brandi Rose Owens."

For all the pain of his childhood, he'd never doubted he'd go to college. Not once.

"Mom didn't see me graduate. Neither did Ms. Jenkins." She was shredding her napkin, tearing and tearing it again as she spoke. "I'm not a religious person, but I hope they saw. I hope they knew. I wanted them—"

She stopped. Swallowed back a raw, rough sound. "I wanted them to be proud."

Against all his instincts, he didn't try to touch her. Didn't fold her into his arms and rock her like the mother she'd lost so long ago.

She didn't need his comfort right now. She needed him to listen.

Her head ducked down, and she gathered all those shreds into a little pile. Tidied them. "With AP U.S. History, I get to use my academic background. I get to explore our history in so much more depth than when I teach regular or honors classes, and I wouldn't give that up for anything. With Honors World History, though, more of the students are like me as a teenager. Smart but poor kids who may not expect too much of themselves, and who may not have anyone else expect too much of them, either. But they have time to change all that before graduation. They have time to raise their GPA and make a good case for college admission, if that's something they want."

He'd like to think that was still possible for juniors and seniors too, but in reality, he didn't know. One or two years of newfound academic success might not sway college admissions committees. Again, he'd never had to worry about such matters for his own sake, or even for Bea's.

Jesus, his thoughts seemed fuzzy. Weird.

Her eyes blazed with emotion when they met his. "For me, the best moment in the entire school year is always, always, when I see next year's AP U.S. History roster. When I get to watch some of my honors kids reach for more, like I did. Some of them won't succeed in such a high-intensity class, and I understand that. But others will, and that success can change their lives for the better. Forever. I know that for a fact, Martin."

Conviction firmed her jaw, but tears roughened her voice as she finished her story.

"And on the most selfish level, I'm so proud those kids trust me enough to take a chance. To take on hours of extra homework each week, hours they could be sleeping or working for their families, all to keep me as a teacher. All because I helped them believe they could do more. Be more." Her throat worked. "It's the greatest accomplishment of my life. By far."

She angrily knuckled away the wetness shining on her cheeks. "When Dale took that away, it fucking gutted me. I found out literally minutes before I met you the first time, Martin. I know I was a cold bitch to you, and I'm sorry. None of it was your fault, but I was so angry and hurt I could barely stop myself from crying." She choked out a laugh. "Like I am now."

He waited, but she'd finished. Was staring down at her plate with livid stripes of color on her cheeks as she sniffed back more tears.

Which meant he could finally speak. Finally hold her.

"Rose..." He started up from his chair, eager to provide whatever solace and understanding she'd allow. But as the room swirled and his legs turned to Chef Boyardee spaghetti beneath him, he sat right back down. "Fuck."

After one last sniff, she looked over at him, emotional

devastation gradually replaced by wry amusement. "The pills started kicking in, huh?"

"Yeah." He had to think. What did he need to tell her? "You're amazing. You have to know that. Amazing."

Her lips tucked inward in a small smile, and she rose to her feet with enviable ease.

"When you start sounding drunk, I figure it's time for bed." At some point, she'd maneuvered herself beneath his arm, and it seemed he was standing again. "Upsy-daisy. There you go."

They made halting progress toward his bedroom, which seemed much further away than he remembered. And there was something he needed to tell her. Oh, right. "Amazing. So pretty. Soooo pretty."

"At least you're a happy drunk," she muttered. "But you're heavier than you look."

Oh, no.

He dropped his chin to his chest and halted. "Sorry. Pills...hit me hard."

"No, no. Don't stop moving now." She tugged him back into motion. "No need to apologize. It's kind of fun to see buttoned-up Mr. Krause undone."

Wait! That was what he needed to say. "Want to see *you* undone."

"I think you just did." Another few feet. "When you're feeling better, you may get another chance. This time without drugs or tears. Or clothes."

With a few gentle pushes and nudges, she got him onto his mattress, and he sank a mile deep. Oh, yeah. That felt good.

Was she speaking?

"—sleeping on your couch, and I'll probably be gone before you wake up. But I'll check on you in the afternoon, and if Bea doesn't come to take care of you, I will." Something warm and soft brushed his closed eyelids, then his cheek. "Sweet dreams, Martin."

In a blind grab, he caught her hand. "Dream of you."

Another tender brush against his cheek.

And that was the last thing he remembered until morning.

THIRTEEN

A WEEK LATER, MARTIN PACKED UP HIS SECOND-period materials and eyed Rose with both admiration and frustration as she greeted her AP students at the door.

"Good morning, Vonnie." She smiled at the slight young woman. "Last day before the exam. How are you feeling?"

Vonnie sagged in the doorway as other students edged around her. "Tired. But that horrible review packet helped. I feel more comfortable with the Gilded Age now." Her mouth tipped up in a slight smile. "I kind of want to kick Vanderbilt in the nuts, though. I'd forgotten how awful he was."

Rose snorted. "I'm pretty sure most of his business competitors felt the same way. And I'm happy to hear the packet did its job. Sometimes the most horrible things are also the most effective."

As Vonnie began to wander toward her seat, Rose laid a gentle hand on her arm. "Honey, don't stay up late studying tonight. You need your sleep more than anything else right now."

The young woman's back straightened, and she looked up

at Rose with her heart so exposed, Martin almost looked away.

Her face soft with affection and absolute trust, she reminded her teacher, "You said the same thing last year in honors, right before the state test."

"And you aced that test, didn't you?" At Vonnie's nod, Rose gave her a gentle push toward her desk. "That's why you need to listen to me again. I'm always right. Now sit down before you fall down, and no energy drinks after school. Just sleep."

The girl saluted and dropped into her chair. "Yes, Mom."

Vonnie's halfhearted snark didn't conceal the connection between the two, and it wasn't intended to. They understood one another perfectly.

This. This was the bond Rose had formed over two years with these students.

This was what Dale had stripped from her. From kids like Vonnie.

In that moment, Martin decided it wasn't going to happen a second time.

Reluctantly, he prepared to leave the room, even though he was hungry for any glimpse of Rose's stubborn chin and shining, bitter-coffee hair. Starving to claim the privileges she'd promised him in the dimness of his bedroom, the chance to render her unclothed and undone under his hands. Desperate to tell her how her attention, her tenderness toward him, had transformed him into the man he'd always dreamed of being.

No. That wasn't quite right.

She hadn't changed him. She hadn't *wanted* to change him.

But her total acceptance had changed everything around him, cleared away the fog, until he could look at himself in the mirror over his bathroom sink and see himself for what he truly was.

Not Mute Boy or Old Sobersides.

He was a man who would sacrifice anything to protect Rose, even though she didn't ask for protection from him or anyone. Even though most people wouldn't even see that she sometimes needed it. He'd dive into frigid dunk tank water. Make her coffee suitably dark and bitter. Insist to Dale, an all-too-familiar bully, that she reclaim her Honors World History classes next year.

He was a man who paid attention. Who understood her thick, gleaming armor and could help her shed it whenever it got too heavy for her. Who nevertheless appreciated its beauty and the reasons she'd donned it.

He was a man who made her snort with laughter.

He was a man she trusted to keep her secrets.

He was a man who adored her intelligence, her will, her wit, and her beauty.

Above all: He was a man who could make Rose happy.

That is, if they were ever alone again.

By the time he'd woken the morning after her visit to his home, she'd left for school hours before, leaving only a neatly folded blanket and a note as reminders of her recent presence.

Relax, Martin. I've got this. Talk to you this afternoon. —R

When she'd phoned him after school, as promised, Bea had already arrived to take care of him, and he'd had to cut the call short.

Each night he was absent, he and Rose had talked at some point, but he'd always remained too aware of Bea's presence somewhere in the house to share anything more private than test strategies.

And once he could move comfortably enough to return to classroom duty, he and Rose were working almost around the clock to prepare their students for the AP and state tests, and neither had the time or energy for any sort of intimate conversations or encounters.

So, yeah. It was fair to say that he was a bit frustrated. In the sense that a tornado was a bit breezy, or Dale a bit dickish.

The bell rang for the beginning of the period, and Rose closed the door.

Dammit. It didn't matter how much he wanted to bask in her presence. He needed to vacate her room before he got in her way.

But once he got halfway to the door, the intercom blared to life.

Tess's voice rang out, clear and authoritative. "Attention, all faculty, students, and visitors. We are conducting a scheduled lockdown drill. Please follow standard lockdown procedures, rather than Run, Hide, Fight procedures. I repeat, this is a drill."

With a final crackle, the intercom went silent.

Fuck. He'd completely forgotten. Now he wasn't going anywhere anytime soon, and Rose had one more person in her classroom to consider during the drill.

She spoke over her shoulder as she jogged to the door. "Chase and Ariana, get the blinds. Everyone else, either squeeze into the closet or get in the corner behind my desk, just like we practiced. Leave room for Chase and Ariana. No talking, not even whispers. Phones on silent. Understood?"

The kids, well-versed after years of these drills—a fact that never failed to hurt him—went about their business quietly as Rose threw her deadbolt, flicked off the overhead lights, and covered the window in her door with the appropriate laminated sign. Green to indicate the safety of the room's inhabitants, rather than yellow to indicate injuries or

—God forbid—red to indicate the presence of a shooter in the classroom.

A black sign would tell authorities to expect fatalities inside.

The blinds descended one by one to the windowsills, and the room turned gray and dim as Chase and Ariana finished their task and joined their classmates.

Most classes had at least a few giggling or whispering kids during lockdowns, since the unimaginable had somehow become banal in the last decade. But Rose's kids remained in absolute silence, their eyes following her.

Slipping off her heels, she carried them in her hand as she hustled barefoot toward her desk. Given the number of students in her class, though, there wasn't much room for a woman her size to hide behind it, and there certainly wasn't enough space left in the closet.

He might be able to squeeze into the empty area underneath her desk, but not her. If a shooter burst into the room, she'd have nowhere to hide.

Several other kids hadn't found a large enough hiding spot, either, and he knew without asking Rose what that meant. She wouldn't duck behind a desk or into a closet while any of her students crouched there in the open, exposed.

Come what may, she'd remain in front of that desk, chin tipped high and proud as she shielded the students with her body. Just as she was doing now.

Without a word, she'd nudged the unprotected kids behind herself. They glanced up at her after obediently moving into place, faces drawn as they realized what her position implied.

What she'd do for them, if she could. What she'd sacrifice.

Footsteps down the hall slowly grew louder. Doorknobs rattled.

Rose waved him behind her too. When he didn't move from her side, she tried—gently—to push him back to the only shelter she could provide him.

He didn't budge, and her flared-nostril glare should have incinerated him on the spot.

That's when he knew.

He loved her.

And AP exam or no AP exam, he was done waiting.

———

As soon as Rose noticed Martin in the doorway, she frowned at him.

He really should have been grading review packets. Or dreaming up new ways to remind his students about thousands of years of world history before their AP and state tests later in the week. Or, best of all, sleeping, since Nosferatu would take one look at those bags under Martin's eyes and feel comparatively well-rested and fresh-faced.

Instead, however, Martin was lounging in the entrance to her classroom at nine o'clock at night, tie uncharacteristically loose around his neck, as if he had nothing better to do with his time.

"What's going on?" He tilted his head in the direction of her classroom's back counter, where she'd laid out just under one hundred brown paper lunch bags. "You decided to run a meal delivery service in your spare time?"

"Ha-ha," she said. "These are for my kids tomorrow. They'll come by here right before getting on the bus for the AP test."

He edged around the student desks to reach her side. "You've done some shopping."

After her last students had left for the day, she'd stopped at the local big box store for supplies, then returned to the classroom to put together her offerings. Given her limited funds, she'd done the best she could.

He nudged the top of one of the store's plastic bags. "May I?"

"Feel free."

If he was investigating, she was sitting. Bared feet aching, she plopped into the closest blue plastic chair and watched him sort through her loot.

"Black pens. Number two pencils. Water bottles. Granola bars. Peanut butter crackers. Apples." He directed a questioning look her way. "Beef jerky?"

"Alternate source of protein."

He nodded. "And, of course, sticky notes. Many of which you've filled with personalized praise and encouragement for each student."

That was everything. She'd distributed the water bottles, pencils, and pens into each bag already, but the rest of the job lay before her. Composing individual messages for each sticky note took the longest, she'd found. Especially once her hand started cramping.

He settled into the seat next to hers and quirked a brow. "I'm surprised a heart as black and bitter as yours can still beat."

She threw an extra pen at him. "Shut up, Krause."

"So you're making sure they can write their test answers. But you're also feeding them." After scanning her bags a second time, he turned back to her. "Carbohydrates and protein and water. Not to mention love."

Some of them don't get their recommended daily allowance of that.

Nope. Too sappy to say aloud.

"They can eat on the bus to the test, or during the testing break." She spread her hands. "I can't afford to feed them every day. But I can afford to feed them tomorrow, so a year's effort doesn't go to waste because they're too hungry to concentrate."

With his typical deliberateness, he thought for a minute before responding.

"Don't get me wrong. I think this"—he gestured to the bags—"is wonderful. Beautiful, actually. But don't needy kids have access to free breakfast and lunch at school?"

"Even some of the kids who can afford breakfast might forget to eat." Her arms ached from carrying the bags from the parking lot, and her head had begun to throb an hour or so ago. She was too tired to prevaricate, and she didn't need to. Not with him. "Besides, if they're anything like me, some of the poorest kids in my class haven't applied for free breakfast and lunch in the first place."

He closed his eyes in understanding. "Pride."

"It's humiliating. And as much as staff members try to be discreet, other kids usually find out at some point." She shrugged. "Most days, I had an off-brand Pop-Tart in the morning and didn't eat again until Mom came home for dinner. I imagine many of my kids do the same. Tomorrow, they won't have to."

In a minute, she'd have to get going again, so she could head home and grab a few hours of much-needed sleep before returning early in the morning.

But first, she needed to make sure Martin was okay.

She heaved her chair ninety degrees, until she was facing him. "Bea told me she made her final decision about schools last week. How are you holding up?"

"I'm happy for her." His attempt at a smile hurt to witness. "I know she misses her old friends in Wisconsin, and UW-Madison is a great school. I think she'll love it there."

She rested her elbows on a nearby desk and propped her

chin on her hands. "Okay, let's try this again. How are you holding up?"

He deflated. "Well, I'm not delighted at the prospect of paying out-of-state tuition for a school located ten miles away from our old house. But that's what the college fund is for, I suppose."

"And?"

"And I'm kind of..." He cleared his throat. "I'm kind of devastated that she'll be living a thousand miles away from me."

Oh, fuck. She hadn't even considered... "Will you move back there to be closer to her?"

"No." He abruptly straightened in his chair, his face no longer quite so drawn in misery. "One, I can't afford to do that again, not with closing costs and moving expenses. Two, Marysburg is my home now." His eyes met hers. "Everything I want is here."

Her pulse tripped at that look, but she wouldn't be distracted. Not if he needed to talk more. "Except Bea."

"Except Bea." He sighed. "Parenting is a real bitch, Rose. Anyone who tells you otherwise is trying to sell you wet wipes or formula."

They were sitting in her classroom. This wasn't the place for any sort of intimacy, no matter how innocent. Still, she reached over to stroke her knuckles down his bristly cheek, unable to keep herself from giving him some sort of physical comfort.

"I'm sorry you're hurting. What can I do to help?"

The line between his brows smoothed under her touch, and he reached up to catch her fingertips. Bring them to his mouth for a kiss.

This smile looked more genuine, and he squeezed her fingers. "You're already doing it." After a long, slow breath, he returned his attention to the plastic bags. "Let's knock this out so we can get you home. You're squinting like you have a headache."

How in the world had he noticed that, especially while steeped in his own misery?

When he offered his arm, she let him help her to her feet. "You're willing to help?"

He shot her a chiding look, which was answer enough.

For an hour, he helped her fill the bags and waited as she wrote notes to all her AP kids. When she'd finished, and all the bags were labeled and resting in neat rows on her back counter, he hoisted her briefcase alongside his and walked her to the parking lot.

Theirs were the only two remaining vehicles. By that time, she could barely see straight, and Martin had devolved from Nosferatu to Crypt Keeper. But his presence had turned the evening from torturous to tolerable.

More than tolerable. Companionable. Exciting.

Especially when they'd tossed her bags in her passenger's seat, and she was leaning against the driver's door, too tired to stand upright without support.

"Good night, Martin," she said.

He didn't respond verbally. Instead, he took a step closer. Another. Until his pants brushed the thin flounce of her skirt, his breath mingled with hers, and he became everything she could see. Everything she cared to see.

His blue eyes didn't stray from her face. Didn't flicker away in indecision or embarrassment. Instead, he watched his own fingers trace her cheek. Brush along her lower lip like a whisper. Stroke the line of her neck so slowly and gently she shivered.

He leaned closer. Smoothed her hair back from her ear, making her skin prickle everywhere. Spoke with low, unhurried intimacy into that sensitive ear, like a man who intended to savor the way their bodies fit, the way their oxygen mingled.

"I want to kiss you," he said. "May I?"

She nodded.

One more step forward, and all that lean strength pressed into her softness. Backed her into the cool metal of the car door. Her breath hitched at the immediate heat against her breasts and belly, the forest scent of him, the way he let her take some of his weight. He didn't try to hide his arousal, but he didn't impose it upon her either, and when her thighs parted to allow one of his in between, he didn't immediately accept the offer.

Instead, his sensitive fingers cradled her skull, sliding through the hair she'd loosened from a twist once her headache began. His thumbs slid along her cheekbones and followed the line of her jaw. Tipped her chin downward a tiny bit.

She felt surrounded. Sheltered bodily in the same way she'd tried to shelter him earlier that day, in her classroom.

Then his mouth settled over hers, and her world became velvet.

Soft. He was so soft with her. Careful in a way she'd never experienced.

There was no demand. Only invitation. A quiet offer of pleasure as his lips nuzzled hers, exploring the plush give of her mouth and the slickness just inside. Encouraging the low hum in her throat as her tongue met his for the first time.

Oh, this was luxury like she'd never known.

She teased his inner lip, sucked on the tip of his tongue, and he took that final step forward with a rough moan. So carefully, his thigh fitted between hers. Pressed.

When her head fell back, he trailed his mouth down her neck. Deliberately took a bit of flesh between his teeth and tugged. Just a little, until she arched into him and let his thigh ease her ache for a moment.

His hands left her face, slid down her sides in a lingering caress. Then they were on her bottom, hitching her forward. Hitching her tighter against his leg, rocking her, until the slow, easy rhythm had her short of breath, clutching his shoulders, and remarkably, damnably close to orgasm. She was tightening between her legs, swollen and trembling in little spasms.

In the past, she'd had to fight for her pleasure.

There was no struggle here. Only a man who paid attention, determined for her to have everything she wanted.

Another slow slide of that thigh over her clit, and she'd come. Here. At school.

She managed to rasp out two words. "Parking lot."

He let her go, but not quickly. His hands tightened on her bottom for a moment, and only released her with a final, savoring stroke of the generous curves. And his mouth didn't lift from her neck until he'd had one more lingering suckle of her tingling flesh.

He licked a path up to her ear. Bit her earlobe gently.

Whispered, "Were you about to come, Rose?"

Oh, he was pleased with himself. Which was fair, because she was rather pleased with him too.

"Yes." She scratched her nails down his back, just to see his satisfying shudder. "About five seconds away, if my calculations are correct."

He laughed softly into her ear, and her second countdown began again with that warm tickle. "Me too. You saved me from a ruined pair of pants."

She turned her head to press one last, light kiss on his mouth. "I'd invite you home, but I need to be back here in about eight hours. That's not enough time for what I have planned."

"You've made plans?" He looked delighted. "Again, me too."

"Let's save those plans for one night soon, then." She fumbled for her keys with unsteady fingers. "Maybe after our AP and state tests are done, a week when you don't have Bea."

"It's a date." When she moved to swing open her car door, he caught her hand. "Hold on. One more thing."

For the first time, those worry lines appeared on his brow again, and he adjusted his weight from foot to foot. But why in the world would he be nervous now? They'd already made out, already proposed plans for actual, full-on sex within the next several weeks.

"I haven't done this before," he began, and she couldn't help but snort.

"I don't think that's true." She patted his cheek. "Unless you really did pluck Bea from the cabbage patch. And based on your performance tonight, you'd have to be a prodigy of some kind. A sexual wunderkind."

He took a moment to bask in the praise. Smugness looked good on him.

Then he sort of shook himself. "That's not what I meant. When I said I haven't done this before, I wasn't talking about sex. I was talking about prom."

Poor thing worried way too much. "You haven't chaperoned before? That's okay. It's not for another month or so. I'll fill you in before then." A yawn caught her by surprise, one so big her jaw cracked. "But I should really get g—"

"No, Rose. Please let me finish." His hands clasped her shoulders in a gentle hold. "What I'm trying to say is that I've never asked anyone to prom before."

She blinked at him, too tired to make sense of it.

"But I'm asking you. Now. Will you go with me to prom as my date?"

Prom. In front of the entire school. Teachers and students and staff, all suddenly aware of her relationship with Martin. All suddenly able to speculate. Gossip.

Pity and mock her if everything fell apart.

She cared about him too much. She wouldn't be able to hide her devastation if they broke up, and then all her armor wouldn't help her fend off the scrutiny and judgment of others.

No. Never again.

His thumbs stroked her skin through her blouse. "We'll still have to chaperone, of course, but we could talk. Dance. Spend the whole evening together without a single paper to grade or parent call to make."

His blue eyes were so earnest, so sincere. So nervous. So beloved.

She had no clue what to think. What to say.

God, her head hurt. For a moment, in his arms, she'd completely forgotten.

He brushed a tender kiss on her temple. "Please, Rose."

"I don't know." The words emerged in a tumble. "I just... don't know. My headache is getting worse. Can we talk about this later?"

And then, like a coward, she got into her car and drove away before he could request a more definitive response from her. Because the only answer she could give right now was one he wouldn't want to hear.

FOURTEEN

MARTIN SAT AT HIS SOCIAL STUDIES DEPARTMENT office desk and opened a new document on his laptop. Then stared at the white screen, unable to remember what he'd wanted to write.

At some point this morning, he was going to have to stop last night's encounter with Rose from tumbling over and over in his mind, but he hadn't found that off switch yet.

Another mug of heavily-sugared coffee didn't help. Neither did a perfunctory check of his e-mails. Five minutes later, he closed the blank document with a disgruntled mumble and gave in to his need to obsess over, replay, and analyze everything that had happened.

In his past, he could claim exactly one previous girlfriend. One previous lover.

Sabrina. His ex-wife.

So on the one hand, his ability to arouse Rose almost to orgasm in an empty school parking lot—up against the side of her car, for Christ's sake—seemed somewhat miraculous. A gift he hadn't even dared request, given the decidedly temperate nature of his union with Sabrina.

He'd expected awkwardness. Fumbling. Possibly apologies on his part.

Instead, Rose had melted like marshmallow fluff under his hands and mouth. And in return, she'd kept him aflame the entire night with the memory of her nails in his back, the heat between her thighs.

He could only count that as a win.

On the other hand, asking a woman to prom for the first time ever and having her plead a headache and speed away as if pursued by ravenous, educator-eating zombies didn't feel great. Especially since she wasn't just any woman, but Rose. Gorgeous, brilliant, fierce *Rose*. The culmination of every desire, every longing, he'd never let himself acknowledge.

It had simply never occurred to him that she might be willing—no, blessedly *eager*—to have sex with him, but leery about dating him in public. Sabrina's preferences had tended toward the opposite.

But he should have known. Dammit, if he'd thought about it for more than five minutes using an organ not located in his boxer-briefs, he *would* have known.

A woman who guarded her privacy like jewels and wore pride like armor wouldn't want her personal life made public, especially when that personal life involved a colleague. Not unless she knew—*knew*, with the sort of certainty that had built and toppled monuments—her relationship with that colleague would never damage that pride, never leave her exposed and humiliated before the unkind gaze of near-strangers.

He'd pushed her too hard, when she was already hurting and exhausted and worried about the AP exam. From the social studies department window that morning, he'd seen her wave off the buses full of her kids, all of whom were carrying brown paper bags filled with concrete manifestations of her love for them.

She'd stared after that bus, hands on her hips, for a minute before returning inside. No doubt to keep working on review prep for the state exams, which occurred later in the week.

She needed more time. He could give it to her.

Maybe more time would coax her to share what exactly had happened in her marriage and what sort of scars its collapse had left behind. Maybe more time would allow him to share his particular iteration of that story too.

Now was not the moment to become impatient.

Now was the moment to become clever.

Bea clutched a black washed-silk dress close and petted it, her blue eyes—so like Martin's—alight with wonder and lust. "I have enough money for this. And it fits perfectly."

Annette drifted to the young woman's side and began a lecture Rose had heard before. Had received before, from the very same source, approximately two decades ago.

"My dear, the fit and the price tag alone don't tell you everything you need to know about whether you should buy an item of clothing, especially when you're on a budget. Which, unfortunately"—Annette directed a glare at Martin, who pretended not to see it—"it appears you are. Since your father deprived an infirm old woman very close to death the pleasure of buying a wardrobe for such a lovely girl."

Rose snorted, while Bea giggled.

Martin bit his lip and eyed the nearby café longingly.

Annette's nimble fingers located the care label sewn into the inside seam of the skirt. "There are other factors to consider. The care instructions, for example. I imagine your dorm won't offer dry cleaning services?"

Not unless dorms at public universities had been taken over by the Rockefellers since Rose graduated. Although she probably shouldn't mention that, since Annette and Alfred might be tempted to sponsor Bea's housing in some round-about way.

Next thing they all knew, Bea would have a private loft with an espresso bar.

Bea's face scrunched. "Uh, I don't think so?"

"Then you'll want something easy to wash and dry. This dress doesn't fulfill that requirement." When the younger woman drooped, Annette continued soothingly, "But that's not the only other factor. We also need to consider cost-per-wear, a calculation that takes into account not only how many times you're likely to wear a garment, but also how many wears that garment will withstand before becoming unusable. Better-quality clothing lasts longer, and so do sturdier fabrics."

"I...don't know how often I'd wear this." Bea's hand lingered over the jet detailing at the neck. "How sturdy is silk? It doesn't snag or anything, right?"

Annette pursed her lips, then decided to move on. "And finally, there are the intangibles."

Rose stopped idly flipping through a rack to watch her favorite bit of the familiar lecture.

"When you're wearing the garment, do you feel confident? Do you feel powerful? If looking beautiful is important to you, do you feel beautiful in it? Does it bring you joy? Will there always be some niggling doubt in your mind about its fit or color, or does it seem made for you? You don't want to buy something you're always readjusting." Annette glanced at Rose. "As Rosie and I know, a good tailor can fix many sins, but not everything."

That was the end of Annette's very informative lecture, except for one small detail.

"I feel amazing in this." Bea slowly put the dress back on the rack. "But it's almost half the money my grandma gave me. I probably wouldn't wear it often, and it needs dry cleaning." The girl forced a strained smile. "Let's look at other stuff."

Rose waited for it.

"There's one last factor I forgot to mention," Annette announced. "Whether an elderly woman who's barely able to walk some days might wish to give a graduation gift to a wonderful young lady."

And there it was. The part where Annette ignored all the sensible advice she'd just given and bought the damn clothing anyway.

But when Annette's hand reached for the dress, Martin's hand got there first. For a fraught minute, the winner of their silent tug-of-war remained in doubt, but he emerged victorious. Brandishing the hanger well over Annette's reach, he took a moment to catch his breath.

Annette eyed him balefully, nursing her hand as if he'd broken it, when Rose knew for a fact Martin hadn't hurt her. Wouldn't hurt her. Not in the slightest, not ever.

He shook the dress, his spoils of battle. "Sweet Bea?"

"Yeah, Dad?" His daughter's disappointment had shifted into muffled hilarity at the sight of her father and Annette fighting over a hanger in the middle of a classy department store. "Congratulations on your victory, by the way."

He gave a little bow. "Thank you. I had a worthy opponent."

"Fierce. Committed." Bea kept a straight face. "One might even say vicious."

Annette appeared mollified, although she kept eyeing the stack of discarded clothing in Bea's dressing room in a way Rose recognized all too well.

"I haven't chosen your graduation gift yet. If you really

want this, I'll get it for you. Save your grandmother's money for a more"—he read the price tag with a sigh—"practical college wardrobe."

Bea had ceased breathing. "Really?"

"Really." He leaned over to kiss her forehead, and she didn't even try to stop him. "If this dress makes you feel confident and powerful and beautiful, then you need to have it. And then we need to leave this store. Immediately."

After he'd paid for the dress, handed the hanger to Bea, and headed for the door—minus one member of their group, although Martin apparently hadn't noticed that yet—Rose leaned over to whisper in his ear. "I told you to stay at the other end of the mall, no matter what Annette said."

He threw up his hands. "When we arrived, she told me she only felt comfortable using the facilities in this store. That they had stalls equipped for women who needed extra support to stand. What kind of monster would refuse her?"

Annette was a marvel.

"Do you remember her using the bathroom?" Rose asked. "At any point while we were here?"

He stopped dead. "Hold on. Maybe she...no. No, she never left Bea."

"She really didn't."

His mouth had dropped open. "Oh, God, she played me. She totally played me."

She really shouldn't smile. Martin had been so patient all morning as Annette and Bea dragged him to makeup counters and jewelry displays and racks upon racks of gorgeous, expensive, midnight-black clothing. To Bea's credit, though, she'd been thrifty with her maternal grandparents' birthday money to this point.

And shortly, if Annette had her way, Bea was going to discover she had very few items left to buy.

"She definitely played you," Rose agreed. "You don't know the half of it yet."

When Rose had asked Martin about the origin of this little expedition, he'd lifted a shoulder in a casual shrug and said Bea and Annette must have exchanged numbers at some point over dinner.

"My daughter admires Annette's style," he'd said. "Yours too. When she got the money for a new wardrobe, she wanted guidance from both of you, and she called Annette to plan a group shopping trip."

Then he'd changed the subject very quickly. Too quickly.

Hmmm.

Maybe Martin wasn't the only one who'd been played. Rose had the distinct impression that he—and maybe even Bea and Annette—had been trying to make a point today. Trying to demonstrate how well the four of them meshed as a group.

As a kind of family, even.

She swallowed, hard.

Clever. Very clever.

When it came to subtle maneuvers, however, he'd just been outclassed.

His head suddenly jerked in a frantic scan of the store. "Where *is* Annette?"

"If I know my former mother-in-law, she's back in the dressing room, deciding what to do." Rose nodded in that direction. "She'll want to buy all the items Bea admired but discarded for being too frivolous. But she won't want to upset you or hurt your pride, so she'll be considering her options. Maybe calling Alfred for advice."

"Really?" Bea's brow furrowed. "I...I don't know if I can accept that sort of gift. Dad?"

"We're not letting Annette purchase an entire wardrobe

for you. Sorry, sweet Bea." He turned to Rose. "If I don't let Annette buy something, though, what will she do?"

"Look pitiful." She considered. "Acquire a decided hunch. Discuss her nonexistent rheumatism."

His groan was low but heartfelt.

"I know how you feel. For the first few years of my marriage, I told Annette not to buy me anything." She shook her head. "Pride, you know."

His mouth quirked. "I know."

"Yet somehow I ended up wearing cashmere capelets and sleeping on silk bedding. Because if I didn't, she'd shoot me this *look*, like I'd selfishly snatched away her only source of pleasure in life, and the trauma of it all might very well kill her on the spot."

He snickered a little at that.

"It's her way of taking care of the people she cares about. It brings her genuine joy." She laid a hand on his arm. "That said, only you get to choose what she can and can't buy for your daughter. Whatever you decide, I'll support you."

His lips pursed in thought. Then, finally, he came to a decision. "Bea, if you pick one more item, I'll let Annette buy it for you as a graduation gift. Everything else, she'll need to return to the dressing room. If she argues, send her to me, and I'll deal with it." He caught his daughter's eye. "Later today, you'll send her a handwritten note of appreciation. And you'll also be calling her on the phone to chat and find out if there anything, *anything*, we can do for her in return."

Bea's uncertainty transformed into a beam. "No problem!"

When she caught sight of Annette in the distance, staggering under a mountain of garments on hangers, she sprinted in that direction.

Martin watched the two of them, his forehead creased. "Was that the right decision?"

"Remember the context here. Annette and Alfred have more money than they can possibly spend, even with all the charities they support. And they like both of you." A quick glance established that Bea and Annette were occupied looking through the clothing options, so Rose dared a soft kiss on his cheek. "You made two good women happy, and you also maintained your boundaries. I think you handled the situation just right."

His fingertips pressed lightly at the small of her back, where Bea and Annette couldn't see. Traced up her spine in a slow, lingering caress.

"I'd like to make another good woman happy," he murmured. "Soon."

They hadn't been alone in almost two weeks. State tests had followed hard on the heels of the AP exams, and during that stretch, they'd been too exhausted to do anything more intimate than exchange the occasional heated glance. Bea's week at his house had begun the day after the Honors World History state test, so they'd continued to wait.

But that night, Bea was heading back to her mother's, and Rose fully intended to take advantage of Martin's wide-open schedule.

Martin, it seemed, had been thinking along the same lines.

"This good woman plans to make you happy too." She flicked him a glance through her lashes. "Several times. At least once with her mouth."

High color glazed his cheekbones, and those fingers on her back tightened. "Funny. I was thinking the same thing."

Another glance. Still no one within hearing distance. "That you wanted a blowjob?"

"That I wanted my mouth on you."

The bolt of pleasure between her legs nearly staggered her.

Before she could respond with anything more than a small, shaky gasp, the sound of Bea's chattering drew nearer, and Martin's touch disappeared.

"Tonight?" he whispered, his voice low and raspy.

She smiled in anticipation. "Tonight. My house."

FIFTEEN

After Martin pulled into Rose's driveway that night, he double-checked the number above the garage, then the text she'd sent earlier that day.

Yup. He'd found the right place.

But it didn't *look* like the right place.

He'd pictured her in an impeccably maintained, black-painted Victorian mansion. Or some sleek, uber-modern, urban loft, never mind the fact that Marysburg didn't actually contain any uber-modern urban lofts. At the very least, he'd counted on turrets and a moat.

Instead, she appeared to inhabit a one-story bungalow with dove-gray siding and dark green shutters. All neat and well-painted, but also so...normal. Middle-class.

No moat. No arrow slits. No chrome or black paint to be found.

When she answered her doorbell, her feet delectably bare, he tapped the trim around her entrance. "Green instead of black? This seems so unlike you."

"HOAs are a bitch." Her hair swayed around her shoulders as she turned. "Sorry for any disappointment. My next home will be enormous and dark enough to blot out the sun, if that's any consolation."

"Some." He stepped inside and removed his shoes. "I'll look forward to purchasing a tasteful plant and several evil henchmen as your housewarming presents."

She snorted. "Don't bother with the plant. It'll just die without sunlight, like the rest of you mere mortals."

"Black and bitter." He shook his head. "Black and bitter."

Her laughter trailed after her as she headed toward the kitchen, and he looked around her home for a moment before following her.

Ah. He recognized her here.

Other than a hallway off to the right, the house boasted open sightlines, her kitchen flowing into the living room and dining area. The furniture was surprisingly sparse but unsurprisingly elegant. Mahogany bookshelves along the deep blue walls, lined with paperbacks. A couch and chaise in pewter velvet, separated by a sculptural glass table. A thick, subtly patterned rug underfoot. Heavy curtains—metal-shot silk, he'd guess—framing her windows. A gleaming metallic dining room set, and veined marble countertops. All the other necessary pieces for daily life, also stylish and of unmistakable quality, but nothing extra.

In a hammered silver vase on the glass table, calla lilies provided a splash of contrasting ivory, severe and spare in their beauty. Perfect for this home.

Only the enormous television in the far corner seemed out of place. At least until he remembered the story of her mother and their ever-disappearing TV fund.

His heart twisted at the reminder, and he hurried after Rose.

"Does everything pass inspection?" She donned oven mitts to remove a tray of little pancake-like things from the oven, using her foot to close the door. "Or do I need to start over?"

Irony freighted her voice, but she wasn't looking at him as she deposited the tray on the stovetop and removed her mitts. Her bare toes began tapping against the dark hardwood planks underfoot.

She cared what he thought of her home.

"It's you," he told her. "Which means it's gorgeous and impeccable."

With a gentle hand on her arm, he steered her a few safe inches away from the hot pan. Then he wrapped her up tight and simply held her as the weeks-long tension in his body released. After a few seconds, she relaxed into his embrace, leaning into him enough that he gladly bore some of her weight.

She was here, in his arms, bare-faced and dressed in slouchy black clothing, with her hair down, no heels anywhere in sight. In short, wearing no armor.

He loved her, and she cared about him.

They were going to spend the night together.

His life had definitely taken an upswing in recent months.

"Did you fix silver dollar pancakes for me?" He spoke in her ear, remembering how she'd reacted last time. And sure enough, her arms tightened around him in an entirely satisfying manner. "How domestic of you."

She lifted her head from his shoulder, amber eyes heavy-lidded. "Blinis. I have crème fraîche and caviar to put on top."

Dear Lord. Either she'd gone all out preparing for his visit, or she must spend twice her salary on food alone.

He could only imagine she'd gotten one hell of a divorce settlement. Although if she was so wealthy, why was she staying in such a decidedly middle-income neighborhood?

"Ah. Caviar-and-crème-fraîche blinis." He kissed an especially adorable freckle on her cheek. "Like the kind Little Debbie makes."

When she pinched him lightly in the ribs, he groaned piteously.

"I needed a snack." She sniffed, lifting that narrow-tipped nose high in the air. "But I suppose I can share with a philistine."

She'd made the blinis for him. They both knew it.

And he couldn't wait any longer. "Thank you, ma'am. Let me properly express my gratitude."

Her mouth was salty and sweet, open and eager under his. Without hesitation, her hands slid down his back to his ass, taking a firm, possessive grip, and he moaned as her tongue glided along his lips. His own hands stroked her upper arms, the silky length of her hair, the curve of her waist. Then she bit his lower lip, her teeth a bee sting, and his pulse echoed in his ears as blood turned to flame.

He backed her into the counter, hard enough that he was poised to apologize. But she gasped into his mouth in response, parting her thighs, her fingernails sunk deep into his ass, and he discarded the apology in favor of mouthing down the length of her neck, nipping and sucking her tender flesh along the way.

His hands slid beneath her thighs, prepared to help boost her to the countertop, but she spread her hands on his chest and gave a breathless laugh.

"First of all, you'd give yourself a hernia. Second, I'd rather do this somewhere we can spread out. Like a bed."

She was so fucking clever, his Rose. "What about the blinis?"

The skin of her shoulder slid beneath his tongue, so smooth and hot, and he wanted to take that silky tee and tear it into two. But it had probably cost more than his month's salary, so instead he nudged the neckline aside with his teeth, traced her bra strap with his nose.

She tilted her head to the side with a moan. "I was keeping them warm in the oven. But they taste good at room temperature too."

Clever beyond belief. "Then let's go."

She led him by the hand down her hall and into her bedroom, where an enormous slab of a mattress waited for them, lit only by a dim bedside lamp. A dark-wood headboard curved above the expanse, arching back in a way that sparked a new fantasy.

But he had a few things he needed to say first.

By the bedside, he let go of her hand to cup her face and turn her molten eyes to his. "I brought condoms, but if you want to use your own, no problem. Anytime you want me to stop, I will. Anything that doesn't feel good, tell me." Despite his nervousness, he had to grin. "Anything that *does* feel good, tell me. I may be too preoccupied with not coming to notice."

Her swollen lips curved. "Same goes. Tell me what works for you and what doesn't, so I can make this good for both of us."

He almost laughed.

"Unless you somehow transform into a different person, there's no way this won't be good for me." One more question, and then he could kiss her again. "Is there anything you want me to know ahead of time?"

She thought for a moment. "My breasts aren't particularly sensitive. Play with them if it gives you pleasure, but maybe not for too long. After a while, I get bored or uncomfortable." Turning her head, she kissed his palm. "What about you?"

Oh, God. Was he really going to tell her? When he hadn't told his wife of twenty years?

"I, uh..." His face flushed with heat. "I like a little bit of pain. Not much. Not like a whip or paddle or anything. Just a little pinch, or—"

Her eyes flared. "A bite?"

He nodded.

She traced his lower lip, her finger rubbing over the mark of her teeth. "I got that feeling earlier, against the counter. I'm the same way. Do you enjoy hair-pulling and nail scratches too?"

"I think so." The admission would reveal entirely too much about his marital sex life, but he had to tell the truth. "I don't know for sure."

Her slow smile poured over him like heated syrup. "Then let's find out."

MARTIN DIDN'T REMEMBER HOW HER CLOTHES HAD come off, or his.

He didn't remember climbing up onto that enormous bed, or when exactly he'd maneuvered up against the headboard and coaxed her onto his lap, her back against his chest.

His few available brain cells were entirely preoccupied by the tremble of her thighs as he urged them open, draped them on either side of his own legs. The smooth curve of her shoulder and her gooseflesh as he sank his teeth into that muscle. The way she squirmed against him, her ass providing welcome friction against his cock. The silky fall of her hair. The heady smell of her arousal when he raised his knees and opened his own legs inch by inch, stretching her wider and wider, until she was spread before him.

There. That's what he'd pictured when he'd seen the arch of that headboard. Her back arched the same way, her head on his shoulder, her neck bare, her thighs wide.

His hands slid down the outsides of those soft, dimpled

thighs. Slowly, slowly, spread over her inner thighs and inched upward. Then all that wetness and heat lay under his fingertips, and her breath caught as he petted her there. Smoothed her hair aside. Traced the furrow of her sex, each delicate fold entirely new. Entirely fascinating.

She was so slick, so sweet as she pressed into his touch, gasped at the edge of his teeth on her neck. Her fingernails bit into his thighs, and he gave a helpless rock of his hips, grinding himself against all that softness.

A stroke down her center made her sigh, but a slow circle of her clitoris elicited little gasping whimpers. When he spread two fingers, rubbing softly on either side of that peak, she raised her arms and gripped his hair with both hands. Tugged sharply, until the throb of his cock nearly blinded him.

Fuck. She needed to come first.

But God, she was straining now, her back in that lovely bow, her neck exposed.

With his tongue, his teeth, his lips, he worked the flesh there, but kept his fingers slow, slow, slow. Steady. Stroking until her clitoris had swelled, slick and sensitive, and her pussy pulsed in occasional little clenches. Not orgasms, but not far away either.

Her little puffs of breath came faster, and her sounds became harsh. Guttural.

She fisted his hair, pulled, and gasped that she needed harder. More.

He rubbed harder, pressed deeper, in little circles, until her head was tossing on his shoulder, and he couldn't keep his mouth on her neck.

With another, louder gasp, she stiffened, and then her sex began pulsing beneath his fingertips, her slickness coating his hand, as she ground against his touch and moaned and came and came and came.

As she rode his hand, her nails dug into his scalp, the grip of her fingers in his hair tight enough to make his eyes water.

God, it felt amazing.

When she finally collapsed back against his chest, sweaty and still, he whispered into her ear. "Do you think you can come a second time? With me inside you?"

With that murmur into her sensitive ear, she twitched against his fingers again.

"We can try," she said, her voice hoarse. "But if I don't, I won't feel deprived. Believe me."

She got up on shaky knees, her round ass jiggling in a way that made him bite off a groan, and he rolled on the condom. Then she was sinking down onto his cock, her sex gripping him tight as he pressed deeper and deeper.

She wriggled a little, adjusting her position, and took more of him. All of him.

With a sway of her hips, she began a gentle rocking motion. A slow grind of her ass in his lap as she pursued her pleasure. Bracing himself against the headboard, he pulsed his own hips up and down, working his cock deeper and rubbing himself inside her again and again.

"This feels..." Her moan vibrated in her throat. "It's so good, but I can't..."

"Can't come like this?" he managed to gasp out.

She shook her head.

Gently, he tipped her forward, easing out from inside her. Urged her to her knees, her head against the mattress.

Then he ate her from behind, licking into all that slickness and those swollen, plump folds. Flicking against her clitoris until she started those telltale little clenches again, the not-quite-orgasms.

He rose to his knees and pushed deep once more. She shoved herself against him, taking him to the root, and snapped her hips forward and back again. Fucking herself on him. He gripped her hips, fingertips tight, and fucked her right back, until he was breathing in harsh inhalations and making helpless sounds of pleasure as he watched all that tight wetness stretch around his cock, enveloping him even as he sank inside her over and over again.

This white static of agonizing pleasure...he had no context for it. No—

She reached between her legs. Rubbed. And then she sobbed out a breathless *fuck*, and her pussy locked down on him, squeezing and convulsing until he thrust one last time and held. His throat strained as he made a sort of strangled howl and let go, let himself come inside Rose in furious spasms of release and teeth-clenching ecstasy.

She was tightening around him, working her internal muscles to draw out his pleasure, and he fell forward, barely able support his weight on his hands, as he kissed her spine. Kissed her shoulder. Kissed anywhere he could reach.

Jesus, he'd had no idea. Had always thought books and movies exaggerated.

If anything, they'd undersold sex. Maybe because those books and movies weren't about Rose, and she was the crucial bit. The crux of everything.

His unsteady hand covered hers at her sex. "Want more?"

She straightened her legs until she lay flat beneath him, and he slipped out of her body. But she didn't protest as he rested atop her, a human blanket. Their hands remained pressed beneath them, cupped between her legs.

Her voice was a breathless tease. "I thought older men needed more recovery time."

"Some parts do." He grinned against her damp neck. "But our fingers and tongues don't."

He couldn't move his hand much, not with so much weight atop it, but he managed to trace the slick seam of her. Tease her entrance with his fingertip.

She made a little hum of pleasure, but shifted minutely away from his touch. "I'm a bit sensitive right now, but give me five minutes. Then let's test that theory."

He knew just what he wanted to do. How he wanted to bring her more pleasure. "Are you—"

He cut himself off, unsure.

Never in his life had he even attempted to talk dirty. What if he sounded like a fool?

With a heave of her body, she rolled to the side and out from underneath him.

She nudged his chin until she could see his expression. "What?"

"How do you feel about a little...um..." He looked at the pillow for a moment. "Are you okay with dirty talk?"

Her grin should have been a suspension-worthy offense, it was so wicked.

"Oh, I'm more than okay. I'm downright enthusiastic." Her voice was nearly a purr, velvet in the darkness. "Let me have it, Krause. I want to hear all about what you want."

Okay, then.

He thought for a moment, then steeled himself to say it. To do what he'd envisioned.

His breath teased her ear as he nudged her hair aside. "Are you going to come all over my face, Ms. Owens?" He licked her earlobe. Bit down. "How about if I finger-fuck you? Are you going to squeeze my fingers and soak my hand again?"

She drew back and stared at him for a moment, silent, and he regretted everything. Everything. Even his birth.

Then she spoke, those amber eyes aglow with what he could only interpret as lust. "I certainly hope so. Because as far as I'm concerned, your five minutes are up."

Dirty talk fucking rocked.

SIXTEEN

Rose slid Martin's plate in front of him and waited for the inevitable teasing.

He considered the crème-fraîche-and-caviar blinis for a moment, straight-faced. "Well, it's not a Pop-Tart, but I suppose it'll do."

And there it was. Smartass.

Rose rolled her eyes and filled her own dish. "Pearls of caviar before swine."

"I'm on board with the pancake part. I'm just not sure fish eggs are a breakfast food." When she deposited her food onto the table, he tugged her into his lap, even though she had to be crushing him. "You, on the other hand, I consider a nutritious and delicious part of any balanced—"

"Forget it." She tickled his neck until he stilled his wandering hands. "I need coffee before foreplay. Before conversation too, preferably."

He relented. "I forgot you hadn't yet consumed your two-liter vat of coffee."

"The Mug of Caffeinated Glory waits for no man." She

patted its porcelain surface fondly as she took a sip. "And it doesn't hold two liters. Not until I refill it, anyway."

Because he was a considerate man, as well as a wise one, he retreated to the entertainment of his phone while she drank her coffee and consumed her blinis. Which were freaking delicious, whether he appreciated them or not.

But it appeared he did, because after eyeing them suspiciously and taking the world's tiniest bite of the closest one, he began popping the rest into his mouth in quick succession.

When he finished everything on his plate and peered longingly at the contents of her own, she transferred a few more blinis to him. By that time, she'd finished her first mug of coffee and started her second, and was feeling human-adjacent once more.

"Any interesting news?" She slung her bare feet into his lap, and he gave them a squeeze. "Or were you checking your e-mail?"

He laid his cell on the table. "Work e-mail, actually. Keisha says we'll finally get initial class rosters for next year's preps in another week or two. Apparently there was some sort of computer malfunction."

In other words, she'd find out soon just how extreme her drop in AP enrollment really was. Keisha might even tell them which preps they'd be teaching.

Rose expected bad news in both cases.

"I wanted to talk to you about something." His fingertips gently rubbed her arches. "I don't think you're going to like what I have to say, though."

Please let this not be about prom. Please let this not be about prom.

He'd let the subject slide for a couple weeks now, but her grace period couldn't last forever. At some point, he'd want an answer, and she still wasn't sure which one she could give.

He leveled serious blue eyes on her. "I think you should sic Annette and Alfred on Dale."

Whew.

"If they worked their rich-person magic on the school board, he'd be lucky to keep his job." The prospect of an unemployed Dale appeared to cheer Martin. "Even if he managed to stay employed, he'd lose any power he had over you. You know that."

She inclined her head. "I do."

Lines scored across his forehead once more, his momentary levity gone. "So I don't understand why you aren't fighting him with every weapon you have. He's a sexist, arrogant ass who's punishing you for your success and your refusal to make yourself smaller than you are, not for anything problematic you've done. If you enlisted your former in-laws, it wouldn't be because you were trying to avoid some sort of punishment you actually deserved."

"Martin..." She nudged his flat belly with her toe. "I refuse to meet with him one-on-one. I walk out whenever he says anything obnoxious. I threatened to cut off his balls and serve them as our school lunch special if he kept hugging me every time we met. He has plenty of reasons to discipline me, even if he's an ass."

He let go of her feet and threw his hands in the air. "But the reason for those infractions is because he *is* an ass!"

She caught one of his hands. Held it. "On that, we agree."

There was something especially seductive about a man who defended you to yourself. Who was determined to see your least-professional behavior as justified at worst, an actual virtue at best.

He lowered her feet to the floor so he could move closer and take her face in his hands. "Rose, you should be teaching those Honors World History kids. For their sake, but also for yours."

The pain darkening his eyes was for her, and she had no idea how to handle it.

"They do just as well with you," she told him with complete sincerity.

"Maybe for this year." He cradled her face so carefully, like an artifact almost too precious to touch. "But by not getting you in tenth grade, they don't know what an amazing teacher you are. They don't know they can trust you. They don't know they should follow you to AP U.S. History." He paused, giving his next words extra weight. "Which means in eleventh grade, they're missing out on an opportunity to do more. Be more."

He was echoing her own words. Her own past. Her own triumph and her own grief.

Sharing herself meant being seen, being understood, even when she'd rather not be. Even when she'd rather pretend icy indifference and nurse her pain privately.

It hurt.

"Sweetheart..." He brushed the wetness from her cheeks so tenderly, she couldn't even feel embarrassed about crying. "You need those kids. You love those kids."

When Vonnie—or Chase, or Ariana, or any of them— walked across the graduation dais in a little over a year, she'd do the same thing she did every spring. Smile. Congratulate them. Praise them to their loved ones. Then she'd go home, throat aching with unshed tears, and hope her kids never forgot they were loved and capable of greatness, even after she could no longer remind them every weekday.

In a small way, she imagined it was the same pain Martin was experiencing when it came to Bea. A necessary loss didn't hurt any less for its necessity.

"For that matter, Annette and Alfred love *you*. Let them help you." He kissed her closed eyelids. "It would make them happy. It would make you happy. It would make your future students happy. Depending on what happened to Dale, it might even make your fellow social studies teachers happy."

He wasn't wrong, but…

But.

"It's a matter of pride, Martin." She opened her eyes and covered his hands with hers, desperate for him to understand. "As long as I'm not in danger of getting fired, I want to outmaneuver Dale on my own. I don't want him to know I needed help to defeat him."

He considered that for a moment. "Is your pride more important than your happiness?"

The question was unfair. What's more, he should know it was unfair, because she'd shared her past with him.

She scooted her chair back, and his hands fell away from her face. "Pride kept me from drowning in poverty. Pride got me scholarships to college and a 4.0 GPA in graduate school. Pride helped me survive my marriage and my divorce. Pride deprives Dale of satisfaction every time he insults me and waits for the hurt to show."

Because he was Martin, he didn't interrupt. He didn't compose his own response in his head while she was still speaking. He listened.

Which was good, because she wasn't done yet. "Because of my pride, I survived long enough to have any chance at happiness now." She spread her hands flat on the table and met his gaze directly. "And you're telling me to set it aside? Disregard it as if it has no more use?"

He waited to make sure she was done.

Then he spoke slowly. Carefully. "As Bea and I have discussed many times, women are told again and again to swallow their pride to appease others, while men are celebrated for standing strong and remaining defiant. I'd have to be a sexist prick to want you to disregard such a fundamental aspect of yourself."

He reached out for her, then paused for permission. When she didn't stop him, he traced the tight line of her jaw. Measured the angle of her chin.

"And on a personal, selfish level, your pride was the first thing I noticed about you. The first thing that drew me to you. I would never want you to abandon it. I find it admirable, and I find it intensely, painfully arousing." He flashed a self-deprecating smile. "But this isn't about me. It's about whether that sexy, stalwart pride—in this one, very specific instance—is keeping you from what you want, rather than helping you get it."

She tried to picture doing what he'd suggested. Receiving what she wanted so desperately, but at such a steep cost. Seeing the knowledge in Dale's smug face that she'd once again had to recruit people richer and more powerful than she was to thwart him, that she hadn't been able to stymie him on her own.

Could she make that sort of compromise when her entire career wasn't at stake?

She didn't know. She just...didn't know.

"Let me think about it," she finally said.

Until recently, she'd considered herself a decisive person. But now, with Martin in her life, decisions no longer seemed separated into right and wrong halves, the division crystalline. Instead, right and wrong flowed into one another, amorphous and impossible to decouple.

Martin didn't insist on a clearer answer. Instead, he pressed a kiss to her nose—he loved her freckles, as he'd demonstrated the previous night—and sat back in his chair. Cell phone in hand once more, he gave her time.

One last blini remained on her plate, and her stomach churned at the sight of it.

"Do you want this?" She pushed the plate in his direction. "I'm done."

"Are you sure? Because those were amazing." When she didn't change her mind, he popped the little pancake into his mouth and swallowed with a look of utter bliss. "Rich-person food is the best. I had no idea what I was missing."

Wait. Did he think she was rich? Or just that she ate expensive food?

"You realize I'm not actually rich, right?" She waved a hand around the open kitchen area. "I mean, look at my house. It's not precisely a villa in Tuscany."

His face creased in confusion. "Well, I know you weren't rich growing up. But given what I've seen of Alfred and Annette, your ex-husband is definitely wealthy. From what you wear and what you eat, I assume you received a decent amount of money in the divorce settlement."

She had to laugh. "I didn't take a penny from Barton in the divorce. Not even when his parents badgered him into offering me a good settlement."

For a moment, those blue eyes just blinked at her, and then he heaved a groan. "Pride." He dug two fingers between his eyebrows. "Of course. Of course you didn't take any money from your obscenely rich and apparently dickish ex."

As far as she remembered, they'd never talked about her marriage. His either, for that matter, except in the most roundabout terms.

Now she was the one confused. "How did you know he's a dick? I mean, he is, but how did you figure it out?"

"First of all, he let you go." He held up a finger. "Which means he's either a fool or a dick, and you wouldn't marry a fool. I wouldn't have thought you'd marry a dick either, but it's easier to disguise dickishness than foolishness, at least long enough to trap a woman into marriage."

Another finger. "Second, while you were in the bathroom at Milano, Alfred said something that implied his son tried to change you. Once more, I have to err on the side of dickishness. Although one could also argue that only a fool would want to change someone so amazing, and only a fool would expect you, of all people, to change for a man. Even your husband." He nudged her hand on the table. "Don't worry. I made certain Alfred didn't say any more than that. You'll tell me whatever you want me to know about your marriage in your own time."

God, she could love this man. Maybe already did.

She didn't need to keep secrets, because he'd keep them for her.

"Do you want to know what happened?" She got up to put the plates in the sink. "I'll tell you. It doesn't bother me."

Anymore.

"Of course I want to know." He raised his brows in emphasis. "But only if you want to tell me."

Her desire to share everything with him...it disoriented her. But she couldn't deny the urge, just as she couldn't deny the relief she experienced afterwards. "I had no idea you thought I was rich. So it's probably good for me to explain some things."

As always when she spoke about anything personal, he offered her his complete attention. Cell turned off and pushed away, eyes on her and nothing but her.

She kept it snappy. "I met Barton when I was in the master's program for American history at Marysburg University. He was getting his MBA. Mom had just"—she took a sip of water, hiding her face for a moment—"died, and I was kind of...lost. And that's when Barton swooped in."

Without even knowing the full story, Martin cringed a bit at that.

"At first, he thought I was rich too," she said.

Martin nodded. "Because of how you carry yourself."

"I have a talent for finding quality clothing at thrift stores. Mom did too." On weekends when her mother didn't work, they'd take the bus to wealthier neighborhoods and comb through secondhand shops for hours, searching for undiscovered treasures. "I was also very well-educated by that point, and I made a point of sounding like it. I didn't have any desire for people to know where I'd come from or judge me for my upbringing."

His mouth opened, and then he shut it again. Kept it shut.

"But at some point, I told him about my past. I thought he'd be horrified, but instead he was…" The memory of the avid glee on Barton's face made her squirm, even now. "He was excited. I thought because he wanted to help me, wanted to give me everything I needed. Social polish. The tools to make sure no one ever looked down on me again. I still thought that after we both graduated and got married."

She controlled her exhalation. Made it slow.

Martin was suddenly crouching by her side. "Sweetheart, it's okay. You don't have to talk about this."

"No. I want to." After she'd tugged him upright, she didn't let his hand go. "You need to know this to understand me."

He settled back into his chair, mouth tight with concern. "Okay."

"He had Annette and Alfred assist in teaching me what to wear for different occasions. How to eat. What to say in different types of company." She didn't want Martin to get the wrong idea about her former in-laws, so she hurried to add, "They did it because they knew I needed that knowledge in their social circles. So-called upstarts were mocked and insulted even as people smiled to their faces and accepted their dinner invitations. It had happened to Annette and Alfred, and they didn't want it to happen to me. They were trying to protect me."

He gave his empty blini plate a vaguely accusing glance,

as if it were responsible for such polite viciousness. "That sounds terrible."

"Their social circles are not for the faint of heart." Her lips tightened. "The two of them also knew I'd always wanted an impeccable appearance and flawless manners, and they actually cared about my getting what I wanted. Unlike Barton."

Trepidation weighted his next question. "What did he want?"

"He considered himself the Pygmalion to my sculpture. The Henry Higgins to my Eliza." She smiled without an ounce of humor. "In short, he wanted to mold me. Form me. Pare away the excess clay and sculpt me into his preferred shape. Which was fine in the beginning, because I'd always intended to take that shape one way or another."

Martin let the story play out, the hand not holding hers curled into a fist on the table.

"But then I'd changed as much as I wanted to. I was the person I'd intended to become. If he pared away any more, I'd lose my essential form. My structural integrity, I guess." She rolled her eyes at herself. "Sorry to belabor a metaphor. Anyway, once our goals no longer aligned, I slowly realized he'd never wanted to help me. Not really."

Martin's jaw could have been used as a carving implement itself, it had become so sharp. So stony. And all that outrage —on her behalf, always on her behalf—helped her finish the story.

"He wanted to control me." That simple truth had taken her a ridiculously long time to see. "Once I was the perfect hostess, the perfect dinner companion, he started talking about my size. The weight-lifting I did wasn't enough, because he suddenly wanted me thin, not strong."

Martin dropped his chin to his chest. Stared down at the table, that iron jaw working.

But his hand held hers as if an ounce too much pressure might fracture her.

"He started complaining about all the time I spent at school and all the time I worked at home planning and grading, because he'd only ever seen my teaching career as a conversation piece. Something to indicate our humanitarian impulses, rather than an actual job." Now they were getting to the best part of this particular tale. "At some point, I had enough. I told him I wanted out. And oh, God, Martin, he accused me—"

She choked back a laugh that sounded suspiciously like a sob, and Martin's thumb stroked the back of her hand.

After a moment, she regained control of herself. "He accused me of marrying him for his money. I told him to keep it. I'd already gotten everything I wanted from him."

Martin didn't let that stand.

His voice was as soft as her silk comforter. "Not everything."

"No, I suppose not." She swallowed back the thickness in her throat. "I wanted him to love me."

"I know," Martin said. "I know you did."

SEVENTEEN

THE MORNING SUN STREAMED THROUGH HER BAY window, bathing them both in warmth as she let her emotions settle once more.

"What happened after the divorce?" Martin finally asked.

"I haven't heard from Barton since, except concerning necessary legal matters." That wasn't the painful bit, really. Rose had never missed her actual ex, just the possibility of what she'd once thought him to be. "I tried to keep in touch with the few people I considered my friends. But maintaining relationships with a teacher's schedule is tough during the school year. You know that."

He spoke quietly. "I do."

"Besides, our lives were so different suddenly. I couldn't go on vacations to Europe or Bermuda. I couldn't pay thousands of dollars for a table at a charity dinner. I didn't have time, I didn't have money, and I didn't have the same interests. So those friendships faded. And others..." After so many years, it still stung. "Most of them weren't really my friends at all. When Barton and I split, they spread rumors about me. Said I was a gold-digger and Barton had found me fucking the gardener. Someone of my own class, as they put it."

She'd known almost from the start that they'd use her childhood poverty as a weapon against her at some point. But knowing that hadn't stopped their malice from hurting.

"They watched everything I did and judged me for it." She lifted a shoulder in a carefully nonchalant shrug. "At that point, I stopped trying to fit into those circles. The only people still in my life from that time are Annette and Alfred, because they refused to let go."

Not that she hadn't tried to discard them, her grief and anger blinding her to their sincere sympathy. To the love they'd always, always shown her.

Time to wrap up story time and return to her initial point. "I'm not rich. At all. I have nice clothes because I take good care of the wardrobe I acquired during my marriage. I have a nice but aging car that Barton deemed too old to be of any interest to him in the divorce. I eat nice food because I enjoy it, and I don't spend much money on anything else. I don't have a child, unlike you, so I don't have to save for a college fund."

She waved a hand at her sparsely decorated living room. "Even decorating the house doesn't cost much, because I'm only willing to buy good-quality pieces I absolutely love and can afford without too much scrimping."

As usual, he waited until he was sure she'd finished before speaking.

"A lot of things make much more sense now." He raised her hand and pressed a kiss on her palm. "Thank you for telling me all that."

This morning-after could use a bit of levity.

"I can't be your sugar mama." She flicked his earlobe. Leaned forward to lick it, then whispered in his ear, "I hope you're not disappointed."

For once, he didn't respond to the overture.

Instead, he drew back but kept her hand in his. "My story is a lot less dramatic than yours."

Apparently, they were covering all their combined rough ground today. At long last, she'd discover whether she needed to locate Sabrina Krause and make that woman regret ever laying eyes on Martin. Because if Sabrina had hurt him like his family hurt him, a supernova's explosion would seem quaint in comparison to Rose's fury.

"Sabrina and I met in college. She was my first girlfriend, and my last." He squeezed her hand. "Until you, that is. We were never a particularly passionate couple, but I loved her. I thought she loved me. We liked and respected one another."

Rose braced herself for the inevitable *but*.

"But at some point, that changed. For her, not me. She hated the long hours I spent at school. Hated how often I brought home grading. Found any discussion of my teaching boring." His throat worked, and he looked down. "She found *me* boring. Full stop. And all the little comments about how serious I always looked, how I cared about my students more than her, how I had no sense of humor, didn't feel affectionate anymore. They weren't jokes. They were jabs. But I didn't see that until this past year."

From her conversations with Bea, Rose suspected his daughter had recently experienced a similar revelation. And others, too—about her parents' marriage, about the kind of father she truly had, about the sort of respect he deserved.

All long-overdue insights, in Rose's firm opinion.

Her anger, however, she reserved for Martin's ex, the adult in the situation. The woman who'd vowed to love and honor her husband, and then proceeded to rip him to shreds for being the sort of man he'd always been. The man she'd chosen to marry.

Martin was still talking. Still offering up a ragged wound, one that clearly continued to pain him, for Rose's inspection.

"I would have spent a lifetime like that, probably." The admission sounded reluctant. "Then about three years ago, I accidentally spotted some text messages she'd exchanged with a college friend of ours. I filed for divorce the next day."

She waited, but that seemed to be it. The end of his story.

Jesus, this man could break her wide open.

He'd left so much unstated. How the blow of his wife's infidelity must have staggered him. What immense strength must have been required—from *Martin*, of all people, a man whose family had denied his worth again and again—to tell himself he deserved better. To leave, instead of blaming himself for his wife's disdain and betrayal. To watch as his ex got engaged and moved his beloved daughter halfway across the country, and then uproot his entire life for one more year with that daughter.

How he could sit there by Rose's side, holding her hand, full of so much love and kindness, she had no idea. He'd somehow managed to keep his heart open, even as the people he loved proceeded to damage it, one after the other.

He had to know. She had to say it.

"You're a marvel, Martin Krause," she told him. "Look at you. So many people you loved didn't value you like they should have, but you're still whole. Still loving and vulnerable and...amazing beyond words. A marvel, like I said."

She was more than ready to elaborate, more than ready to listen if he wanted to share more. But in typical Martin fashion, he took the compliment and turned it around. Made it about her, when he deserved so much more recognition than he'd ever received.

Leaning forward, he shook her hand gently. "But that's exactly what I wanted to say earlier. You're so sure people will judge you for your past, and I don't get it. Look at *you*."

His gaze caressed every inch of her, from top to bottom. "Everything you are, you made yourself. I don't understand why that isn't a source of pride for you. Why you wouldn't expect the people who matter to admire you for it, not criticize or judge you."

Her back snapped straight in startled affront. "I *am* proud of who I am. What I've become."

"But you don't trust anyone else to feel the same." His brows rose. "Is that it?"

Somehow, he really *had* turned this conversation around on her. And not in the sweet, safe way she'd originally envisioned. Now she was scrambling for answers, for justifications, for anything that would nudge this discussion back into calmer waters.

"I trust Annette and Alfred. I trust some of my college friends. I, uh"—she forced out the words—"trust you."

That admission didn't seem to be as big a revelation as she'd expected it to be. It certainly didn't distract him from his intended point.

He gave his head a little shake, and his lips firmed in determination. "Then come to prom with me, Rose. Make our relationship public. Trust me not to hurt you. Trust me not to expose you to the judgment or ridicule of others."

And there it was. They'd circled back around to the topic she'd been dreading. The topic they'd both carefully avoided, for fear of cracking a still-fragile connection.

It seemed that avoidance had ended.

Unfortunately, she still had no idea what to say.

When she didn't respond, he continued. "If that's asking too much right now, trust your own ability to handle scrutiny and brush off any unkindness you might experience. Especially since I'd have your back the entire time. I promise."

Words. She needed words.

"I want..." Jesus, why was a direct statement about her

emotions so fucking hard? "I want you. I want a relationship with you. More than you know. I'd just prefer our colleagues not find out about it."

"For how long?" He wasn't backing down, and she respected that, even as she feared what it meant for her. For them. "At what point would you be sure enough to risk exposure?"

She had no idea. None.

Before she could fumble through an inadequate answer, he continued speaking. Continued tearing her foundations out from under her, one by one, as she scrambled for balance.

The rare hint of anger in his voice had disappeared, leaving only tenderness and sadness, which were somehow much, much harder to take. "I don't want to hide how I feel about you, and I'm too old and tired to sneak around for long, even to keep someone I want as much as you." So gently, he smoothed her hair behind her ear. Stroked her cheek. "I get your scars, Rose. I respect them, and how you've chosen to deal with them. But I have scars of my own."

Of course he did. Why hadn't she considered them before, except as a source of rage on his behalf? Why hadn't she understood how they'd shape her relationship with him?

He pressed a kiss to the bridge of her nose. Her temples. The center of her forehead. "Above all else, I need to be with someone who's proud of me. Proud enough to claim me in public, rather than hiding me like a dirty secret."

She'd never, ever considered him a dirty secret.

Her time with him, their relationship, was a jewel she'd wanted to protect from damage, to tuck into a box and keep safe. The same way she'd kept herself safe all these years.

He held her gaze, his steady and solemn. "I know it's too soon. I know it's not entirely rational of me to demand so much of you right now. But I am who I am. I need that public acknowledgment. I need to know the woman I love is proud to be with me."

Love. She'd suspected, of course. But she hadn't let herself acknowledge it.

"Of course you do." She should have known that. Should have realized this impasse would arrive long before she was ready to confront it. "And you deserve everything you need. You deserve the world."

She just didn't know if she could give him what he deserved and remain intact.

The silence between them stretched, and she eventually realized he was done. He had nothing more to say. He was waiting for a more definitive answer from her.

About prom. About them.

Her thin, halting words barely pierced the still air of the sunny kitchen. "Can you give me more time?"

He nodded, but those lines on his forehead carved deeper.

Pretty soon, he'd respond differently, and they both understood it.

HE'D PUSHED HER AGAIN. MAYBE TOO HARD.

This time, Martin wasn't so certain it was a mistake.

Especially as one week passed. Then two.

When he didn't have Bea, he and Rose spent every night together. They discreetly arrived at school in separate cars and left the same way, but every other non-working moment belonged to them as a couple.

She taught him to cook cassoulet. He reintroduced her to the wonders of Pop-Tarts.

They talked for hours about various nerdy history topics, about their families, about their pasts, about everything. His chest still expanded with a surge of triumph every time he made her snort with laughter, and she didn't seem to be guarding any more secrets from him.

They graded next to one another. Read the news next to one another. Loaded plates into the dishwasher next to one another. Slept next to one another.

And in between all those conversations and the tasks of daily life, they had startling amounts of passionate sex.

No. That didn't quite capture it. Their lovemaking wasn't just passionate. It was literally mind-altering.

In bed—or on a countertop, a table, the couch, the floor, etc.—what he'd understood about himself as a man and a lover fell away, replaced by the reality of Rose gasping above or below or beside him, her sex quivering as she bucked in orgasm.

He could give pleasure. Lots of it, as long as he had the right woman.

The tepid sexual response he'd accepted as normal for so long seemed to exist in another, sadder lifetime as well. Because how could he remember any other lover when Rose scratched him up, wrung him out, and made him come so hard, he couldn't stand afterwards?

It was more than he'd hoped for, in bed and out. More than he'd ever imagined he'd have.

It wasn't enough.

They hadn't gone out on a public date. No one other than Bea knew they were together, not even Annette or Alfred. She hadn't mentioned prom—now less than a week away—again.

And he was done accepting less than what he needed, even from those he loved. Even when he knew his needs weren't necessarily reasonable.

Jesus, he loved Rose with all the devotion his battered heart could muster, and that was a lot. A lifetime's worth. Maybe more.

But he was through waiting.

He found her in her classroom late in the afternoon, her shoes and jacket discarded as she sorted through her students' end-of-year projects. When the door quietly clicked closed behind him, she looked up with a welcoming beam.

"Hey, babe. Let me just put this grade into the computer, and then I'm ready to go." A few quick keystrokes, and she began shutting down her laptop. "What do you want to do for dinner? And no, I'm not having bologna again. M-A-Y-E-R isn't *my* second name."

Her bitter-coffee hair gleamed in the lamplight of her desk, and she was eyeing his silk tie with an expression that indicated she was remembering a particularly adventuresome night last week. When she gathered up her briefcase, it bulged with the end-of-year letters she wrote for her students, each one personalized, each one sweet enough to turn lemons into lemon-flavored Starburst.

She was incredible. Everything he wanted.

Was he really going to do this?

Yes.

What he needed mattered. He mattered.

"I'd like to talk for a minute," he told her.

Immediately, a crease appeared between her brows. But she settled back into her desk chair, her eyes studying him with care. "Martin? Are you okay? You look...I don't know. Conflicted."

He could only offer her the truth. "I don't know if I'm okay yet."

"Well, that's ominous." She leaned her elbows on her desk, clasped her hands, and gave him her full attention. "What's going on?"

His swallow didn't ease any of the dryness in his throat. "I don't want to badger you, so I won't ask this again."

He saw the moment she realized the purpose of this conversation. The stakes.

Her face paled from ivory to paper, and her fingers started to fidget in that very un-Rose-like way. She fiddled with her stapler. Straightened a stack of folders on her desk. Lined her green pens—her favorites for grading—in a tidy row.

If he didn't ask now, he'd never respect himself again.

"Prom is this weekend. Saturday night. Will you be my date?"

Her amber eyes immediately filled with tears, and he knew. He knew.

But he let her say it in her own time, because this was it. The last intimate conversation they'd ever have. So he allowed himself to memorize that beloved face, now crumpled in grief. Allowed himself take in Rose Owens, magnificent and stalwart and too damaged to give him what he needed, one final time.

But that was unfair. Her needs didn't match his. That was all.

He could just as well say he was too damaged to give her what *she* needed.

"I..." Her breath shuddered hard enough to shake her shoulders. "I don't know what to tell you."

"Okay." The light of her lamp spangled in his vision, and he concentrated on blinking back the aching press of his own grief. "I understand."

He did. But that didn't mean her decision wouldn't pierce him for the rest of his life.

The smile she attempted through her tears didn't convince either of them. "I take it that means we're not having dinner together."

Unable to speak, he shook his head.

Someday, the sound of her quiet little sob would stop echoing in his skull. Not anytime soon, though.

"I'll be..." Another hitching breath, and she blindly snatched at a tissue. "I'll be thinking of you and Bea. Tell her to have fun at college but remember her future. And when you g-get"—he'd never heard such an ugly, wrenching sound come from another human's throat—"l-lonely, c-call one of your old friends."

He bit his lip and looked up at the tiles on the ceiling until he'd gotten himself somewhat in order. "I will."

Silence wedged between them, driving them further and further distant from one another.

Her voice was tiny. Cracked. "May I kiss you one last time?"

He circled her desk. Bracketed her with a hand on each chair arm, because she loved being surrounded by him. It made her feel safe, although she'd never admitted it, not out loud.

Her lips were soft beneath his, trembling and salty.

He supposed his were salty too.

One sweet, tender brush. One more.

When he raised his head, he let himself kiss away a few of those gut-churning tears before walking off. She didn't protest or reach out for him. Instead, she simply watched him go, her hands balled into shaking fists.

At the door, he stopped and turned around. Hesitated.

Then he said it anyway.

"Rose..." He tried to smile. Failed. "Please let someone love you. Even if it's not me."

Then he left for good.

EIGHTEEN

"Ms. Owens. Precisely the woman I've been trying to locate." Keisha poked her head out of her open classroom door as Rose passed by. "Come see me in my room after school."

Rose attempted a cool, disinterested lift of one brow. "Do I have detention?"

Her department chair didn't appear impressed, probably because cool, disinterested brow lifts were easier to pull off when one's eyes weren't red and swollen as fuck. But dammit, it was Rose's planning period, and the school day was almost over. She could cry in the faculty restroom if she wanted to.

However, she was composing a sternly worded online review for Annette's favorite eye cream, because its de-puffing guarantee had proven laughable.

Or it would have proven laughable, if Rose could actually laugh anymore.

Keisha shook her head. "Just come here after the final bell."

After a nod of acknowledgment, Rose fled to the safety of the social studies department office, currently empty of all other teachers. Thank Christ.

Before yesterday, she would have been working quietly in the back of her own classroom—with Martin's permission, of course—to get all her end-of-year papers in order. But not now. Even the passing, mumbled greetings they'd exchanged as he entered and left her room gutted her. An entire period spent in his presence, watching him teach and move and breathe and *exist*, would likely leave her catatonic.

Two more weeks of school remained on the calendar. She had no time for complete emotional breakdowns. Incomplete ones, she'd discovered last night, were hard enough.

So instead of getting necessary tasks done in her classroom, she was staring into space and trying her best not to cry again. Not productive, but it did pass the time.

When the final bell rang, she rushed to Keisha's room, unwilling to encounter Martin in the hall as he left Rose's own classroom. Dodging students as they streamed toward the exits, she plopped down in a random vacated chair and waited for her department chair's attention.

Once all the kids had gone, Keisha closed the door behind her.

Uh-oh. Never a sign of good tidings.

After a quick stop at her desk, she sat in the seat next to Rose's, handed over a tissue box, and got to the point with her typical directness.

"I told you I wouldn't interfere in your personal life again, and I won't. It's not my business." She peered at Rose over the top of her glasses, her eyes slightly crossed. "But there are people at Marysburg High who care about you, and you need to know that. I'm here if you want to talk, Rose. Always."

Dammit. No wonder Rose's eyelids were completely unable to de-puff.

She reached for the tissue box. "Th-thank you."

"I'm not the only one concerned. Tess took me aside this morning to find out if you were okay." Keisha heaved an exasperated sigh. "And this afternoon, Candy Albright threatened to put a hit on whoever had made you look that way, then another on you for making her worry."

"That's sweet. Kind of." Rose frowned. "Also concerning."

Keisha waved a dismissive arm. "Don't worry. Candy's too busy with her annual Wuthering Heights is *Not* a Romance Initiative to murder anyone right now."

That was...sort of comforting.

"Not even you or Martin," Keisha added. "Despite your murder-convenient location just down the hall."

Oh, God. Who else knew about Rose's relationship with Martin?

Deny, deny, deny.

"Why..." Rose blotted her cheeks. "Why do you mention Martin?"

Keisha's dramatic eye-roll was magnificent up close. "Come on, Ms. Owens. I've been teaching for over thirty years. I know when two teachers are indulging in some extracurricular activities."

If that had been the extent of it, Rose wouldn't have been stemming yet more tears with a balled-up tissue. "Martin isn't just an extracurricular activity."

"No." Keisha laid a gentle, consoling hand on her arm. "No, I imagine he's not. And I don't think anyone else knows it's him, if that's worrying you."

Rose didn't move from beneath that hand, allowing the comforting gesture to blunt the biting edge of her grief, if only for a moment. Especially since fifteen years of working together had taught her that Keisha didn't gossip or ridicule her colleagues, so whatever the other woman had witnessed before, whatever she saw or heard today, would go no further than this room.

Please let someone love you.

"I appreciate the offer to listen." After blowing her nose, she offered her supervisor a weak smile. "I'm not sure that's a great idea, though."

"Then find someone you trust and talk to them. Because, honey"—she shook her head, lips pressed together in sympathy—"you look like your world just collapsed beneath you."

It had. That world had only been created over a single school year, but it was the warmest, safest home Rose had ever known.

She tested out the words. Found them true. "I trust you."

Keisha's eyebrows flew to her hairline.

"I just think there are some things you'd rather not know about members of your department." Rose took one last tissue and pushed the box back toward Keisha. "But maybe…"

In the face of Rose's grief, her department head had offered sympathy, not pity.

Keisha hadn't asked a single intrusive question. She'd only pledged her support.

Nothing about her expression indicated anything but sincere worry. Rose couldn't find a hint of glee or prurient curiosity.

And Rose should have been able to predict all that after fifteen years spent working alongside a good woman. Why she hadn't was something to ponder that night.

"Maybe," she began again, haltingly, "we can go get dinner one night soon."

At that, Keisha's brows caught a ride on the International Space Station. But she overcame her shock long enough to give Rose's arm another consoling pat. "I thought you'd never ask."

LATER THAT NIGHT, ROSE PEEKED THROUGH HER classroom blinds to watch Martin walk slowly across the parking lot, his steps heavy. Once he'd driven away, she locked up behind her and left too.

She should go home and fix something simple but delicious. Shakshuka, maybe.

But she didn't want to go home. Didn't want to eat at the table where Martin had pulled her into his lap and they'd completed the crossword together. Didn't want to read in the chaise where he'd coaxed her legs open and nuzzled her so sweetly, she'd cried when she came, then sobbed when he fucked her deep into the cushions and made her come again.

Above all, she didn't want to smell him on her sheets, even as she refused to wash those sheets. It wasn't the scent of sex that hurt so much. It was him. Martin. Clean and piney and dear.

Instead, she drove to Annette and Alfred's mansion along the Hanover River. When she got close, she saw lights blazing through their endless windows and exhaled in relief. Then tensed again upon remembering how they instructed the butler to make the house look welcoming whether they were home or not.

But when she rapped on the enormous front door with their ornate wrought-iron knocker, the butler immediately opened that door, ushered her into the front parlor, and told her to await the imminent arrival of Mr. and Mrs. Buckham.

While she lingered, unsure why she'd come but loath to go home, a cluster of photos on the eighteenth-century Chippendale table caught her attention.

When she'd married Barton, Annette and Alfred's only child, they'd littered the house with impeccably framed pictures of the newlyweds. At first, she'd found it odd and a bit ostentatious. Then endearing, as the sincerity of their excitement about having a daughter-in-law became unmistakable. Then sad, when the joy in those photos no longer existed in the actual marriage, and she knew her in-laws would have to replace the contents of those frames sooner rather than later.

She hadn't visited them at their home in years. Maybe a decade.

Whose photos they now considered precious enough to display, she no longer knew.

She should know.

She should know.

The table held five pictures now, rather than the dozen or more from before. Off to the side, they'd included a generic photo of Barton in his favorite pose, looking up in faux-surprise as he faux-adjusted his shirt cuffs and flexed discreetly. He'd aged well, which came as no shock, given how much effort and money he devoted to the task.

Did he ever call his parents? During their marriage, she'd been the one to remember birthdays and anniversaries, the one to select Christmas gifts and ensure Annette and Alfred had company at Thanksgiving.

She should have known from the beginning who and what he was, simply from the way he treated his parents. Sure, he'd told her they were clinging and querulous, but hearing that should have been like hearing a man call his ex a crazy bitch: a reflection on him, rather than anything revelatory about the object of his contempt.

She hoped his second wife had taken some of his money in the divorce, unlike Rose.

Two more pictures featured Annette and Alfred themselves. One had been taken when they'd been attending some sort of charity ball. Annette could have been a queen, her posture regal in black satin and lace, her silver hair swept into lush waves, as Alfred—an aging James Bond in a formfitting tux—gazed down at her in admiring devotion.

In the other, Annette was laughing and batting her sweaty husband away as he hauled her into his arms at the finish line of a 5K.

They swam with piranhas, but their happy marriage had remained entirely inviolate.

Barton's mother had taught Rose all about donning an icy-calm demeanor to deter human predators and protect her privacy, but Annette had never let that knowledge stop her from loving Alfred, Rose, or even her awful son. Never let it stop her from displaying that love openly, whether through expensive dinners and designer clothing, or through calls to the school board and photos on her Chippendale table.

Annette loved in full view of the public. Which meant she could be hurt there. Had been hurt there.

Definitely by Barton. Probably by Rose too, and the way she'd continually forced Annette and Alfred to chase her company after the divorce. To scheme and maneuver, all for the dubious pleasure of her presence.

Others had surely seen Annette's pain, including unfriendly witnesses.

But Alfred would have comforted her. And had anyone dared feel sorry for her, dared mock her, even for an instant, she'd have poured the liquid nitrogen of her scorn over the schadenfreude of her detractors and shattered them with a flick of her elegant finger.

Why hadn't Rose learned that lesson too?

Because—Jesus, she was going to need to buy stock in lotion-soft tissues—the last two pictures were of her.

Her in-laws didn't have any recent photos, so these originated during her marriage. But Barton was nowhere to be found in either image. In the first, she was twenty-five again, a Christmas bow slapped off-center on her head as she posed, beaming, with a black cashmere sweater-dress they'd given her. Then she was maybe twenty-eight, dignified and resplendent in ebony satin for an arts charity event, standing in the middle of Annette and Alfred.

By that point, her marriage was already falling apart. But the evening had been wonderful anyway, especially once Annette had one glass too many of champagne and kept hiccupping through her giggles, while Alfred rolled his eyes in fond exasperation.

She'd forgotten the event.

She'd forgotten this picture.

In it, both of them were looking at her like...

Well, like Martin looked at Bea. With affection and pride and ineffable sadness, as they watched someone they loved slipping bit by bit out of their immediate orbit.

Please let someone love you.

"My dear, we had no idea you were—" Alfred stopped in the doorway. "What happened? Are you ill? Hurt?"

"I—" She stifled a sob. "I'm sorry. I'm so sorry, Alfred."

Then he was holding her tight, that familiar expensive-cologne smell a blanket surrounding her. "Shhhh. Rosie, dearest, stop crying. Calm down, and tell us what's wrong."

Us. Because Annette had arrived too. Was holding her too. Was whispering that everything was fine, Rosie dearest, she didn't need to keep apologizing, if she could please stop crying they'd both be very relieved, please please *please* stop crying.

When Rose resurfaced, she was sitting on a silk brocade

settee, one former in-law on either side of her, still apologizing in a cracked voice.

"—basically had to buy my company, and I'm so sorry. You've always loved me, and I love you, so why I can't seem to show that, I don't—"

"Enough," Alfred interrupted sternly, and Rose hiccupped into silence.

"Alfred is right." When Rose opened her mouth, Annette shook her head. "No. Let us speak for a minute while you calm yourself enough to tell us what's wrong."

More tissues. So many tissues.

Annette raised an elegant forefinger. "Point number one. You've never wanted us to pay for you. We have to enact a Cheltenham tragedy each time we meet to spend money on you, so acquit yourself of making us buy your company. That's unfair. To all of us, not just you. Do you really think we'd be fools enough to love you like we do if we had to purchase your affections?"

When Annette phrased it like that, it did seem a bit insulting.

Rose hiccupped loudly, as she often did after crying, and Alfred patted her back.

"Well said, Nettie." Alfred cast a fond look over his wife, but his expression turned stern once more as he faced Rose. "Point number two. We've never doubted your love for us. Whether or not you said the words, you've behaved toward us with clear affection from the start. Do you think we didn't know who bought our gifts? Who sent us cards? Who forced our son to call weekly?"

Annette sighed. "All that started when you married Barton, and all that ended when you divorced Barton."

Barton Buckham: total dick. How he'd emerged from the DNA of such wonderful parents, Rose had no idea.

"After the divorce, yes, you were hard to reach sometimes," Alfred admitted. "But our son hurt you. You needed time. We understood that."

They were being kind to her, as she might have expected. Too kind. "But we never just...hang out. And you're always the ones who call me about getting together."

"My dear, *hanging out* is all well and good, but I need a shopping partner." Annette plucked at the fluted hem of her black linen jacket. "Without your help, how could I keep upstaging those other biddies?"

"And if I'm going to *hang out*, I'd much rather do so at restaurants with tasting menus." Alfred sniffed. "You would not believe the inferior canapés I've consumed while *hanging out* with our country club acquaintances at their homes."

They used that phrase as if it were in quotes, or italicized for its foreign origin.

Annette slipped an arm through Rose's. "You could call us more often, though. We know you're busy with the school year, but we miss your voice."

"And we are getting quite old," Alfred added.

Annette's hunch reappeared. "Also feeble."

"Quite, quite feeble." He raised his voice. "Rogers, my cane!"

The butler hovered near the door. "Sir, you don't own a cane."

"Then find me one." Alfred nodded in gratitude. "Thank you, Rogers."

Before poor Rogers was tasked with procuring a wheel-chair and possibly a coffin as well, Rose put aside her tissues and made herself clear. "No need for theatrics. From now on, I'll call more often. I promise. I'm sorry I haven't done it before."

"Unnecessary apology accepted." Annette's gaze turned searching. "Now tell us what's wrong, Rosie. Is it about your young man?"

Rose hiccupped out a laugh. Bless them for calling a divorced dad in his mid-forties a *young man*. Martin would be so tickled when she told—

Oh, Jesus. She couldn't tell him what Annette had said. She couldn't tell him anything.

Because she'd let him walk away.

She'd fucked up. And if she ever stopped crying, she was going to have to explain to Annette and Alfred exactly how badly.

AN HOUR LATER, ROSE WAS STILL SITTING ON THAT settee, flanked by her former in-laws. Her tears had slowed now that she'd reached the end of her story, but she figured that was a temporary respite. Her body seemed to contain untold stores of salt water and mucus.

The couple was taking a minute to consider what they'd just heard.

Then Annette tsked. "My dear, your social armor was meant to protect you. Not keep everyone out at all costs, for fear they might damage it."

Alfred reached across Rose and gently tapped his wife's hand. "Dearest, Rosie's history isn't ours. Not her childhood. Not her marriage and divorce. I believe she's had some justification for her concerns."

The couple's eyes met, and Annette conceded the point with a silent sigh.

"Still, I think we're all in agreement that our Rosie has"—she blinked at Alfred—"how did she put it?"

"Fucked up," Alfred supplied.

"Ah, yes. Fucked up." Annette scrunched her powdered nose. "Normally, I don't approve of such crude language, but the phrase does seem to fit her present situation."

How comforting.

"How are you going to fix this, my dear?" Alfred sounded entirely convinced that Rose would, simply curious about the means she'd employ. "Do you need our assistance?"

Slowly, the bare outlines of a plan were assembling themselves for her.

It would have to be heartfelt.

It would have to be—goddammit—public.

And given the circumstances, it would have to be soon.

"Thank you for the offer." She squeezed Alfred's hand, then Annette's. "But I think this is a problem I have to solve on my own."

They seemed unsurprised.

"Let us know if that changes," Annette said.

"However…" Rose gulped, pushed through the panic, and continued. "I may need your help with something else."

Annette's eyes went as round as the asparagus tarts they'd consumed several minutes before, even as her face crinkled into a huge smile. "Really?"

"Really. But that can wait until our conversation tomorrow. When I call you." Rose got to her feet. "I need to head home now and make some plans. But thank you for welcoming me tonight. Thank you for listening and supporting me. And—"

Annette and Alfred had risen as well, and they both lunged for the tissue box as Rose's tear ducts proved functional once more.

She choked out the rest of it. "And th-thank you for loving me."

Annette's arm around Rose's waist provided support in multiple ways. So did Alfred's loving kiss on Rose's forehead.

"You may not have gotten a penny from our son in the divorce, but you kept us." Annette blinked back her own tears. "We're not going anywhere."

During all her years as Barton's wife, Rose had never felt so rich.

Not once.

NINETEEN

As his students labored quietly on their end-of-year research projects, Martin checked his work e-mail for any procedural updates, which tended to arrive regularly as summer break approached. When a new message, one sent to the entire social studies department from Keisha, caught his attention, he braced.

The class rosters for each prep next year had arrived.

He and Rose—God, he could barely even think her name without doubling over—had tried their best to convince his honors kids to take her AP class next year, but it wasn't the same as having her as their teacher for almost ten months, and they both knew it.

The attachment opened with a quiet click, and there it was.

Dale had fucked Rose over, just as he'd intended.

She had enough students for two classes of AP U.S. History next year, rather than three. A handful of Martin's honors students had signed up, but not enough. Not nearly enough.

She was already missing the emotional connection formed

through two years with those kids, the ones who reminded her of herself. The ones whose trust and willingness to push themselves—with her steadfast encouragement—she valued so intensely. The ones whose affection and respect brought meaning to her teaching career in a way that even her love of her other students, her love of her subject matter, didn't.

And now Dale had damaged her AP program and possibly endangered its funding.

Before the school year ended, Martin was setting up a meeting with that asshole. Right was right, no matter the wounded state of his heart. Rose deserved better than Dale's petty revenge, and Martin refused to let himself remain a bludgeon used against her.

Against Rose. Christ, Rose.

He rubbed two fingers between his brows as the analog clock on the wall ticked and ticked. All week, he'd been hustling out of her classroom at the end of second and seventh periods, much more quickly than he had the rest of the year. In return, Rose had been arriving much closer to the end of the five-minute gap between classes than she usually preferred.

They'd barely passed within spitting distance of one another for days. Not that he hadn't seen her in the halls, chin high, makeup immaculate, eyes swollen.

Well, early in the week, anyway. The last day or two, she appeared to have recovered her normal equanimity. He supposed he was glad, since he didn't wish suffering on her, especially not the sort of gut-twisting longing he was currently experiencing.

But shit, having the woman he loved get over him in three days kind of blew.

And now he was going to have to linger in her room, have to see her calm acceptance of their relationship's end up close, because he couldn't let Keisha's e-mail go unremarked.

Rose needed to know he understood the pain of such terrible news, and he needed to tell her he was sorry.

They'd tried, but maybe he could have done more.

The bell rang before he figured out exactly what he wanted to say. He distractedly sent his students on their way with a reminder of their project's due date, and while he was still speaking, Rose walked in.

She hadn't delayed long enough to avoid him. That was... surprising. Maybe seeing him didn't hurt her anymore?

The prospect stung worse than when Kurt had deliberately rubbed him with those horrible nettles by the river. Worse even than having her within arm's length but a half a world away, and that was saying something.

Or maybe—he clung to the possibility—she wanted to say something about the rosters too? Despite how much his presence pained her?

"I saw the e-mail," he said quietly, as soon as the stragglers had neared the door. "I can't tell you how sorry I am."

Her high brow crinkled. "What e-mail?"

Fuck. The sight of him definitely didn't hurt her anymore.

She angled herself behind her desk and started pulling papers from her briefcase, but her work area was still mostly covered with his laptop, his grading, and other detritus. Double fuck.

And triple fuck, because now he was going to be the one to tell her horrible news.

He gathered his papers in a hasty stack and shoved them into his briefcase, eyes averted from her as he considered what to say.

"You missed a few." She passed over another pile. "Here you go."

Her hand brushed his arm, and she didn't even flinch. Not like he did.

Yeah. She was completely over him.

He tried to think past the ache. "The class lists for each prep are finally out."

"I assume my AP numbers are way down." Her lips tightened, but other than that, she might have been discussing marker colors for the whiteboards. "Two classes, huh?"

He nodded. "Like I said, I'm sorry."

"That's okay," she said, and she even sounded sincere.

Damn, she put up a good front.

"Maybe we can try something new next year." He fumbled for something more to say, but found nothing. "I'll think over the summer."

"Trying something new." She seemed to taste the words, turn them over in her mouth. "Sounds like a plan."

If she'd only recruit her former in-laws for help, but...

Rose would do what Rose wanted to do. Pride above all.

With an awkward bob of his head, he gathered his shit, dumped it on his cart, and escaped into the hall before his own pride abandoned him and he begged her to forget everything he'd said and just take him back. Take as much time as she needed before going public with their relationship.

For such a new relationship, he'd demanded a lot. Too much, too soon, especially for a woman like Rose. A different man—the right man—would have had more patience.

He wished he could be that man.

But his past had shaped him, just as her own history had transformed her into the glorious, prickly, loving woman she was. Rational or not, he needed more than she was willing to give right now, and he was going to hold out for it. Even if it felt like dying by inches, every second of the day.

Once he'd returned to the sanctuary of the social studies department office for his planning period, he parked his cart and slumped into his chair, face in hands.

The last two weeks of school were going to hurt like a motherfucker. And there was no telling how he'd feel when he showed up again next fall, and there Rose was, calm and gorgeous and perfect and completely unaffected by him.

Maybe he should move back to Wisconsin after all.

When he finally reopened his laptop, he'd received another new e-mail message. This one, oddly, from Rose.

I think I accidentally dropped an important letter, and it got mixed up with your stuff. It's notebook paper, made into a kind of envelope. Could you look through your papers and try to find it?

Which meant he'd have to see her again to return it. Damn, what a shitty day.

But he started rifling through his mess. Drafts of student projects on the UN. Others about the current refugee crisis. Lesson plans. Memos.

The lined notebook paper, shaped and folded into a triangle, fell out of a pile of essays about global warming and its international effects.

He hadn't known students these days still passed notes like this. He hadn't seen one tucked so carefully into an envelope since his own high school days.

He'd rolled back his chair, ready to return the letter to Rose, when he noticed the writing.

Specifically, Rose's bold green scrawl on one side of the note.

He couldn't misunderstand the message. *FOR MARTIN. PLEASE OPEN.*

It was his name. The note was for him.

Why was the note for him?

No matter how long he stared at it, no extra information revealed itself. No clue as to why she'd apparently slipped this folded triangle into his papers and sent him searching for it.

When he started plucking at the note's edges, he realized he'd underestimated the artistry involved in its creation. In true Rose fashion, she'd ensured no one else could accidentally see its contents, and either one of them would know immediately if someone had intercepted and pried open the message, unless that person had a goodly amount of time and patience to burn.

He supposed he had enough of both.

Half an hour later, the note lay spread before him, unripped, creases delineating the neat folds Rose had made. The message was simple. Direct—again, in true Rose fashion—but filtered through a girlhood she'd left behind long ago.

Do you still like me? As in like me, *like me?*

She'd drawn three little checkboxes below. One for *NO*. One for *YES*. One for *NOT SURE*. Stars and hearts decorated the expanse of paper, and she'd signed the note with a tiny, terrible sketch of a rose.

It was a perfect recreation of the type of note he'd never, ever received in high school, but had always wanted to find slipped into his locker. The only contradiction of early-1990s teen custom was a little addendum toward the bottom of the note.

P.S. Please place your answer in my department mailbox before the end of third period.

He didn't know what she wanted or what she intended, but he wouldn't lie to her. Wouldn't dishonor his own emotions by denying them. He put a clear, neat check in the *YES* box, and then attempted to recreate her folds to close the note.

Nope. Not even if he had a year.

He brought out the department stapler and made certain no one else could see the note's contents, unless they wanted to rip the edges of the paper to shreds or spend a lot of quality time with a staple remover.

His hand shook as he deposited his answer in her box.

The rest of his planning period, he spent trying not to

look at that box. Trying not to think about the implications of that note. Trying not to hope.

He failed miserably.

By the end of the school day, Martin was beginning to wonder if he'd hallucinated the whole note incident. Since then, he hadn't received another message, either via college-rule paper or e-mail. She hadn't stopped by the office to talk to him, although his stapled response in her box had disappeared before lunch. She hadn't even waited around for him between sixth and seventh periods, when he'd arrived to take over her classroom.

He'd spotted her at the end of the hallway right after lunch, talking with Candy Albright and Principal Dunn.

But that was it. Otherwise, she'd become a ghost.

At the after-school faculty meeting, he kept sneaking glances toward the back of the cafeteria, where she was sitting beside Candy. Which seemed like a dangerous choice of company, to be honest. But both of the women appeared absorbed by the various end-of-year announcements and updates, and he didn't detect Rose's eyes on him. Not even once.

She wouldn't fuck with you, he reminded himself. For all her queenly demeanor, she was a marshmallow over a campfire with those she cared about. Covered with black and slightly bitter on the outside, sweetly gooey within.

So what was she doing? His heart couldn't handle much more suspense.

Then, halfway through the meeting, he looked behind himself for the umpteenth time, and she was gone. Nowhere to be found.

When she failed to return within several minutes, his

fevered brain started spitting out various theories. Maybe she was terribly ill and had written his note in a hallucinatory stupor? Maybe she planned to quit because of Dale's machinations, and the message was a sort of weird goodbye?

"That's everything for today, but keep checking your e-mail for any further instructions. We're in the home stretch now, everyone." Tess smiled out at the crowd. "This meeting is officially over, but if you have time, you might want to stay a minute longer. I believe we have a bit of entertainment planned."

Martin barely heard her. Instead, he stared blankly down at his untouched legal pad.

Rose hadn't come back, which was very unlike her. Should he call to check that everything was okay? Maybe Annette or Alfred had injured themselves, and she needed—

A whiffle ball smacked him directly in the chest, its impact slight but shocking.

What. The. Actual. Fuck.

Instinctively, he jerked to his feet. Scanned his surroundings for the source of the ball. Only to see—

No. That made no sense. Maybe *he* was the one hallucinating.

For some unknown, unholy reason, Bianca appeared to be strolling toward him, black feathered wings fluttering behind her, a plastic bow-and-arrow set slung over her shoulder, more whiffle balls at the ready. And before he could do more than blink in confusion, she promptly nailed him again.

"Hey!" He ducked a third ball, which bounced off a nearby cafeteria table. "Stop that!"

"Consider this payback for the Tim Burton comments." Her evil grin stretched her elfin face. "FYI, I got permission from my mom and Principal Dunn to throw stuff at you, so anytime Ms. Owens wants me to play Goth Cupid, I'm here for it."

He took a breath. "Bianca, what in the world are—"

The next ball bounced off his shoulder, and he narrowed his eyes at her.

"Bullseye." Bianca blew on her hand, as if it were smoking-hot from her pitches. "I'm out of arrow balls, so quit giving me the stink-eye and look at them already."

Wait. Goth Cupid? Arrow balls?

Keeping one cautious eye on Bianca at all times, he picked up the nearest ball.

Someone had used Sharpies to draw little black arrows on it. And red hearts.

"My work as Goth Cupid is done," Bianca announced, and then glided serenely out of the cafeteria, her black wings—attached via some sort of harness, he thought he saw—bobbing above either shoulder.

His colleagues had stopped shuffling toward the exits. Instead, they were jostling each other and whispering and getting out their cell phones. Within a minute, he'd be on YouTube, and he still had no idea why.

Rose had to be involved, but what *was* all this? Punishment for loving her?

As soon as Bianca disappeared, Candy Albright marched toward him with martial intensity, her horn-rimmed glasses gleaming under the fluorescent lights.

"I'm coming for *you*, Martin Krause," she boomed.

Yes, Rose clearly did want him dead, although he wasn't entirely sure why.

Candy's echoing pronouncement had prompted the appearance of yet more teacher cell phones, all aimed in his direction.

She paused for effect, then roared, "I'm putting a hit on your heart!"

Wait. Was Candy saying—

Her nose wrinkled, and her voice lowered. "Or, rather,

Ms. Owens is. I told her she needed to work on her phrasing, but she insisted the original iteration would have more impact. This is why I teach English, while she languishes in the gutters of history."

Candy Albright flounced away, but Martin knew better than to relax.

His coworkers' whispers came to a halt, and their cell phones reemerged when—

Jesus Christ. There was his daughter, clutching two signs with a huge grin on her face. But she didn't say anything, just entered the cafeteria and stood to the side.

Then, at last, Rose appeared, serene as ever, gliding into the room with her chin high and her heels higher, as if nothing had just occurred.

Only...

Only...

Only she appeared to be wearing a puff-sleeved monstrosity of a gown, black and impeccably fitted but shiny and adorned with a huge bow across her ass. As far as he knew, dresses like that hadn't been sold in at least twenty years. For good reason.

Her gorgeous hair rippled over her shoulders in odd, sharp angles.

Crimped. She'd crimped it.

From somewhere, she produced a hand-lettered sign, her Sharpied scrawl unmistakable. She held the sign high and let him read it. Let their colleagues record it for posterity with their cell phone cameras. Let potentially everyone in the world with internet access know what question she was asking him.

WILL YOU MAKE PROM A NIGHT TO REMEMBER? IN A NON-TITANIC SORT OF WAY?

Arrow-riddled hearts bordered the sign, as well as other doodled hearts with—

Yes, that was *RO + MK* written inside each of them.

He swallowed back his emotion.

At that point, Bea moved closer and brandished her own signs, one in each fist. "Pick your answer, Dad."

The first sign featured an image of Jack and Rose—oh, his beloved was so clever—dancing happily down in steerage. The second showed another iconic image from the movie, this one of the famous ship broken in two, vertical and sinking.

Love and dancing or disaster and heartbreak.

His choice.

There was no question. Absolutely no question.

He snatched the appropriate sign from his daughter and held it high.

"Yes." He held Rose's gaze and spoke clearly. Proudly. "Yes, I'll go to prom with you."

She let out an audible breath, those strong shoulders lowering a fraction beneath her puffy sleeves. Then she opened one hand to reveal a flower. A black calla lily, elegant and gorgeous. Just like her.

Her fingers trembling, she put down her sign and pinned the boutonniere to the pocket of his button-down.

When she'd finished, he covered her hand with his. Moved it until her palm lay flat against his heart. "Rose. All this was for me?"

Her amber eyes turned glassy, to his horror. "You deserve a woman who's proud to be at your side, in private or in public. I'm sorry, Martin. More sorry than I can say."

"Shhhh." He brushed away her tears with his free hand. "I'm sorry I demanded so much, so soon. Especially since I know all this"—he tilted his head to acknowledge the roomful of teachers watching them, as well as Bea and various staff clustered in the cafeteria doorway—"is hard for you."

"But you'll help me through it." Her smile was shaky but genuine. "Right?"

Be damned with professionalism. He had to kiss the quivering curve of her lush mouth. Once. Again. "Every second. I'll have your back every second for the rest of your life, Rose. And if anyone tries to make you feel small, go subarctic and hand them their asses. But do it in front of me, because I want to watch."

A small gasp and titters, as several teachers repeated *asses* to one another.

He supposed he could always find a new line of work.

"Annette's tailor made me this replica of a vintage nineties prom dress in black." She glanced down at herself. "Do you like it?"

Another kiss on her temple, and he rested his lips there, where the skin was thin and soft, and the smell of her shampoo surrounded him like a nimbus.

"Like isn't, uh...quite the word. I love it." Or at least what it represented, so it wasn't really a lie. "I love you, Rose. I'll always love you."

A vein beneath his lips was throbbing, throbbing, throbbing. But she didn't hesitate.

"I love you too," she said, loud enough for everyone in the cafeteria to hear.

He wanted to memorize those words, the certainty in them. Bask in the sound of his Rose setting aside her protective armor and announcing their relationship to the world, because she knew he needed the public declaration.

Because she loved him.

She loved him.

If he wanted to experience this moment again, he supposed he could download the YouTube clip. Problem solved.

A gentle hand landed on his shoulder. "Congratulations,

Dad. I have to go, but I'm so happy for you both, and I love you. More than you know. I'll call tonight."

His daughter's eyes were bright with tears, but her smile seemed sincerely happy. Proud.

"I love you too." His voice was a choked rasp. "Talk to you tonight, sweet Bea."

With a little wave, Bea edged out the door and vanished.

He squeezed his eyes closed, doing his best not to cry in front of his coworkers.

"If this promposal doesn't go viral, I'm going to be pissed," Rose whispered. "Do you know how much Annette's tailor charges per hour? We need a new profession, Martin."

He huffed out a laugh. "I imagine we will, after Keisha hands us our asses for making a spectacle of her department."

"Thank you for the reminder," Keisha called from a nearby table. "Please see me in my classroom in ten minutes, Mr. Krause and Ms. Owens."

"Detention?" Rose murmured.

He nodded. "We'll pass notes."

She snorted, and everything in his life turned bright.

EPILOGUE

Rose surveyed her prom date with satisfaction.

Martin's black tuxedo looked damn fine on him. Which it should, given the amount of money Alfred had no doubt spent to purchase and custom-tailor it overnight.

Because of Martin's eagerness to wear a well-fitted tux to prom, he hadn't even tried to resist Annette's Decrepit Hunch of Doom, not to mention Alfred's repeated demands for his nonexistent cane. Her former in-laws had been delighted by his acquiescence, bordering on smug.

Eventually, Rose figured Martin would get quite a few uses out of that tux. Her man wouldn't prefer a casual wedding. Instead, he'd want the world to witness their formal commitment to one another, and he'd dress accordingly. Besides, all the future proms they'd chaperone together should bring the cost-per-wear down a notch, from Heart Attack to merely Eye-Popping.

After prom ended, Martin and Rose were meeting the older couple—at Rose's invitation—at Milano for a late dinner. The bill there would also no doubt be Eye-Popping, and Martin would insist on paying for himself and probably for her too, so Alfred and Annette's smugness was doomed to be short-lived.

But before then, Rose fully intended to make Martin's first prom date amazing.

For the moment, she was sharing him with another, younger woman. Bea had dragged her father out on the floor for a slow song. And as he carefully held his daughter for their dance, her right hand clasped in his left, he was quite simply the most handsome man Rose had ever witnessed. Because of his ass in those tuxedo pants, sure, but also because of the expression on his face as he regarded Bea.

Soft. Loving. Proud. Grief-stricken.

His girl was leaving in less than three months. But at least she was giving him this moment to cherish first.

Rose wasn't quite certain whether he'd realized his daughter's intent yet.

Bea was claiming him in public, showing how proud she was to be his daughter, and she was doing it in front of her friends and teachers and everyone else. So now he had two women in his life who loved him like he deserved.

It was enough to make an Ice Queen melt.

Especially since Bea was wearing that beautiful washed-silk dress from her shopping trip with Rose and Annette, its jet beads reflecting the light from the mirror ball overhead. Her back was straight, her pride evident in that tipped chin.

Annette was going to be a formidable grandmother to that girl.

Rose's mother would have been the same.

She wished to God her mom could have lived to see all this. To be proud of how Rose had taken Margie's legacy of hard work and pride and used it to find a profession she loved. A man she loved. A family who loved her as much as she did them.

She had a family again. Her. Brandi Rose Owens.

Her mother wouldn't have wanted Rose to be alone. Had never wanted Rose to be alone, even when she'd been forced from her daughter's side by work or death.

Her mom wasn't around the corner or in the kitchen, just out of sight. But Rose didn't need a high fever and hallucinations to talk to her.

Thank you, she silently told her mother. *Thank you for working so hard. For loving me so hard for as long as you could.*

"Ms. Owens?" A tentative voice interrupted Rose's reverie. "You look nice."

"Thank you," she automatically responded. Then she blinked and truly saw the couple in front of her. "Oh, how lovely you both are."

Sam, one of her favorite students from Martin's classes this year, stood by their date. A young woman named Carla, if Rose remembered correctly.

Their dresses shone in the light, each perfectly suited to its wearer. Sam's flattered the slim lines of their body, while Carla's emphasized the nip of her waist and flare of her hip. The two were holding hands, and Sam looked as happy as Rose had ever seen them.

After introducing herself, Carla headed for the restroom, and Sam looked up at Rose.

"When I saw your promposal on YouTube, I finally got up the nerve to ask her. Finding dresses at the last minute was a b—" Sam paused. "I mean, a pain."

Wait. Hadn't she seen Carla in each of the school's major drama club productions that year?

"Is she the reason you stayed late at school all the time? Because you wanted to see her after play rehearsals ended?" At Sam's nod, Rose leaned down to admire their corsage. "Mr. Krause and I were a little worried about that."

Sam's brow wrinkled. "Why?"

"Not every kid has supportive parents." Rose kept her tone gentle. "And Mr. Krause wasn't able to get in touch with your father. You also seemed unhappy a lot of the time."

Understanding dawned on Sam's face. "My dad is great, but he works two jobs and doesn't check his voicemail much." They shrugged. "Since I was doing fine in school, I told him not to worry about contacting teachers."

That shouldn't have been Sam's choice to make, but at least Rose and Martin finally had an explanation. "And all that unhappiness?"

"I'm sixteen, Ms. Owens." Sam suddenly grinned. "Dad says being mopey and whiny is kinda my job. Besides, I was pining but too scared to do anything about it."

Rose returned their smile. "Fair enough."

When Carla emerged from the bathroom and waved from across the room, Sam straightened from leaning against the wall. "Gotta go. But I'll see you next year in AP U.S. History."

"I can't wait," Rose said.

The couple reunited and disappeared into the crowd. But before she could locate the punch bowl, Candy Albright had appeared on one side of her, Bianca on the other.

Jesus. She was going to die at prom, wasn't she?

"I've decided not to put hits on you and Mr. Krause." Candy looked pleased with herself, which was always terrifying. "As long as you're willing to help with my George Eliot Was *Not* a Man Initiative next year."

No one in Candy's orbit had ever actually been murdered, as far as Rose knew, but better safe than corpse-y. "Fine, fine, fine."

Candy marched away in triumph, no doubt headed toward her next victim.

Rose turned to Bianca. "Those boots look amazing with your dress."

"Yeah." Bianca scuffed the toe of one of her heeled boots against the polished wood floor. "Listen, tell Mr. Krause the vendetta is off."

Rose blinked. "Okay. May I ask why?"

Two years. *Two years*, Bianca had harbored a vendetta against Rose. And Martin got a mere six months? Pfffft.

"Mom says no more vendettas, or else she's putting bleach in my laundry the day before I leave for college." Bianca scowled. "I have to inform everyone by the end of the school year."

"Life is difficult sometimes." *Don't laugh. Don't laugh.* "Thank you again for helping with my promposal, Bianca. Even though I specifically told you to throw those arrow balls underhand. *Gently.*"

"He insulted Tim Burton."

Apparently, that was all the justification Bianca felt necessary.

"I hope you have a lovely summer." Rose helped the girl straighten the filmy black sleeve of her dress. "And give 'em heck at Virginia Tech next year."

"Yeah." Bianca swallowed. "I, uh, wanted to thank you. You made school fun."

Every year, a few kids who'd seemed to loathe every moment in Rose's class came up to her and said something similar. And every year, surprise and unexpected emotion left her fumbling for words.

One hard blink. Another.

There. She was under control again.

"Same goes." After a silent moment, Rose couldn't help herself. "So are we going to hug it out, or what?"

"You wish." But Bianca was smiling as she stomped away.

Moments later, a warm arm slid around Rose's waist, and her body recognized the gentle affection in that touch before she even looked. Martin. Always, always Martin.

"Coward." She leaned into him. "Don't think I didn't see you hiding from Candy and Bianca."

He grinned. "Discretion, valor, etc. Besides, I know you can handle those two with one elegant hand tied behind your back. Especially since they both obviously adore you."

She dipped down to whisper in his ear. "You want to try restraints, huh?"

Amazing. Against her lips, she could actually feel the flare of heat under his skin.

Then he muttered a quiet *fuck*, and she looked up to see Dale making his way across the room in their direction.

Perfect timing.

"No need for coarse language, Mr. Krause." She straightened, but let his arm remain around her waist. "Only yesterday, you said you wanted to see this."

It took him a moment to remember. But once he did, his stiffness slowly relaxed, and that Expensive Cologne Model grin returned as Dale drew within a few feet of them.

Oh, this was going to feel *gooooooood*.

"Brandi," Dale greeted her loudly. "I saw your numbers were low for AP U.S. History next year."

She drew herself up straight and looked down her nose at him. "Good evening to you too, Mr. Locke."

His step stuttered, but he recovered himself and came closer. "Don't know yet what's going to happen with your funding, but it depends on enrollment. Be a shame if you lost money for training or supplies."

Her smile, she knew, would gleam under the dance floor lights, and its absolute chill should freeze him in place.

Sure enough, he stopped dead.

"If our AP program lost funding, that would certainly be a shame." She cast a sidelong look at Martin. "Dearest, have you heard? I'm sure Dale already knows, since all the important people in administration do."

Dale's mouth worked, as he attempted to conjure a suitably crushing response.

Currently, only the superintendent—who'd answered Annette and Alfred's call Wednesday morning—was aware of the news, because the details were still being determined. But Dale couldn't know that.

She let her smile spread. Become terrifying.

"Anonymous benefactors have offered to fully fund our school system's AP programs for the indefinite future." She paused. "Under one condition."

Martin's arm spasmed around her waist, and she heard his indrawn breath. He didn't say a word, though. Instead, he let her have this moment, since he knew exactly how difficult arranging it had been for her.

She wasn't accustomed to asking for help. But she'd learn.

The seconds ticked by, and she waited.

Anticipation only sharpened the pleasure.

Finally, Dale gave in. "What condition?"

"From now on, social studies department chairs will determine which preps their teachers receive and which classrooms they're assigned. The head of secondary-level social studies no longer has a voice in those decisions." She tilted her head in feigned confusion. "For some reason, the AP program's benefactors were very insistent on that point."

"I see." His face had turned ruddy, and his lip lifted in an unconvincing sneer. "Apparently your ex-husband's rich friends didn't leave you when he did."

The comment might have hurt a month ago. Not now.

Nevertheless, Martin had become stone beside her, his rage at Dale's cruelty hardening his lean frame.

She found his hand. Squeezed it. Paused to let him regain control of himself.

As if spurred by the movement, Dale swung on him. "I

can't believe she finally wore you down. Have some pride, man. What are you doing with someone like her?"

She almost laughed. As if Martin would take advice from Dale—*Dale*—because they both had dicks. That misogynistic buddy-buddy shit didn't fly with her man.

"Someone like her?" Martin enunciated each word with the care of a drunken man in front of a cop, his voice gravel. "I don't understand. I'll need you to explain precisely what you mean by that."

But Dale couldn't say much more, or else—as he was now realizing—he might be writing his own dismissal letter. So he seethed in silence, his watery eyes bugged out in anger.

"Oh, Martin." She turned to her back to Dale, a deliberate insult. "I forgot to mention one other development. It also involves Mr. Locke."

"Please tell me." Martin's voice was calm, his eyes aflame with rage on her behalf. "I'd like to hear all about it. In detail."

Annette and Alfred hadn't approved of the next bit. They'd wanted to descend on the school system and fix everything in one fell swoop, but Rose needed to do this her way. A way that felt fair for everyone involved, including other teachers who lacked her connections.

A way that required some trust on her part, a willingness to make her private concerns public, and the ability to request assistance from strangers and colleagues.

God help her.

One. Two. Three.

She let Dale hang for a full thirty seconds before speaking again, a move Martin rewarded with a caress at her waist.

"Come Monday, I'm registering a formal complaint with Superintendent Jones and human resources about Dale's use of derogatory terms for our students, his abuse of supervisory authority, and several instances of unwelcome physical contact with a coworker and subordinate. Namely, me. Next week, I plan to visit other secondary social studies teachers and discover whether they have similar complaints to make." She stroked the corner of Martin's mouth, which had dropped open in shock. "I've discussed the matter with the teachers' union, and I've consulted with a lawyer, in case any retaliatory measures result from my actions."

Annette and Alfred's attorney was prepared to represent additional complainants too. And given what the woman charged per hour, law was yet another line of work Rose and Martin should have considered. Not that she or the other teachers would be allowed to pay for any necessary legal services.

When that subject had arisen, Annette had swooned onto a settee in a very unconvincing faint, while Alfred clutched at his chest and called out for heart medication. Rose had told them they were both ridiculous, and then agreed to let them cover all legal fees, because a teacher's salary couldn't pay for a lawyer as sharp-eyed as theirs.

As Dale sputtered, Rose kept speaking to Martin.

"I suspect that during the investigation, Dale will no longer have any supervisory authority over me whatsoever. Tess and Keisha will have to ensure I'm acting in accordance with all reasonable rules and regulations promulgated by the school system." She paused to let Dale steep in his fear and rage, his hands balled into shaking fists. Then she cast him a desultory, dismissive glance. "Fair warning, Mr. Locke. Prepare for stricter oversight at best, unemployment at worst."

Someone had come up alongside her. When Rose turned her head, Tess was eyeing Dale as if he were a cockroach they'd found in Wednesday's chili special. Her tennis coach boyfriend loomed next to her, mouth tight as he regarded Dale with equal disfavor.

"I'm delighted to hear all this, Ms. Owens," the principal said. "I've had concerns about Mr. Locke's conduct for years, especially in reference to you. I'd already planned a long conversation with our superintendent this summer. It appears that conversation will occur sooner rather than later."

Tess smiled then. It wasn't pleasant.

"We've interrupted Mr. Krause and Ms. Owens enough for one night, I believe. They're here to chaperone our students, not chat with administrators." She tilted her head to the side. "Besides, Mr. Locke, you should meet one of my teachers. She's not in the social studies department, but I'm sure she'd appreciate talking with you."

Then Tess and her boyfriend herded a fuming, red-faced Dale toward—

Oh, Rose loved their principal.

Candy Albright. Tess had brought Dale to Candy Albright.

Rose turned away and exhaled slowly. The first confrontation—the most satisfying—was done, but she had more confrontations to come. Many of them would also play out in public.

There would be gossip. Judgment. Snide comments.

A different woman wouldn't give a fuck. Rose did.

But she had the unwavering support of people who loved her. Their affection would cushion the forthcoming blows and help heal her inevitable bruises. And both Margie and Annette had taught her well. Rose could quash the pretensions of the cruel through sheer, stony pride or with a single, icy stare.

She'd survive.

No, more than that. She'd thrive.

"You didn't need me at your back, but I was glad to be there. And that's where I'm staying during the whole complaint process, no matter what happens." Martin tugged her into his arms and surrounded her with his body, a protective gesture of the sort he'd had to stifle in front of Dale. "Rose, I can't imagine how hard all this has been for you. You're incredible."

"It's only going to get harder, once the news becomes fodder for school gossip." She ducked her chin to rest it on his shoulder, and he rubbed slow circles on her back. "But you'll be there to help. So will Keisha and Tess. Annette and Alfred too, of course."

"I will be there. Always." Martin's chest vibrated against her with each quiet, firm word. "Annette and Alfred must have been delighted to assist you with the AP program. Beside themselves, actually."

Delighted undersold their reaction. In their glee, they'd even let Rose pay for dinner that night without any argument, as a thanks for requesting their help.

It was a landmark moment in her relationship with them, really.

"Pretty much." Beneath Martin's tender touch, her muscles released their tension, and she let him bear some of her weight. "Frustrated too, though. Annette wanted to march into the superintendent's office and get Dale fired on the spot, to spare me hassle and preserve my privacy. But I managed to convince her I should go through the system instead."

She grinned and pressed a kiss on Martin's jaw. "If Dale's getting fired, I want to play a larger role in the process."

"I love it when you go Absolute Zero on that asshole." Martin's breath tickled her ear. "You in that silky dress and those heels, gorgeous and in complete control. A queen freezing out the pretender to her throne. It made me want to drop to my knees, push up that skirt, and—"

She couldn't get turned on in the middle of prom. She couldn't.

"Work function," she reminded him breathlessly, tiptoeing her fingers up the placket of his tux. "But when we get home, please share your insights, Mr. Krause. In depth."

He dipped his head and kissed her knuckles. "I should warn you: I spent a lot of time at the tailor this morning without much to occupy my attention. I started a mental list of dirty-sounding pedagogical terms. *Rigor* and *high-impact* are at the top."

No, she couldn't get turned on at prom. But did the prom really require their presence?

A quick glance around the dance floor revealed plenty of chaperones.

"I think there's just enough time for a rigorous, high-impact assignment at home before dinner." She eyed him under her eyelashes. "Interested?"

His fingers laced through hers. Without a word, he gently but insistently tugged her toward the exit.

"You're an eager pupil," she teased.

He grinned, his stride loose and confident. "From now on, I plan to live every week like it's Teacher Appreciation Week."

When she snorted, he slowed his pace and glanced her way.

His blue eyes had turned solemn. "I love you, you know."

"I do know. You've never hidden it, so I've never doubted it." She lifted their entwined fingers to her cheek. "I love you too."

"Good," he said. "Good."

She pushed open the door to the outside, releasing them into the muggy June night. "Now let's go home and experiment with homebound teaching. And maybe conduct some oral presentations."

He laughed and broke into a near-run. "Best. Prom. Ever."

THE END

THANK YOU FOR READING *TEACH ME.* ♥ I HOPE YOU enjoyed Rose and Martin's story! Please consider leaving a brief review where you got this book. Reviews help new readers figure out if a book is worth reading!

If you would like to stay in touch and hear about future new releases in this series or any of my other series, sign up for the Hussy Herald, my newsletter:

https://go.oliviadade.com/Newsletter

And turn the page for a list of my other books and a suggestion on what to read next!

ALSO BY OLIVIA DADE

LOVESTRUCK LIBRARIANS

Broken Resolutions

My Reckless Valentine

Mayday

Ready to Fall

Driven to Distraction

Hidden Hearts

THERE'S SOMETHING ABOUT MARYSBURG

Teach Me

Cover Me / Work of Heart

LOVE UNSCRIPTED

Desire and the Deep Blue Sea

Tiny House, Big Love

PREVIEW OF DESIRE AND THE DEEP BLUE SEA

CHAPTER ONE

Callie stared down at her dumbphone with even more loathing than usual.

It couldn't connect to the internet, of course, but that wasn't why she hated it. God knew, she didn't need constant reminders via e-mail and social media notifications of everything she should worry about, not when some days she was already worried from the moment she woke up in the morning to the moment she made herself quit reading and turn off her bedside light. The cell's limited functionality was a feature, not a bug.

No, she hated her phone because she hated making calls and sending texts. Period.

And above all else, she hated it because she didn't want to make this particular call.

Just last month, she'd been given the numbers for Irene and Cowan, her intern contacts at Home and Away Television. Irene was kind of scary, to be honest. Cowan, though, had always seemed kind and reasonable, a model representative of America's most popular cable channel devoted to all matters home- and travel-related.

He'd also proven much less likely than Irene to sigh loudly whenever Callie took too long to respond to questions.

She needed patience and understanding right now, so she was calling Cowan. Maybe he could figure a way out of this mess for her, a path that would allow her to film her episode of HATV's *Island Match* without a boyfriend.

Even though that would violate the entire premise of the show.

Dammit. She didn't want to tap his name on her contacts list. But the breakroom door was closed, she was alone, and she couldn't delay any longer.

When he answered his cell, she used her Professional Librarian Voice. Tried to exude calm and competence and confidence in every syllable, despite her anxiety.

"Cowan? This is Callie Adesso. I think we may have a slight problem." She put the phone on speaker and laid it on the table in front of her, so she didn't have to hold it up with her trembling hand. "I wanted to let you know ASAP."

"Okay." His deep voice sounded cautious. "What's wrong?"

Before Callie could answer, she heard a distinctive and aggrieved female voice over the line. "Oh, Jesus, what now?"

Irene. Lord help them all.

"For God's sake, woman, you can't just snatch my—" Cowan made a sort of growly noise, and Callie could decipher the faint sounds of a scuffle. "My apologies, Callie. Hold on just a moment, please."

Everything went silent, as Callie blinked at her phone in befuddlement.

"We're back." Cowan sounded breathless. "And just so you know, you're on speaker phone so both Irene and I can hear what's going on. We're here to help. *Without any complaint.*"

Callie had a feeling that last bit wasn't directed at her.

A glance at the wall confirmed the sad truth. After dithering for so long, she only had ten minutes left of her break. She needed to get back on the desk with Thomas, much as she wished she didn't. There was no time to prevaricate or stall further.

"Andre and I broke up this morning," she told them. "He won't be able to film our episode of *Island Match* next week."

She could have sworn she heard Irene mutter *I told you so*.

"Callie…" Cowan's tone softened even further. "I'm so sorry. Are you okay?"

What would be the point of pretending? "Please don't worry. I'm not heartbroken."

Not about that, anyway.

Over the last couple of months, a relationship that had seemed promising if unspectacular had devolved into mutual dissatisfaction. Andre had stopped even pretending to listen to her, his bored gaze going unfocused whenever she tried to talk to him about her day or her worries or anything other than their dinner plans. And on the rare occasions he *did* pay attention to her, he'd begun responding to her concerns with increasing impatience. Telling her they were stupid and unfounded, and she just needed to get over them.

As if it were that easy. As if she hadn't already tried telling herself that thousands of times.

In return for his impatience, she'd begun responding to his amorous overtures with indifference. So she'd spent the last several weeks in a sexless, tension-filled relationship with a boyfriend whom she barely saw.

She should have ended things last month, probably. But starting a conversation about how and why their relationship had gone bad was way beyond her capabilities, as was a conversation about ending that relationship. If Andre hadn't broached the topic himself, she had no idea when it would have happened.

For someone like her, that kind of awkwardness and conflict could cause hives, and she wasn't inviting more Benadryl into her life.

So she'd stayed with Andre to avoid confrontation. Even more than that, though, she'd stayed with him for *Island Match*. For the beach.

Not Virginia Beach. Not even Myrtle Beach or Nags Head. After one too many jellyfish stings, she shied away from any body of water where she couldn't see her feet below the surface.

No, she needed clear Caribbean water. Sun-warmed sand beneath her soles. Lapping waves, their soothing rhythm carrying away her thoughts and leaving her brain in blissful peace.

And now she wasn't going to get any of it.

She blinked away the wetness blurring her vision.

"I'm glad you're not upset." Cowan sounded relieved not to have to comfort a grieving near-stranger over the phone. "Don't worry about the show. We'll take care of cancelling all the travel arrangements, including—"

His words failed to register as she swallowed a sob.

She'd considered the trip her reward. Not for earning her MLS and landing a good job at the Colonial Marysburg Research Library, or at least not entirely. Instead, for waging an endless war with her doubts and her frustrated loneliness at work. For the way she kept putting one foot in front of another and answering calls on the desk and helping patrons and pretending to be okay even when she wasn't, and the way she kept doing all of that until she *was* okay again.

In pursuit of that trip, she'd overcome her reluctance to be on TV. She'd convinced a resistant Andre to fill out the *Island Match* application. She'd filmed an interview alongside him. She'd talked on the phone countless time to Irene and Cowan, even when her library shifts had left her weary of people and conversation. She'd braced herself for limited cable-television fame and notoriety. She'd accepted the presence of new worries and uncertainty as the trip grew near.

Because she wanted that week on the beach. Needed it.

But she couldn't afford the trip on her own, not with her MLS-depleted savings, and she refused to ask for charity from her better paid and more successful family members.

So if she didn't speak now, she wouldn't go to a gorgeous Caribbean beach, not for months or years to come, and she'd never know what might have been. She'd always wonder whether she could have done something, said something, advocated for herself and gotten what she wanted.

God, speaking up was so hard.

Still, she was going to do it.

Maybe she could go on the trip by herself. Maybe she could substitute a friend or family member for Andre, and the show could proceed as normal. But she wouldn't know unless she asked.

"Cowan?" The word was thin and shaky. She could no longer summon Professional Librarian Voice. Instead, all she could muster was a frayed thread of sound.

Still, Cowan stopped talking immediately. "Yes?"

She squeezed her eyes closed and tried to breathe, but her brief, bright burst of conviction was already fading, even as a familiar fiery prickle spread across her chest.

Literally every episode of *Island Match* involved a romantic couple. No exceptions. Why would she think they'd alter the entire premise of the show just for her?

If she kept bothering them, Cowan and Irene were going to hate her, if they didn't already, for delaying the inevitable. For asking questions and causing them more effort and trouble instead of simply disappearing into the ether.

Besides, no one *owed* her a beach vacation. Someone else deserved this opportunity, and Cowan and Irene deserved to get off the phone so they could deal with the aftermath of Callie's problems.

She needed to keep her mouth shut. Avoid confrontation. Keep forcing a smile and wait until the pretense of being fine became reality.

Yes, speaking up was so hard.

Too hard for someone like her.

"I'm sorry," Callie whispered.

Cowan's voice was gentle. "It's okay." After a moment, he spoke again. "Like I said, you have nothing to worry about. We'll take care of all the cancellations on our end. Do you have any other questions?"

No. Everything seemed clear. Terrible, yes, but clear.

"I—" Callie gulped back another sob. "I don't—"

At that moment, when her personal history would have predicted that she would acquiesce to the inevitable, choke out a goodbye to Cowan and Irene, and never bother HATV again, a dark head of curls crowning a concerned face appeared through the little window in the breakroom door.

Thomas.

So tall. So handsome. So smart. So kind.

Such a pain in the ass.

He must be stooping, because otherwise she'd only see his chest in that square of glass.

His dark brows had furrowed above those ocean-blue eyes, and he made some sort of weird chin-jerk at her. Oddly enough, she could translate that gesture.

He'd heard something that worried him, even through the door. Which seemed impossible, given both the ambient noise in the library and the single-minded, damnable focus he normally displayed on the desk.

However improbably, though, he'd detected something

amiss. And now he wanted to know if she needed help. As if he, the architect of her current despair, the main reason she needed a freaking beach vacation to begin with, could solve her problems.

She sniffed back more tears and waved him away.

When he didn't budge, she waved him away again.

At that, he pressed his lips together, horizontal lines scored across his high forehead, and slowly, reluctantly, left the window.

She stared after him for a moment.

Single. Thomas was single. Charming in his own way. Exceedingly telegenic, she'd guess.

And she'd seen his upcoming schedule. As soon as the spreadsheet came out every month, she immediately compared her shifts to his. Out of morbid curiosity, of course, and also to confirm once again just how thoroughly she was fucked.

Their schedules were always in sync. Always. No matter how fervently she wished they weren't, or how late she entered her schedule requests. Somehow, even if she waited until the very last hour, his requests still came in after hers, and whatever he put would mean the two of them were on the desk at the same time.

It was inevitable. Unavoidable. Like choosing the slowest checkout lane at the grocery store.

This month was no different. They were working together almost every shift. And for some bizarre reason, he'd even taken vacation next week, the same week as her.

Maybe it was all a huge coincidence. Or maybe he knew her work ethic would allow him to function as he preferred on the desk—i.e., at the pace of a molasses-coated sloth—and he was gaming the system.

The latter possibility had caused her no small amount of rage over the past few months.

But before then, back when she'd first started at the library, she'd searched for his lean, handsome face in the breakroom and sighed happily when she'd found it. She'd arrived early at work to talk with him about whatever she was reading that day. She'd showed him pictures of her nieces and nephews, and he'd smiled down at the images with such gentleness she'd nearly gone liquid.

She didn't want to remember. It *hurt* to remember. But she couldn't seem to help herself.

And at that moment, something in her brain shorted out.

She cleared her throat. When she opened her mouth again, Professional Librarian Voice rang out, loud as her heartbeat and clear as the Caribbean.

"I do have another question, Cowan." Inexplicably, her mouth had said that. Her voice. "What would you say if I told you I had a new boyfriend?"

As soon as the last word emerged from her mouth, her face twisted into an instinctive wince, her stomach began to roil, and her skin might as well have burst into flame.

Oh, Jesus. What had she done?

She never spoke without thinking. Ever. So why had she done it now? To representatives of a cable television network, of all people? The two of them were in the entertainment industry, for God's sake. Savvier and way more sophisticated than a woman like her.

They *had* to know she was lying. But they weren't saying anything.

If they remained quiet much longer, Callie was going to throw up.

Confronted with such a brazen falsehood, maybe they'd lost the power of speech. Maybe they'd muted the phone or were communicating via carrier pigeon or semaphore flags about how much they hated her. Maybe they were preparing to hang up on her. She didn't know, and the uncertainty was killing her.

Finally, Irene broke the silence.

"My, my, my. Callie Adesso, total dark horse." For the first time in Callie's memory, the other woman sounded highly entertained. "Didn't you say you broke up with your ex earlier this morning?"

"Yes." Callie paused. "It was a long time coming."

"I'll bet," Irene said.

"But just to be clear," Callie rushed to add, "Thomas and I didn't get involved until after I was free."

She was already a liar. No need to make herself sound like a cheater too.

The other woman snorted. "You're telling me you didn't stray while you were with Andre, but you *did* find a new guy before lunchtime on the same day you became single? Is that right?"

Lying wasn't as easy or fun as she'd been led to believe.

"Umm..." Callie bit her lip. "Yes. That's right."

A gleeful laugh crackled through the cell's speaker. "I don't know whether to check your pants for flames or congratulate you for finally kicking that asshole to the curb."

At that, Callie's eyes widened. "You thought Andre was an assh—"

Cowan didn't let her finish. "I'm sorry, Callie. The timing of your relationships is none of our business. Also, HATV and its employees would never call one of our applicants an asshole. Ever. Not under any circumstances. Please excuse us for a moment."

They must have muted their conversation again, because she couldn't hear anything for a few seconds. By the time they returned, she was nibbling on a thumbnail, trying not to scratch her chest.

"Apologies for calling your ex an asshole." Irene didn't

sound especially sorry, and she didn't wait for her apology to be accepted. "We have a few more questions."

"Forgive us," Cowan said, "but how do we know this man is really your boyfriend?"

The true moment of decision had arrived. If she backed out now, Irene and Cowan wouldn't belabor the issue. They'd merely hang up and find someone else for the show.

But if she kept lying, she'd actually have to provide evidence of that lie.

She could either continue on the Dark Path of Duplicity, or she could make a sharp right onto the Rosy Roadway to Righteousness. And she had to make the choice now.

"Ummm..." She closed her eyes and grimaced. "After work tonight, I can e-mail you pictures of us together, and you can judge for yourself whether we look romantically involved. Or you can send someone to interview us, like you did with Andre."

Trundling along the Dark Path of Duplicity it was, then.

And somehow, she was still talking. "All this might seem a bit quick—"

"You think?" Irene said.

"—but Thomas and I have worked together for months now, and there've always been, uh, feelings." Irritation and impatience were feelings, right? "We just didn't act on them before this. Until Andre and I ended things."

Shit, shit, shit. How had the scope of this lie not occurred to her? Did she really plan to create fake pictures of them as a loving couple? Or convince Thomas to memorize and parrot a fictional story about their torrid love affair?

"We don't have time to do another interview before the trip." After a muffled conversation with Cowan, Irene came back on the line. "Tell us about your new boyfriend, Callie."

He makes a tortoise seem speedy. Fails to multitask or retain basic information about checkout procedures. Bumps into the microfilm machines and various desks while deep in thought.

No. That wouldn't do.

Instead of dwelling on her more recent frustrations, Callie conjured up her first impressions of Thomas, back when she'd found him charming. Sought out his company.

This part of the lie would be comparatively easy.

"His name is Thomas McKinney. He's thirty-five and unfairly handsome." Picturing him, every detail of that too-attractive face and long body, was easier than she'd like. "He has dark, curly hair with a little silver just starting at the temples. Pale skin. Eyes like..." She thought about it. "In the Caribbean, you know how the water close to shore is turquoise, but if you go out a bit further, it's ridiculously blue? That's his eye color."

Cowan made a weird choking sound. "Ridiculously blue?"

Engrossed in her description of Thomas, Callie barely heard the intern. "He's tall. Lean, but really strong. When we had to move our encyclopedia collection, he was able to carry these enormous stacks of books." Well, until he'd tripped over a cart and dumped various volumes all over the polished wooden floor. "Plus, patrons flirt with him all the time, and he doesn't seem to notice."

That obliviousness always made her feel just a tiny better during their shifts together.

"Maybe you could—" Cowan started to say.

"Sometimes he wears dark-rimmed glasses, and they suit him way too well. It's like he's a bookish spy or a really sexy professor, which can be very distracting." She hesitated. "Sorry. What were you saying?"

Irene blew out a loud breath. "Can you tell us something else about him? Something that doesn't involve how hot he is?"

Oh. She supposed she had kind of rambled about his

looks for a bit too long. Probably because she didn't have much practice with lying.

"He's very intelligent." Maybe the smartest man she'd ever met, but she would keep that little tidbit to herself. "He started at the library six months before I was hired, so he's been here a year. He has a Ph.D. in American history and knows a ton about different time periods."

"That's plenty of—"

Callie barely heard Cowan. "When he gets a tricky question on the desk, he'll do everything he can to answer it as thoroughly and accurately as possible, no matter how long it takes. He's dogged, he's curious, and he truly wants to help people."

All true. Cowan and Irene simply didn't need to know how all that endless patience and curiosity impacted Callie. How by the time she'd started working at the library, the researchers and interpreters with more interesting and complex questions had already learned to go to him for answers when he was on the desk. How she got stuck with all the basic factual and circulation questions, and her own knowledge of history and the library remained untapped. How she had to deal singlehandedly with any lines at the desk, because he would spend almost his entire shift on one or two people and fail to offer assistance when she was in the weeds. How she was continually forced to calm patrons who were frustrated at the wait for help. How she had to hurry through any interesting questions she *did* receive, because of that line and those pissed-off people in it.

Cowan and Irene didn't need to know that working with Thomas all the time had stopped Callie from forming closer ties with patrons and other colleagues and left her feeling increasingly isolated.

So instead, she tried to remember more of the good stuff.

The reasons she used to rush to work half an hour early so she and Thomas could hang out before her shift started.

"He's kind. Easy to talk to." Somehow, amidst her burgeoning anger and worry, she'd forgotten that. "Not particularly familiar with pop culture but interested in everything. And he has this wry sense of humor with absolutely no meanness to it. No mockery whatsoever."

At first, she'd chatted with him all the time, and he'd always listen intently to whatever she wanted to say. Then he'd ask her questions or offer up his own well-considered opinions with that quiet confidence she so envied, and they'd talk for hours in the parking lot after work. Those chats hadn't been mere water cooler talks or gossip sessions, but the sorts of conversations she'd always hoped to have with her boyf—

Nope. Not ambling down that particular mental road.

It didn't matter how good a conversationalist he was. As her aggravation with him had grown, she'd stopped talking to him unless work required it. Because having all his careful attention, all his decency and kindness, directed her way somehow felt even worse than if he'd been a dick.

If he'd been a dick, her anger wouldn't feel so petty. If he'd been a dick, she might have mustered the courage to complain, either to him or to a supervisor. But he was a good man. She didn't want to hurt his feelings, she didn't want to get him in trouble, and she didn't want to borrow conflict or seem high-maintenance at a place where she'd only worked for six months.

Just the thought of confronting him made her itch.

So she was stuck. Frustrated and lonely and sad, but silent.

Irene interrupted her thoughts. "I think we're good here."

"What..." Callie swallowed, too nervous to hope. "What does that mean?"

"It means you've convinced me. You're into this dude, no question about it. We can make this work."

Wow. She was an *excellent* liar. Who knew?

"Have him fill out the online application tonight. We'll do the interview and take some pictures when you arrive at the first island." Cowan sounded distracted, and Callie could hear a tapping sound, as if he were taking notes. "I'll update the tickets and reservations and send you all the confirmation messages as soon as I can."

Her eyes were swimming again, and she wiped them against the sleeve of her blouse.

She'd done it. Oh, God, she'd done it.

Next week, she'd be digging her toes into white sand and splashing in the surf, allowing the water to erode all her worries as she luxuriated in the best trip of her life.

That is, if she could convince Thomas to abandon his previous vacation plans, lie on cable television, and spend an entire week in close proximity with a coworker who hadn't talked to him for several months.

Oh, God, she *hadn't* done it. Not really. Not yet.

She didn't need to blink back happy tears anymore. Her eyes were as dry and gritty as that imaginary white sand. "Got it. Is there anything else I need to know?"

"One last thing." Cowan was silent for a moment. "I'm choosing to believe that you and Thomas McKinney are a couple, because I like you. And, to be frank, because cancelling your trip would mess up the entire *Island Match* schedule for the rest of the season. But there will be cameras on you almost constantly for days. If you're lying…"

When he paused again, she squeezed her eyes shut, shame suffusing her cheeks with heat.

Finally, he sighed. "If you're lying, Callie, do it well."

CHAPTER TWO

"So I told them you were my boyfriend." Callie fiddled with a strand of her dark hair, her face twisted into a grimace. "I'm sorry. I shouldn't have dragged you into my issues."

Thomas blinked at her, startled and somewhat confused, but not unhappy.

Nope. Not at all.

Callie and Andre had broken up. Finally. She'd said the split was a long time coming, and Thomas had to concur. To him, it had felt like centuries. Millennia.

Apparently, Thomas and Callie were also going to spend a week together in various tropical paradises. While being filmed, from what he understood. And while those weren't necessarily optimal circumstances for wooing such a mercurial woman, they were certainly better than reading in his condo while she cavorted on the beach with her ex.

As far as he knew, he hadn't tossed a coin into an enchanted well, procured a potion from a witch, or fondled a lamp of mysterious provenance. But he could think of no other plausible explanation for these miraculous turns of events, so maybe he'd missed something.

Most importantly, Callie had stopped crying, and that was enough to set his world aright once more. He could wait for clarity on everything else.

That said, he should probably determine a few key facts before they proceeded.

"Let me make sure I understand the situation." He leaned against his hybrid's sun-heated hood in the stifling humidity of the library lot. "Next week, we're flying to three islands for one night each. And then we'll choose one of those islands for the last three nights of our trip."

She nodded. "Whichever one is our favorite."

"And HATV will film us in the belief that we're a couple."

Her nod was a bit more tentative that time. "Yes."

"Did we..." He hated to ask. It made him sound like a dunce, and he didn't think even he could have missed such a crucial development. But he needed to know for sure. "Did we agree to date at some point?"

If so, he had no memory of it happening. And when Callie spoke to him, looked at him, or hell, just breathed in his general direction, she captured his full and utterly devoted attention in a way no other woman ever had.

So he'd probably remember if they'd talked about dating.

Callie was shaking her head so hard, she had to be giving herself a headache. "No. No. God, no. You were just nearby, single, and on vacation next week, so I thought you'd be a good candidate for the job."

Too bad. Learning that he'd won her affections while in a fugue state of some sort would have been convenient. But no matter. He had a week to do the job while completely conscious.

"Thomas..." She was nibbling on that plump lower lip, a

signature gesture that had caused him to fumble various writing implements over the past six months. "I should've asked you before saying anything to them. But I just"—her inhalation turned shaky, her eyes shiny, and he would have torn apart the concrete parking lot with his bare hands to assuage her distress—"I just need this vacation. So badly. Can you possibly play along with me? Or did you already have plans? I know this was meant to be your summer break."

"I wasn't doing anything important." He shrugged. "I'd planned to read about the influenza pandemic during World War I, but that can wait."

Her eyes grew bright in a different, better way. "Last year, I read *The Great Influenza*, and I really appreciated Barry's discussion of—" She stopped herself. "Never mind. That's not the point right now. Are you really agreeing to go along with my stupid plan?"

"Not stupid." Reaching out, he touched her elbow. Just for a moment, through the silky barrier of her blouse, but the contact still dizzied him. "Ingenious, given the urgency of the situation. And yes, I'm agreeing to your plan."

Her lips parted, and she stared up at him for a moment. "I can't believe you said yes."

Any opportunity he could find to spend time with her, he'd take. Even if it meant relinquishing his favorite morning shifts to work in the afternoons and evenings. Even if it meant attending work gatherings at noisy, overcrowded bars. Even if it meant spending a week on camera and possibly making a fool of himself in front of a cable-television-viewing audience.

When Callie Adesso began working at the CMRL, the axis of his life shifted. From what he could tell, that shift appeared absolute and irrevocable.

And she'd been dating another man the entire time they'd known one another, until now.

If that relationship had been going awry for quite some time, as she'd said, maybe that would explain her seeming unhappiness the last few months. Because she didn't smile at him the same way she once did, and they didn't laugh and talk before or after their shifts anymore.

He hadn't understood it. But maybe this unexpected trip would explain everything.

Even better: Maybe this unexpected trip would *change* everything.

"Believe it," he told her.

DESIRE AND THE DEEP BLUE SEA IS COMING JULY 18, 2019! For news and updates, sign up for my newsletter, the Hussy Herald:

https://go.oliviadade.com/Newsletter

ABOUT OLIVIA

While I was growing up, my mother kept a stack of books hidden in her closet. She told me I couldn't read them. So, naturally, whenever she left me alone for any length of time, I took them out and flipped through them. Those books raised quite a few questions in my prepubescent brain. Namely: 1) Why were there so many pirates? 2) Where did all the throbbing come from? 3) What was a "manhood"? 4) And why did the hero and heroine seem overcome by images of waves and fireworks every few pages, especially after an episode of mysterious throbbing in the hero's manhood?

Thirty or so years later, I have a few answers. 1) Because my mom apparently fancied pirates at that time. Now she hoards romances involving cowboys and babies. If a book cover features a shirtless man in a Stetson cradling an infant, her ovaries basically explode and her credit card emerges. 2) His manhood. Also, her womanhood. 3) It's his "hard length," sometimes compared in terms of rigidity to iron. 4) Because explaining how an orgasm feels can prove difficult. Or maybe the couples all had sex on New Year's Eve at Cancun.

During those thirty years, I accomplished a few things. I graduated from Wake Forest University and earned my M.A. in American History from the University of Wisconsin-Madison. I worked at a variety of jobs that required me to bury my bawdiness and potty mouth under a demure exterior:

costumed interpreter at Colonial Williamsburg, high school teacher, and librarian. But I always, always read romances. Funny, filthy, sweet—it didn't matter. I loved them all.

Now I'm writing my own romances with the encouragement of my husband and daughter. I have my own stack of books in my closet that I'd rather my daughter not read, at least not for a few years. I can swear whenever I want, except around said daughter. And I get to spend all day writing about love and iron-hard lengths.

So thank you, Mom, for perving so hard on pirates during my childhood. I owe you.

If you want to find me online, here's where to go!

Website: https://oliviadade.com
Newsletter: https://go.oliviadade.com/Newsletter

facebook.com/OliviaDade
twitter.com/OliviaWrites
goodreads.com/OliviaDade

ACKNOWLEDGMENTS

This is the first book I wrote after arriving in Sweden, and also the first book I wrote with the express intent of self-publishing it. I wanted to get everything right, so I leaned shamelessly on so many of my friends as I drafted, revised, and readied it for publication.

Before I even began, Tamsen Parker generously provided crucial guidance for one of my main characters. Then a glorious cabal of women kept me motivated and writing via Twitter DM, even as I adjusted to life on a new continent: Therese Beharrie, Aislinn Kearns, Melanie Ting, Lynn Shannon, and Ainslie Paton. Once I had a completed draft, Kate Clayborn, Emma Barry, Margrethe Martin, Gwendolen Crane, and Ainslie (again!) read what I'd written and nudged me toward the best possible version of this story. Cecilia Grant, Sionna Fox, and Zoe York ably helped me get the manuscript ready for the world. In fact, without Zoe's patient introduction to and guidance through Indie Land, I'd have been totally lost. And finally, Lori Carter's adorable, gorgeous cover brought my characters to life in a way I hadn't even let myself hope for.

Thank you to all those friends and helpers. I don't know how I would have survived those first, difficult months in Sweden without you, and I don't know how I would have written this book without you either.

And throughout everything, my family loved me and believed in me and supported my writing. That means everything to me. Everything.